GYPSY GIRL
KATHRYN JAMES

Kathryn James has worked with Gypsy and Traveller children, driving around in a converted bus with a rainbow on the side, doing video and photography projects and documenting Travelling lives. She also writes scripts for a local video production company, mostly for children, teenagers and schools. Kathryn lives in Leicester.

Visit Kathryn's website at www.KathrynJames.co.uk or follow her on Twitter, @Kathryn_James.

For the littlest of us all, the adorable Norah-May

First published in Great Britain 2015 by Walker Books Ltd
87 Vauxhall Walk, London SE11 5HJ

2 4 6 8 10 9 7 5 3 1

Text © 2015 Kathryn James
Cover photographs © 2015 Getty Images / Hero Images
Getty Images / JGI / Jamie Grill

The right of Kathryn James to be identified as author of this work has been asserted by her in accordance with the Copyright, Designs and Patents Act 1988

This book has been typeset in Bembo

Printed and bound in Great Britain by Clays Ltd, St Ives plc

British Library Cataloguing in Publication Data:
a catalogue record for this book is
available from the British Library

ISBN 978-1-4063-5301-3

www.walker.co.uk

GYPSY GIRL

KATHRYN JAMES

GIRL

WALKER
BOOKS

The wedding's over.

My beautiful bridesmaid's dress is soaked in blood. Bright crimson patterning the white. The hem ragged and torn. The tulle skirts missing and the strapless bodice ripped. My tiara is long gone. My hair is stiffening with dried blood, not mousse. My legs are crumpled beneath me, unable to move. I'm like a rag doll.

I'm lying in this circle of trees by the black water. They call it a beauty spot. I can't see no beauty today. Only death. The magpies warned us, but we didn't listen.

Gregory is beside me, his sun-streaked, fair hair red with blood, his face white as a ghost. Shocked and injured again. It's my fault. I want to hug him, hold him close, tell him I didn't mean to let this happen to him. But I can't move. Anyway, he probably hates me.

In the distance, I can hear emergency sirens. Has everyone found out? Has me daddy? His name is Samson Smith. He comes from a long line of champion fighters. He'd have been able to stop Gregory from getting hurt. Not like me, even though I'm the only girl to have inherited the Smith fighting skills. Sometimes I love it, but now I hate it. I'm too fast, too strong, even in my Jimmy Choo heels. It's brought me here, to this place of death.

It began three days ago with a fight. Seems that for me, everything always begins with a fight...

High above us the spotlights lanced down, hot and white. Anything beyond the cage was in darkness, except for the faces of the men standing at the bars, hands grasping them, mouths shouting. I couldn't tell whether they were for me or against. Men don't always like girls winning.

The boy beneath me had a cute face and a Maori tattoo swirling around one arm. I think he was around eighteen, a couple of years older than me. Dark hair spiked with matt-textured mousse. Nice hairstyle, but that wasn't helping him. He'd laughed to begin with, when he saw me. Most boys do. I take them by surprise. I don't look like a fighter girl. I don't even look strong. I look like I get all my exercise from going out dancing or shopping for clothes, not the gym.

But now I had him pinned down. His skin smelled of Lynx Africa.

I shifted slightly, our faces almost pressed together, and got a stranglehold at last. He knew he was lost. I felt the last remaining bit of fight go out of him. He was too sweet, he shouldn't be here. He hadn't got the killer instinct. I wondered what had brought him to this gym, in an old warehouse. He gave a final desperate attempt to throw me off him, but I wasn't going anywhere. This was the closest I ever got to boys. So close, wrapped around them, but only in fights. They joked about me afterwards, looking at me in my little shorts and crop top, their eyes hot. But when they were fighting me, all they wanted to do was knock me down.

I tightened my grip on the boy's neck. He held out for a few seconds, until he ran out of breath. He tapped the mat. The roar of the supporters swept over us. I jumped to my feet, and the fight organizer was there, dragging my hand in the air, almost lifting me off my feet.

"The winner is Gypsy Girl!"

That's what they call me, there in the back streets where there's no rules, just fight, fight, fight. They don't ask if you're over eighteen years old. They don't want to know if you've got into trouble because of fighting. It was the only place for me. There weren't many girl fighters, and I was the best.

Boos and cheers echoed around me. The fight was over, and Maori Boy was getting to his feet, peering at me from under his spiky fringe and trying to grin. And my best friend, Kimmy, was coming through the cage doors with a bundle of cash in her hand and saying, "Let's go, Sammy! I got the winnings. Come on!"

We got out of there fast. Kimmy pushed her way through the crowd, kicking anyone who tried to stop us, until we burst out into the dark car park, drinking in the chill night air. Her rusty old Golf started first time, and we roared off down the road, both of us laughing, me with me feet up on the dashboard, pulling off the black fingerless fight mitts before counting out the money. It was a good night. After Kimmy's split, I had enough to buy me sister Sabrina's earrings, the crystal ones that matched her wedding dress.

"I need food," said Kimmy, as we screeched round a corner. "Chicken Caesar wrap, fries and Coke."

"No. Take me straight home." I was starving hungry too, but the sky over the warehouses and industrial units was getting a rosy glow. Dawn wasn't far away. I had to get back before me daddy missed me. He'd go crazy if he knew where I'd spent the night. This was my secret.

"I know where there's another fight tomorrow," said Kimmy hopefully.

"I'll see."

It was Wednesday morning. I had Sabrina's wedding to finish arranging for Saturday. I was the chief bridesmaid, and she'd turned into Bridezilla.

I hardly had time to crawl into bed and get a few winks of sleep before I was woken again. We live behind my father's gym, but because Sabrina's getting married in Langton, our trailers were packed and we were moving to the town for the wedding. So I had to haul my battered limbs out of bed and ride along beside Sabrina.

We parked up on the outskirts of Langton, where there's a little field called Gypsy's Acre. It's this perfect little spot surrounded by trees on a quiet road, where the houses finish and the countryside begins.

We were there because this was the very field where our mother, Maggie Smith, stayed when she got wed to me daddy. She died two years ago, and we all miss her. So when Sabrina said she wanted to stay on Gypsy's Acre before her wedding, we knew why. There's wild roses growing in the hedges around the field – beautiful and snowy white. They were blooming when our mother got married, and she picked them for her bouquet. You can see them in the wedding photos. We were going to do the same for Sabrina, to add into her massive mega-expensive bouquet. That way it would be as if our mother was a little part of the wedding, even though she's gone.

By midday our three Hobby tourers were standing neatly in the middle of the grass. One for my father, one for Great Granny Kate, and one for me and Sabrina. The rest of my married sisters either lived in the town or were staying with me aunties. Last time we came here it was lovely and peaceful, but things had changed. Behind the trees on one side there used to be a big barn that no one ever used. In fact, it looked like it was falling down. Now it didn't. It had been repaired, just like a few other buildings built around it – the type you see on industrial parks, with flat roofs and big doorways. A wide tarmacked drive led to a yard, where several lorries were parked behind a high security fence. No one had seen us arrive, but they didn't have to worry, we wouldn't bother them.

Soon as we'd got ourselves settled, the dressmaker woman arrived with the wedding dress. You'd think that would make Sabrina happy. It didn't. Straightaway she started screaming that the skirt wasn't big enough.

I swear to God it's six feet across and sparkling with a thousand Swarovski crystals. We could hardly get it in through the trailer door. But you try telling that to me sister.

"It's not fair!" she wailed, as she hung up the enormous dress. We were drowning in net underskirts. They took up nearly all the space inside our trailer. "I told the woman I wanted it *covered* in crystals."

I'm never getting married. I'm the youngest of the seven

11

Smith sisters, so I know all about weddings and being a bridesmaid. But I'm the odd one out. I don't want true love. Since I was little I always wanted to run off and play with our boy cousins and go to Muay Thai kick-boxing classes with them. My father says he knew I was special the moment I was born. He was desperately hoping for a boy after six daughters, so he was disappointed to begin with. But then he held out his finger, and I clutched it, and wouldn't let go. I was so strong he picked me up like that and dangled me, and I still didn't let go. That's the test for a new fighter in the Smith family. Which is why I'm called Sammy-Jo. It's the closest me daddy could get to Samson, his own name and the name of all our fighting ancestors.

Being a fighter wasn't helping me with Sabrina, though.

"The dressmaker woman sez if you have too many crystals, the dress'd weigh too much, and you wouldn't be able to walk down the aisle," I told her.

She didn't look convinced and started flouncing about, so I walked outside to get the bridesmaids' dresses. We'd left them on the sunloungers under a tree, near the entrance to the field, and in the end she trailed after me, still moaning.

My father had gone visiting the Quinns, the family of Sabrina's husband-to-be. So there was only me, Sabrina and Granny Kate in our little camp – unless you count the evil-looking magpie sitting on the picnic table, chattering at us.

Once we'd sorted out the dresses we were going to the high street to get our nails done and get Sabrina's earrings. I was in my tight jeans, high-heeled boots and a little top that stopped short and showed me belly.

I gathered up my bridesmaid's dress from its delivery box and held it in the air. It shimmered in the sunshine, its tight strapless bodice was trimmed with crystals, its waist tight and slim-fitting all the way down over my hips until it flared out into a froth of lacy tulle skirts. Sabrina grabbed the flower girl's dress and immediately started going on about the colour of the ribbons not being the right shade of blue. That's why I never heard the two boys coming down the lane past our field, until I looked up and found them standing by the entrance, staring at us in surprise.

They were near enough for me to hear one of them say, "Oh. My. God. Gypsies," like you might say, "Oh my God, Martians." He flicked a strand of his styled dark hair into place and then stood there smirking at us.

For the moment, my mouth had stopped working, which was unusual for me. I stared back, but not at the dark-haired one, he didn't interest me. It was the other boy that had struck me silent. This one had a mop of fair hair that had gone streaky and baby-blond in the summer sun. You'd think that would mean he had blue or grey eyes, but he didn't. He had brown eyes – not dark brown, but golden brown, like clear amber. I remembered the fair hair and the golden brown eyes from the last time we met. He was staring back at me, so I didn't think he'd forgotten, either.

I just stood there, clutching my armful of frothing white duchesse silk and finest tulle. He leaned against the gatepost, his hands in his pockets.

"So what're you doing here?" he asked, eventually.

"Nothing."

It was true. We weren't getting in anyone's way. We were out of sight. The piece of grass we were parked on wasn't being used for anything. The only problem was Gypsy's Acre belonged to the Langtons. The roof of their big house and a couple of windows were showing through the trees, across the fields behind us. The Langtons were rich, and they owned everything round here.

And the fair-haired boy staring at me was Gregory Langton. Their son.

His friend was beginning to grin, thinking he could get cheeky because we're girls and we're Travellers. He didn't know the Smith sisters, obviously.

"What's your names?" he asked.

"Ignore them," muttered Sabrina, pulling me sleeve. "You've got to do something about these ribbons, they're all wrong, honest."

I shook her off. "This won't take long."

"But you have to help me with the dresses!"

"Take yours inside. I'll sort it in a minute." I walked over to the boys. Gregory and his friend took a step back. My sisters say I have a walk like a tiger, like I'm stalking along – if tigers wore heels, that is.

"Our names? As if I'd tell you," I said, as Sabrina huffed and muttered her way to our trailer. "You're gorjers."

"Hey, she called us gorgeous," said Gregory's friend, looking smug.

Gregory peered at me from under his mop of fair hair. "She didn't, Cooper. She called us gorjers, which means non-gypsies."

"Clever," I sez to him.

"I know I am." He paused. "Sammy-Jo Smith."

So he did remember me. He'd grown taller and skinny since I last saw him. And this time he wasn't wearing his school uniform but slouchy jeans and a check shirt. It was two years ago when we first met. I was fourteen and up to no good. He was fifteen, and he did me a favour.

A wind had sprung up out of nowhere and was tugging at the dress, blowing sparkling silk all around me and making me long, dark hair fan out. It blew the sound of an engine to the three of us. A silver Range Rover was heading up the road towards us.

"Come on, let's go," said his mate, watching the Rover, but Gregory ignored him and turned to me.

"I better warn you. You probably can't stop here any more." He pointed over to the smart new barn and its buildings. "That's a business. And the owner is mad about security."

"I don't see anyone around complaining about us."

He gave another quick glance at the Range Rover closing on us. "Wait another minute and you will. His name's Mr McCloud. You don't want to argue with him."

"Does he own this field as well as the barn?" I said.

"No, that's still ours."

"So he can't move us."

15

Gregory was giving me this long, long look. That's what I remembered about him. Most people don't really look. They glance for a couple of seconds, that's all. This boy really looked at stuff, like he wanted to see every atom of everything and work out the truth of it.

"Him and my dad know each other. He could ask Dad to get a court order," he said.

I shrugged, which is not easy when you've got a frothy bridesmaid's dress trying to fly out of your arms.

"He'll be wasting his time, then." I had to say it loudly, because the magpie was squawking like it was warning us of something. It was on the top of Granny Kate's trailer now. "We're here for me sister's wedding on Saturday. A court order will take ten days, and we'll be gone by then. I'll go and tell him that meself."

I didn't need to. The silver Range Rover had turned off the road and parked neatly at the entrance to Gypsy's Acre. The door opened. A man got out.

Gregory murmured, "Oh, shit."

If this was Mr McCloud, he wasn't what I was expecting. The way Gregory spoke about him, I was expecting a thug, but he was a businessman in an expensive suit and steel-framed glasses. Underneath the suit he looked strong, though, and he walked towards us like he owned the world and would crush anyone he didn't like underfoot. I've met fighters like that. They seem calm and mild on the surface, but there's this power and rage inside them, and it's so strong that you can feel it hit you like a blow when you get close to

16

them. I got that from McCloud now as he strode over to us, taking his glasses off and polishing them, before fitting them back on and giving them a push to make them sit right. He gave the trailers a quick glance, but then his eyes fixed on me. He walked right up close. If he expected me to back away, he was wrong.

"What?" I sez.

He looked me up and down through his spectacles. That's when I saw his eyes. They were shark eyes, pitiless and hostile. I shivered. I hoped he hadn't noticed.

"I was told there was a man with you. Your father? Where is he?"

His voice was as cold as the grave. It made my hackles rise, like a wolf's fur rising around its neck when it senses a threat.

"He's not here."

His shark gaze never left me. "I see. When he gets back, tell him I want you all off this land by the end of today."

His words didn't bother me none. I've heard it all before.

"Why? We've stopped here before," I said. "No one ever complained."

"Things have changed." He pointed at the barn and the buildings behind the trees. "This field overlooks my property and my business. I have a right to privacy."

I pointed my own finger round at the grass and trees. "This is Gypsy's Acre. That's always been its name. That's why we stop here."

He should ask Granny Kate about it. She never learned to

read or write, nor did any Smith before her, so her memory is amazing. When you can't write down your history, you make it into stories and tell it to your children, and then they remember it and tell it to theirs in time. And one of the stories Granny told us was about Gypsy's Acre, and how for hundreds of years whole travelling families would stay here while they were picking fruit for the farmers.

"You can't argue with history," I told him.

His glasses flashed in the sunlight as he leaned closer to me. He never raised his voice, or sounded angry, but the temperature around us got even colder.

"I don't care about the past. I doubt you have Mr Langton's permission in writing, which means you're parked illegally. So you will go back to where you came from."

He made it sound like we came from hell. But in fact we live most of the year behind me daddy's boxing gym, in the next town, which is about twenty miles away. We stay put most of the winter, but when summer starts, Samson Smith gets itchy feet and he leaves the gym in the hands of one of our cousins. Off we go, visiting all the other Smiths up north, and there's plenty of them. Only this time we'd come south, to Langton, for the wedding.

I was about to explain that to him, but I didn't get the chance. Our trailer door slammed open and Sabrina gave a terrible screech, as though someone was trying to murder her. She rushed over and barged into the middle of us with a look of horror on her face, waving a crystal headdress in her trembling hands.

"They sent the wrong crown! This isn't mine! Mine's bigger! I can't wear this." Her face crumpled. "Everything's ruined! WHAHHHH!"

Instant Bridezilla again.

You should've seen Mr McCloud's face. He stepped back quickly, out of her way. And Gregory stopped scuffing his trainer about in the dust – like he was embarrassed to hear Mr McCloud telling me off – and backed away, too, straight into his gawping friend. I didn't blame them. Sabrina in full wedding panic was a terrible sight to see. The military should use her to stop wars, or rioters. She takes people by surprise because she's size eight and has legs like twigs, big flirty brown eyes and masses of hair like a Disney princess – until something upsets her, and then her mouth goes trembly, her eyes go into slits and she turns into a Gremlin.

"Sammy-Jo! You have to do something! Now!"

"Shush," I said. "I'll sort it. I'll ring the woman."

She didn't shut up. She threw the headdress to the ground and went off sobbing and screaming. Mr McCloud went to say something, but Gregory was more sensible.

"Erm, perhaps you should leave them alone. My dad's not complained, and I bet they'll be gone soon."

Mr McCloud peered at him as though he couldn't believe someone had just stuck up for me.

"He's right," I said, quickly. "We'll be leaving after the wedding. And it's up to Mr Langton to tell us to get off, not you." Then I turned my back on him and looked at Gregory. These next words were just for him. I said them

19

quietly. "But I haven't forgotten. I owe you."

I wasn't quiet enough, though. His friend looked surprised and then began to grin, and murmured, "What's this? You and her?" He didn't get any further, because Mr McCloud had heard as well. He couldn't have known what I meant, but he pushed past me and started aiming his icy little words towards Gregory this time.

"Does your father know you're hanging around up here?" he said.

When Gregory didn't answer, Mr McCloud gave a small tight smile that was the exact opposite of an actual smile. "Well, maybe I should let him know."

As he turned away, I got one last icy glare.

"I always get what I want," he said. "I have security. They have my permission to deal with potential trespassers."

"Whatever," I said.

But as he drove away, I shivered as though someone had walked over me grave. I'd had angry people yelling at me before, but they'd never made me go cold like Mr McCloud's quiet, snipped-off words did. I watched the silver Range Rover drive along the road for a short distance and then turn into the yard beside the barns. Gregory and his friend were watching him, too.

"Don't worry about him telling your daddy," I said, in case Gregory was anxious about McCloud's threat.

He gave me a smile. "I wasn't," he said. "I can talk to who I want."

His friend didn't look so sure. He was already backing

away, not cheeking us now. I think Mr McCloud had scared him.

"Come on, Greg," he called.

"Wait a sec, Cooper."

But Cooper wanted to be gone. "No. We've got to meet Alice and Ella."

Gregory gave a start and said, "Oh God, yes," as though he'd forgotten all about it. He raised a hand, did a small, awkward wave and followed his friend out into the lane again.

I watched him go. He might say he could talk to who he wanted, but the truth of it is this – the sons of rich men like Mr Langton don't make friends with girls like me. And I shouldn't have been hanging around with gorjer boys either. I owed Gregory Langton a good deed, and I've been brought up to always pay my debts. But once it was paid, I should have forgotten about him. Him and me come from different worlds.

Tell that to me eyes, though. I was still watching him walk away when Great Granny's trailer door thumped open.

"Sammy-Jo, get over here now!"

I gave up on watching Gregory and walked over to Granny. She was standing in her doorway, her long long hair still dark and in a plait down her back, and a bright pink, oversized Calvin Klein T-shirt hanging over her ankle-length skirt.

"What's up, Granny?"

But she could hardly hear me because the magpie had

swooped down onto a little table by her trailer and was screeching worse than Sabrina. I went to shoo it away, but Granny beat me to it. She was down the steps and flapping her hands before I could move. The bird took one look at her and launched itself into the sky.

"Good riddance!" she shouted after it.

"It's only a magpie, Granny," I said.

She turned sharply. "One for sorrow," she said. "A bad omen, that's what it is."

3

Never ignore the magpies.

I know that now, but not then. Three days ago I hadn't time for bad omens. Not with Sabrina still having hysterics and threats coming from Mr McCloud. There wasn't much I could do about him, but I found the dressmaker's number, got her on the phone and sorted the crown. It turns out the woman had already discovered her mistake and was on her way back.

That shut Sabrina up. I told her to go and do her face, and then it would be time for us to go into town and get our nails done, which made her happy again.

Granny Kate wasn't happy, though. She was still going on about bad omens.

"What?" I said, hardly listening. Being the sensible bridesmaid was wearing me down.

She was perched on her trailer steps, eyeing the bird. "Look at it – staring at me bold as brass! Don't you know about magpies, Sammy girl? They foretell the future, that's what they do."

She's ninety years old and knows all the old ways and

sayings. She was born in a wooden wagon, which is called a vardo, and she used to come here to Langton when she was my age, apple picking.

"How can a bird know the future, Granny?" I sez to her.

"You should know, you're the seventh of the seventh."

She means I'm the seventh daughter of a seventh daughter. She says that makes me special, but mostly it just means that I've got too many sisters and too many aunts.

"What's being the seventh of the seventh got to do with it?" I said.

"It makes you smart."

"Ha. Tell that to me teachers."

But she shook her head. "Smiths aren't always school smart, but there's plenty of other ways of being clever. And you're Smith smart."

Maybe she's right. My daddy sez I walked at six months and was talking by a year. And he swears they had to tie me to the trailer steps with a skipping rope because I could open doors and work out locks, and then I'd go wandering off, looking for trouble.

Granny patted my hand and looked at me with dark eyes that were misty and rimmed with milky blue, now she was so old.

"Watch yourself, Sammy," she muttered. "There's trouble ahead."

"Isn't there always?" I said. "We've already got a man called McCloud trying to get us thrown off here."

There was a squawk from the magpie, as if it was joining

24

in. We both looked over at it. It was skipping back and forth along the back of one of the sunloungers, like it was line dancing. It didn't look like a bad omen.

Granny pointed a finger again. "One for sorrow, two for mirth, three for a wedding, and four for a death."

I swear that the moment she said "death", everything went quiet around us. The birds in the trees stopped singing. The traffic on the main road near by went quiet. A silence fell over our camp and held. Even the sun went behind a cloud for the first time that morning. Sorrow, mirth, wedding and death. I shivered again.

"They're just birds, Granny," I said, to break the silence.

She shrugged. "Maybe."

She was staring through the leaves of the trees at the roof of the barn. The whine of machinery was floating through the air to us, when all of a sudden there was a thud – a deep low noise that we both felt through the soles of our feet – and then someone swore. It all came from the same direction.

"That mush with the specs who you were talking to – he came from there?" she said. Mush is an old word for man.

"Yes. It's a business now. He's the boss."

"What's it do?"

"Don't know."

She got to her feet and went inside her trailer. She came out with a couple of mixing bowls.

"There's some good brambles over by that barn. Lots of blackberries. You can come and help me pick some."

25

She smiled a gappy, crafty smile. "We'll have a look. Who's he to tell us to move? The nark."

I followed her bright pink T-shirt through the trees, pushing my way along a narrow, hidden path, going carefully by the wild roses, unhooking their thorns from my jeans and trying not to get my belly stung by nettles. The path stopped at a high fence that was made of thick steel bars twice my height and ending in sharp spikes holding up a strong steel mesh. It was a fence that said, "Don't even try to get over me." It had two signs attached to it. The first said: INTERNATIONAL EXPRESS LTD. SPECIALIST IMPORT AND EXPORT CARRIERS. The second was a warning. PREMISES PATROLLED 24 HOURS BY SECURITY GUARDS.

Beyond the fence was the barn and the new buildings, clustered around a tarmac yard. The barn had been done up. Its doors were wide open, and I could see crates and pallets of stuff stored in there. Three lorries with INTERNATIONAL EXPRESS printed on their sides were parked in the yard with their back doors open, ready to be loaded. The silver Range Rover was by the side of them. Next to it was a battered old Jeep. And beside that, in total contrast, was a bright red Subaru Impreza WRX, the kind that my cousins are always oohing and aahing over. I couldn't see Mr McCloud driving something like that. And anyway it had a personalized number plate, HUDI8, so I bet it belonged to someone else.

A forklift truck was standing in the middle, beside a couple of white sacks and a load of crates tipped onto their sides. One of the sacks had split open. I reckoned that was the thud we'd heard. The forklift must've dropped the whole lot while trying to load the lorry nearest to us. I don't know what it contained, but it had coated the ground in white, and the breeze had blown it around. A big guy was hosing everything down, spraying the lorry and the fallen crates and the ground all around him. He'd taken his T-shirt off, and his biceps were huge. He might've been one of the lorry drivers, but he looked more like he was part of the 24-hour security. He was facing away from me, so he didn't see me. He carried on swearing and cursing at someone, probably the forklift driver, until a voice shouted at him from inside one of the buildings. It sounded like McCloud.

"Pony. Did you save any of it?"

He paused. "No, it's ruined. But he won't do it again, boss." His accent was foreign. I'm guessing Pony was his nickname because his scraggly long white hair was tied back in a ponytail. As he started to spray the ground again, he glanced my way. He stared for a second or two.

"Boss. We got visitors."

Let him tell tales, I didn't care.

I waited a few seconds, but Mr McCloud didn't come out, so I turned my back on the yard and started picking blackberries. Granny Kate was right about them. There were masses of tangled brambles up against the fence and the side of the barn, and they were loaded down with thousands of berries.

I don't know why Mr McCloud was so bothered about us being next to his precious property. It wasn't like we could get anywhere near it because of the security fence. And we wouldn't want to, anyway. Whatever he was transporting in the big lorries didn't interest us. I cursed under my breath when I got caught on a thorn.

"What are you going to make with them?" I said.

Granny was good with hedgerow stuff. When she was my age, the men would go off and catch rabbits for stew and she would go picking berries from hedgerows. She would make puddings and pies, and a famous syrup that was so good you could take it like medicine and any coughs and colds going round wouldn't dare to come anywhere near you.

She threw a few more berries into her bowl. "I'm going to make my special blackberry wine. We can toast the bride and groom at the reception."

"Does it matter that they're dusty?" I said, picking a handful and blowing on them.

Granny squinted at them. "That's not dust. That's bloom. They'll be fine. Just drop 'em in the bowl."

I carried on picking, but my thoughts weren't on brambles. They were on the big house. From where I was standing, I could see the roof through the trees. I remembered the last time I'd seen it, and I'd gone in – uninvited. That was when I met Gregory Langton for the first time. I wasn't doing a very good job of not thinking about him.

"So who was that yellow-haired gorjer boy?" asked Granny Kate, watching me.

Sometimes I think she can read my mind, even though she says all that Romany stuff about reading palms and telling fortunes is nothing but trickery and hanky panky. Let's face it, if we knew the future then we'd all wait for a lottery rollover, predict the numbers and live in luxury. But at times like this, I wasn't so sure.

"He's from the big house," I said, casually.

"I was watching," she said. "He knew you. And you knew him."

It was no good lying to her, so I took a deep breath.

"Remember when we last came to Langton?"

Granny sighed. "I do. For your poor mammy, God rest her soul!"

Two years ago our mother Maggie had died. She wasn't strong like the Smiths – she was always tired – and one day something went wrong with her heart and it couldn't be put right. We came here for the funeral because it was traditional for all her family to be buried in the graveyard in the town.

"Remember how angry I was that day?" I said. "I couldn't even cry."

I hadn't been going to tell her the whole story, but somehow it came rushing out.

I saw it again in my mind like it was a DVD – the carriage, and the horses with their black feather plumes, the crowds of people, what they wore, what they said, and how the cold sun shone on the tears of me sisters and aunts, turning them to diamonds. But I hadn't been able to shed even one tear. I was burning up inside with anger that she'd been taken from us. When it was over I ran off, still in my

29

long black coat and boots. No one could stop me or find me. I wandered across the fields by myself, until I saw a horse straying onto the road through a broken fence.

I love horses and I didn't want to see him get hurt on the road, so I tried to catch him, but he was a stallion and he had his own ideas. Eventually I managed to get my belt around his neck, even though he kept wanting to kick me with one end and bite me with the other, but I'm fast at moving out of the way. In the end I got him back into the nearest field without me being kicked or bitten to death. There was a big house near by, and I guessed he might belong there, so I walked up the drive to tell them what had happened. I didn't know then that it was Langton House.

When I got to the front door, it was open. I shouted, but no one came. I could hear laughter and chatter coming from the back of the house, like there was a whole load of people having a party. I don't know why I did it, but I walked inside. And once I'd done that, I kept on walking and looking around the hall and the front rooms. I'd never once in my whole life lived in a house. I looked at the pictures on the walls and the ornaments on the tables. And then I saw a couple of twenty-pound notes tucked half under a vase. I went towards them like I was hypnotized. I didn't even need the money, but I was angry with the whole world. As my hand reached out and took the notes, there was a noise behind me. I whirled round.

That's when I saw him for the first time, standing there in

his school uniform, shirt untucked on one side, tie hanging loose, ink scribbled onto his hand. He was in the doorway, blocking my escape. Fair hair, golden brown eyes, I never forgot his face. He looked right at me. He didn't look away.

"Who are you?" he said.

I told him my name, I don't know why. Right then I didn't care about anything but that my mother was dead.

We stared at each other some more, until someone shouted to him from the other room. "Gregory! Hurry up, we're waiting."

The whole world went still, and my future hung before me, spinning like a caterpillar on a thread. I was a gypsy girl trespassing in his house. He was the rich man's son. If he told on me then the police would come and my daddy would be shamed that his daughter had been caught thieving on the day of the funeral.

But the boy didn't shout out.

"What are you doing in here?" he asked, like he really wanted to know what was going through my mind. I couldn't believe how cool he was about it.

I put my chin in the air and squared up to being caught. "I came to tell you that the big horse with the white blaze and three white socks got loose. I put him back in the field with the oak tree in the middle."

He gave a laugh like he didn't believe me. "You caught Nero?" Which I guessed was the stallion's name. "No one gets near him."

"I did. I'm fast and strong." He looked at me and didn't

believe that, either. I didn't blame him. I looked skinny in my funeral black.

He brushed his hair out of his eyes and said, "And the money in your hand?"

I put it back down. "I didn't mean to. Don't tell on me."

Someone began shouting his name again – closer this time, as though they were coming through the house looking for him. He could've called out, given me away, but he didn't.

"I'm coming," he shouted, without taking his eyes off me.

Then he stood to one side so that I could reach the door.

I ran. I never thought I'd see him again, but now I had.

"That's why I owe him. And some time soon I'll pay him back."

Granny said nothing. She was still picking berries.

"I didn't take the money, Granny. I never would have done. I was just angry. And I know you're going to tell me to keep away from boys like him," I said. "Don't worry, I don't want to go near them."

She stopped picking and straightened her back. "I remember a boy from round here," she said. "A long time ago when we came here picking fruit. He was from the big house. He's probably dead now." She put a hand to her back again and winced. "Like I will be soon. I'm getting old."

It wasn't like Granny Kate to talk like this. Maybe the magpie had made her feel gloomy.

"You're only ninety," I told her. "That's no age at all for a Smith."

She shook her head. "The old vardo will be coming soon to take me off to my rest."

She always says that when a Smith dies a wooden wagon comes along and carries them away to wherever it is that Smiths go in the afterlife.

"Well, it better not be yet," I said to her. "Or Sabrina will go mad. Don't go ruining the wedding!"

She laughed, and we carried on picking berries until we heard scuffling and curses in the undergrowth behind us. It was Sabrina, making her way towards us, her tears forgotten.

"There you are, Sammy-Jo!" she shouted, tiptoeing through the bushes, hands high, face screwed up in disgust, like she was wading waist-deep through a poisonous swamp. "You're supposed to be me bridesmaid. You have to look after ME! You can talk to Granny any time. But I need my nails doing. NOW!"

"I'll be glad when she's married," muttered Granny, and we both started laughing.

"No time for sorrow here! Only weddings," I said.

But as I handed my bowl to her, I noticed that Mr McCloud had come out of one of the smart new buildings. He was watching us, his glasses two circles of light as they caught the sun.

I gave him a wave to show he didn't scare me. His face didn't change. His hand went to his pocket and he brought out a phone, dialled and then put it to his ear. He began talking.

I turned my back on him and followed Granny and Sabrina back to Gypsy's Acre. I didn't care who he was ringing. I didn't care if it was the police. Let him.

He couldn't move us.

4

The Paradise Nail and Beauty Bar — PARADISE IS JUST A
FINGERTIP AWAY! — was packed with Smiths even before
me and Sabrina arrived. Three of my sisters, who live in
Langton, were already inside, along with a couple of my
aunties. You could hear them chattering and laughing from
out on the high street.

The noise got even worse when we rushed in, and
everyone started shouting and asking the bride-to-be how
she was feeling. The Paradise girls had been hearing about
the wedding for ages. Star, Sadie-May and Savannah are
always in and out, getting their nails done. It was a pity me
other two sisters, Sylvia and Suzie, couldn't be here, but they
were due to arrive the next day from down south.

All seven of us have names beginning with S. I think my
daddy was hoping for a boy each time, and was thinking
of calling us Samson, and couldn't get the idea of a name
beginning with S out of his mind. All of us have the same
sort of looks — "peas in a pod," my daddy says — long, dark
hair, eyes that seem like they've already got eyeliner and
mascara on and skin that gets a dark tan in the summer. Put

that together with the fact that we all like bright clothes and there's no mistaking us when we get together. There's only one thing that separates us. I love training and fighting, while their favourite sport is sitting on a comfy chair and texting.

"Here, take these chocolates off me," hollered Star, waving a big box as soon as we got through the doors. "You know me, I'm a chocoholic and I'll eat them all."

Star's well named. She always wanted to be a star. She's got a good singing voice, and she used to get us all singing and dancing like the Spice Girls when everyone lived at home. I think she had dreams of entering *The X Factor* before she got married and had her kids. She tossed the chocolate box towards us, and I caught it. It was Thorntons soft centres, so I grabbed a couple before Sabrina snatched it from me, declaring she was going to faint if she didn't get some sugar, and tiptapped her way over to sit next to Star.

"Sammy-Jo! Sit here. I saved you a seat!" screeched another voice.

I've got seven aunties, but only two were here. Beryl is always flaunting round in her high heels, nosing out the latest gossip. Her sharp eyes don't miss a trick – she sees and hears everything, and then lets everyone else know. The other was Queenie, big and curvy with huge, glittering, diamond earrings and strings of gold necklaces dangling down her low-cut top.

It was Beryl who'd shouted to me. She was patting the seat next to her, as her girl delicately painted gold and hot-pink polka dots onto her long silver nails. I sat down, and another girl set to work turning my scruffy fighter's nails into something jewelled and silver to match me dress. All around me there was shouting and laughter, but I didn't join in. I had a problem.

Gregory Langton wouldn't get out of my head. I kept daydreaming about him. I kept seeing his fair hair and amber eyes. My daddy would go crazy if I started hanging around with boys. So would me aunts. But daydreams are different. Daydreams are secret. But even so, I felt guilty.

What was I doing dreaming of a gorjer boy?

I love that I'm a Gypsy and a Smith.

I love it when my daddy decides that we're going visiting, and we pack up and we're off along the road, our homes coming with us. We live lightly. We wear our wealth around our necks. We go where we like, work when we like. Not all the Smiths are angels, but there's plenty of people in houses who aren't angels, either.

I love that we celebrate everything. Birthdays? Let's dress up, let's have a party! Weddings? Christenings? Let's get the brightest dresses we can and dance the night away.

"SAMMY! Are you listening to me?"

Beryl's voice brought me back to the present. She and the nail girl were staring at me. "Huh?"

"I said, when're you getting married then, Sammy-Jo? There's just you left now."

I flicked my hair back with my free hand. "You know my rules, Beryl. I'll only go out with a boy who can beat me in a fight."

"That can't be much of a challenge to the boys," said my girl as she filed and shaped my nails. She knew my aunts and sisters because they came in here all the time. She didn't know me.

"Sammy-Jo's our fighter," explained Beryl. "She does kick-boxing and martial arts. She's a champion, she's got medals and cups. A whole shelf full of them – haven't you, Sammy-Jo?"

"Yes. Yes, I have." I kept my face blank as the nail girl's eyes widened in surprise.

Queenie leaned forward, her dangling earrings catching the light. "She's won everything going. British under-sixteens kick-boxing, gold at the UK championships for whats-its-name..." She clicked her fingers, trying to think. "Tie something or other..."

"Tae Kwon do, Queenie," I said.

"That's the one! There's no one left for her to beat." She gave me a proud look. "Until she turns eighteen and she can enter the adult competitions."

My father and all my aunts and sisters were right behind me when it came to me winning trophies. They wouldn't be so proud if they knew about the sneaking out at nights and the secret fights. If they ever found out, they'd lock me up. Luckily, they didn't know, so all I had to put up with was Beryl and Queenie going on and on about me getting married.

"Nothing wrong with being a champion, except that it puts the boys off," said Beryl.

"It didn't put Alfie off," Star shouted from the back of the shop. "He liked you, Sammy."

"Well, I didn't like him," I said, shortly. Alfie was a cousin of a cousin, and he came to train at our gym last year. He did nothing but hang around me and try to get me to go out with him. Until the day he insisted we do some sparring together – and I beat him.

"Alfie's a fine boy, but he's not right for Sammy-Jo," said Sadie-May, joining in. She's the cleverest Smith sister, and she actually liked going to school. So if she says something, everyone believes her. There was a general nodding of heads in agreement.

"I remember now – in the end she frightened him to death," said Savannah. "He ducked every time she went near him." That made everyone laugh.

"So who'd be right for our Sammy, then?" shouted Star.

There was a pause while everybody tried not to say the one name they all wanted to. Until Beryl couldn't stand it any longer.

"It has to be Rocky," she said, and a sly glance went between her and Queenie. I knew it wouldn't be long before someone mentioned Rocky.

Rocky Quinn is the brother of Tyson, Sabrina's bridegroom. And just because his brother and my sister are getting married, my aunties seem to think I'll marry him in a couple of years. So do half his family. They think eighteen is the best age for a girl to get married, and my family are desperate for me to get with Rocky. His family, the Quinns, have got loads of money, and they live in a big house on the other side of town. There's no mistaking it. It's got two rearing stone horses on either side of the gateposts. Gypsies and horses go together, and most of our men have a horse or two as a hobby. So the stone horses are there to remind everyone that they might be living in a house now, but they're still travelling people.

"He's a lovely boy, Sammy-Jo. So handsome." Queenie paused as the Thorntons box got handed to her. Her fingers danced over the chocolates. "Oh, go on, then, I'll just have the one. I can't resist a strawberry crème."

Beryl reached over and took the box off her. "Put it back! You know what you told me."

Queenie quickly stuffed the chocolate in her mouth. "It's only the one," she mumbled, guiltily. Queenie's always on a diet, but she never gets any thinner.

"You won't get in your dress," Beryl scolded. "It's your own fault. I told you not to buy the size sixteen." She rolled her eyes. "Sixteen! As if!"

That started them arguing, as usual, which gave me the chance to relax and pray that they'd forgotten about Rocky. But a couple of minutes later, Beryl turned back to me, her eyes glittering, and my heart sank because I could see she'd not finished with me yet.

"You like Rocky, don't you?"

Before I could say anything, Savannah shouted, "Aw, leave her alone, Beryl!"

Savannah, my second-eldest sister, had finished having

her nails done, and she was sitting on the easy chairs with her feet up, near to our table. "Sammy-Jo's not interested in boys, thank goodness. She should wait until she's older." She glanced at her sister. "Not like Sabrina."

Sabrina whirled round, nearly causing her girl to paint a silver stripe across her hand instead of her nail. "You got married young as well, Sav!" she howled. "So you can shut up!"

Savannah pulled a face. "I know! And I wouldn't do it a second time, I'm telling you that for a fact. I'd have waited a few years."

"I'm not saying Sammy-Jo needs to get married soon, but she could be dating," Beryl persisted. Her eyes narrowed. "And Rocky could do with a girlfriend. A good Gypsy girl, that's what he needs." She and Queenie exchanged glances.

"Don't start," muttered Queenie. "We don't know anything for sure."

I smiled to myself but kept quiet. So they'd heard some rumours about Rocky as well.

Beryl patted my arm, as my girl put the finishing touches to my nails. "Stay here with me on the site for the rest of the summer," she said, eagerly. "You'd like him better if you saw more of him."

Most of my aunts and sisters live in houses now, but Beryl and Star live on the Langton Traveller site. All towns have to have somewhere for Travellers to stop, even though there's never enough places. I pushed Beryl's hand away.

"I keep telling you. I don't want to get married. And Rocky's too old for me."

I used to idolize Rocky when I was twelve. He was four years older. He was handsome. He was rascally. Who wouldn't fall for someone like that? He never even noticed me. I was this fierce little fighter girl who hung around and got in the way. But now I'm grown I don't idolize him any more. I know things about Rocky that my aunties only suspect.

"He's not that much older than you! And he won't wait around for ever," said Beryl, shaking her head. Like most of my aunties, she couldn't believe anything could occupy a girl other than thinking about getting married.

"I don't care." I stood up. My nails were finished, thank goodness. But Beryl wasn't finished with me.

Before I could escape, she gave me this fond but sad look. "Ah, look at you, baby girl. You're sixteen, seventeen soon. You can't spend your time fighting and training and running your daddy's gym for him."

"She can. She can do what she wants," called Sadie–May, sensibly, ignoring Beryl's glare.

I agreed. I didn't see why I couldn't carry on living my life how I wanted, but it's no use arguing with Beryl. So I grabbed the chocolate box that was still doing the rounds and handed it to Queenie. "Here you go. The last chocolate!"

As Queenie reached for it, Beryl's attention left me and homed in on her. "Hey, that's mine. Give it to me!"

Too late. Queenie nabbed it. "It's coffee! You don't like

coffee, so I might as well finish it. It would be unlucky not to!"

While they argued, I made my escape. Sabrina hadn't finished yet. Her nail design was complicated and trimmed with tiny diamonds. It would take another half an hour before she started yelling for me again.

"I'll wait for you in the street," I told her. "Then we'll go and look at those earrings you want."

I thought that outside I'd be able to relax and stop thinking about Gregory. But as soon as I stepped out into the busy, bustling street I stopped dead, as though I'd walked into an invisible force field.

Something was wrong.

I turned round slowly, spinning on my heel, taking in everything. The high street was lined with all the usual shops, Boots, WH Smith, Topshop, Costa Coffee, McDonald's. People were going in and out of them, hands full of bags, or walking along, talking on their phones. Not far away, a *Big Issue* seller was trying to attract customers. So far, so normal. But however normal and everyday it looked on the surface, I could feel danger lurking near by.

All my life I've loved the tingle that comes with knowing that something's about to happen. I live for the moments when the adrenaline surges through my veins, my eyes go as sharp as a wolf's, and my ears hear the quietest footfall – or on one occasion, the tiny *shhhting* of a knife being pulled. When I was little, I used to hunt out the older bullies in the school playground and taunt them. When I was older,

I deliberately walked home through streets where gangs of big boys lurked. I could fight them all.

And now? Now I sneak off and I fight in the "no rules" cage fights. The ones held in the back streets, where a door has to be knocked and you ask for Maltese Joey, but you never get to see him or meet him because he's clever enough to keep himself a mystery, even though he runs a string of clubs where fights have no time limit and no referee. Fighters go there hoping to win big money, while their supporters stand at the cage bars and shout and scream and bet on them. I'm getting to be known in those places. The name of "Gypsy Girl" is becoming famous. Me daddy would go crazy if he knew, but he doesn't. Only one person in the whole world knows what I do – Kimmy. And she would never give me away because she's my best friend and we're closer than sisters. It's a dangerous and thrilling game, and I can't stop.

That's why, as I stood in the street and looked around, I smiled to myself. I could feel the danger crackling like static in the air. Granny Kate was right. There was trouble ahead, and it was aimed straight at me. But until it showed up, I couldn't do anything to stop it. So, for now, I had to wait. I got meself a coffee from the Costa place and perched on the back of a bench.

I checked up and down the street again. To my left there were shoppers milling about, looking in windows, hurrying into shops. Nothing wrong there. Nor with the group of girls sitting on a bench across from me, swinging their legs and whispering to one another.

I looked the other way, towards the little clock tower that marked the centre of the street and – *zing* – straightaway I got an adrenaline buzz.

Three boys were hanging around the steps at the bottom of the tower, hoods pulled up, jeans so low they were nearly tripping over them. They were the sort of feral boys who made people walk in a big circle around them, rather than risk being sworn at, mocked or barged into for no reason. And they were glancing at me but trying not to let me notice. So that's what I'd felt. Most of us can tell when we're being watched. Some animal instinct that's beyond our eyes and ears takes over. They've done experiments, and it's true. But some people are more sensitive to it than others.

The danger was coming from them. No surprise there. I might've gone over to them there and then if a more amazing sight hadn't been coming down the high street. If the feral boys gave off signals of danger, then the boy strolling towards me was giving off signals of, "Look at me, aren't I wonderful?" You couldn't miss him, what with his looks and the fact he was hollering something to Sabrina's boyfriend, Tyson, who was hurrying into Hollisters. People turned to look at him, but he ignored them.

It was Rocky, and it was too late for me to try and get away.

5

What can I say about Rocky Quinn?

I reckon there's two sorts of bad boys. The ones like the feral boys who look like they'd mug a granny and knock her down without a worry. And there's the sort who'd make a girl fall in love with them and then let them down. Or, they'd be your best friend for a while, until they suddenly forgot all about you.

Rocky's the second kind. He's handsome, his eyes sparkle, his shiny hair is cut just right, his smile is cheeky. He looks like he'd get up to all sorts of bad things. He gazes at girls like he'd drag them off to his lair there and then, if the whole world wasn't watching him. But the whole world does look at him when he's out and about. He doesn't just stroll, he swaggers. He looks like he should be banging on his chest like King Kong. I checked the girls on the bench. Sure enough, they'd stopped playing with their phones and were watching Rocky now. He was wearing a tight T-shirt with very short sleeves to show off his arm muscles and abs. He's got muscles because he's a good boxer, like his brother, Tyson. Tyson's gone professional and he's a celebrity in Langton now, which is why there's lots of buzz about Sabrina's wedding and it has to be the best.

But Rocky's different. I grew up watching Rocky fight at me daddy's gym. He's got a rascally streak in him. In the past he's fought as well as Tyson, but he was never dedicated. Sometimes he'd win, but sometimes he'd just forget to turn up or not bother fighting properly if he did. He was like that with his training, some weeks he'd train from morning to night, and the next month lounge around eating junk. Then last year he stopped going to the gym altogether and stopped pretending to compete. He started getting into trouble, twocking cars and stupid stuff like that, even though his daddy makes loads of money and he could've had his own car. We thought he'd be going to the young offenders' prison, but somehow he got away with it. Don't ask me how, because the police don't usually let bad boys like him go. Them going easy on him didn't make him behave, because now he's always going off somewhere on his own, disappearing for a couple of days, saying he's got to meet someone in London. I think he's up to something again, although everyone else is blinded by him being so handsome.

But that's Rocky. He gets his own way with everyone – except for me. It's my mission in life to not give in to him, even though I used to dream about me and him being together.

When he saw me he whistled loudly and bounded over.

"Sammy-Jo! Here's my girl!"

He has plenty of girls after him the whole time, gorjer girls as well as Traveller ones, but everyone always says that me and him would be perfect together. He knows my rule – that I'll only go out with a boy who can beat me in a fight. He's the only one who's ever offered to have a fight against me. And I refused.

Because he's the only boy who might beat me.

"It's ages since I've seen you," he said, giving me one of his special brilliant white smiles. I think he gets his teeth whitened at the Smile Centre a bit further down the high street.

"It was at your sister's wedding a few months ago, that's all," I told him, staying on the back of the bench. "And I'm not your girl. You don't want me as your girl."

Beryl and Queenie could wish as much as they wanted, I knew the sort of women he liked, and it wasn't me.

His beaming smile never dimmed.

"You know what I mean, Sammy. It's just my way of greeting you."

"Well, don't. Now go away."

I stuck my foot out and pushed him away. He laughed, grabbed it and pulled. But he forgot it was me. I kicked and got myself free and tried to kick him again. It didn't put him off. He skipped out of the way and jumped up and sat on the bench next to me, resting his arm on his knee, just so I could notice the expensive watch around his wrist.

"What you doing out here on your own?" he said.

"Getting away from Beryl. She still thinks I should

marry you." I gave him a crafty look. "But then I'd find out what you do when you go off on your mysterious trips to London. I'd know your secrets."

He smirked. "What do you think I do?"

A couple of times when I'd come over to visit me sisters, I'd seen him sitting in a car with a woman, older than him, with spiky, blonde hair, dressed in a leather jacket and her arm flung along the back of the seat behind him. I never told anyone. I didn't want to get him into bother with his father. But she wasn't a Traveller woman, and she was too old for him. I reckoned Beryl or Queenie had seen her, too.

I shrugged. "Maybe you're secretly married to a rich older woman with a BMW who buys you expensive watches."

He threw his head back and laughed. "I knew you'd seen me. That's my probation officer. That's Miss Stroud." I didn't believe him one little bit. "And I don't need anyone to give me money. I've got my own."

He took my hand. I let him. "And talking about marriage," he said, turning it over and dabbing a finger at a long, thin bruise on the inside, just above my wrist. "Have you been fighting before the wedding? Nobody wants a bruised and battered bridesmaid…"

The bruise was courtesy of Maori Boy, and it was the only strike he managed to land. I should've been more careful. But Rocky wasn't finished with me yet. He let go of my hand, fixed me with a look and said, smugly, "Gypsy Girl."

If he'd smiled like that at any of the girls sitting on the bench, their knees would've gone weak. Mine didn't. I didn't even blink. My face never betrayed me at all. Gypsy Girl. He'd emphasized it. My secret fighter name. Coincidence? I hoped so. But he'd never said it before.

"Huh?" I said, keeping my face blank. "Why're you smirking? Why're you calling me that?"

He flicked a strand of hair back in place. "I heard someone talking about girl fighters, and they mentioned one who they all call Gypsy Girl. They said she was the best." He grinned. "So I thought of you."

"Well, you were wrong, as usual. Must be someone else. I don't fight in competitions any more. I've won everything I can for now." I flicked my hair back and smiled at him. "So, mind your own business … Gypsy Boy."

He laughed again. But neither of us said any more. He had secrets, I had secrets. I stole a quick glance at him. I used to imagine him kissing me, his rascally eyes looking into mine, his lips coming closer as he leaned towards me. I tried it again, but all that happened was his face was replaced by another, one with sun-bleached, fair hair that wasn't cut perfectly and amber eyes that drank in everything.

Gregory Langton's face. And I hadn't imagined it. He was actually here, hurrying down the high street. He was with Cooper, the dark-haired boy I'd seen him with earlier, and this time there were two girls as well. Gregory had his hands in his pockets, shoulders hunched, laughing at something one of them had said. He saw me straightaway, and his smile got broader. I gave him a wave, a tiny lift of my hand. He waved back, the smallest of movements.

"Who're you waving at?" asked Rocky, looking round. "Him? Langton?" He gave a tut. "He's a wuss."

"You know him?"

He held out his hands as though he was embracing the whole world. "I know everyone."

One of the girls, the one nearest to Gregory, had noticed his wave and turned to see who it was aimed at. She had super-shiny, fair hair that swung from side to side as she walked, a cutesy, flat face like a Persian kitten, a boring sundress, bare shoulders and flat ballet shoes. When she saw he'd waved at me, she said something to the other girl, who glanced back and laughed slyly. As if that bothered me.

Rocky was watching me as well, his handsome head tilted to one side, his annoying smile getting broader.

"Jeez, I'd love to know what you were thinking just then, Sammy-Jo," he murmured.

"It wasn't about you," I said, quickly.

He carried on looking at me. "So have you knocked any more girls out these days?"

I knew what he meant. It's why my father's glad there's no more under-eighteen competitions for me to take part in, because I've won them all. I'm too strong. But the knock-out didn't happen in a competition. It was in the street. A girl got hurt. I never meant it to happen, but it did. It was kept quiet, so I don't know how Rocky got to hear of it.

"It's none of your business what I do." I jumped off the bench. "So shut up."

Which made him laugh because he knew he'd rattled me.

I rounded on him, hands on me hips. "Haven't you got anything better to do except hang around here? You're the best man. You're supposed to be helping Tyson, not going on at me."

Luckily, there wasn't time for him to argue because we both saw his brother coming out of Hollisters with a carrier bag. I took hold of Rocky's arm and gave him a push towards Tyson.

"See! That's what happens when you're not watching him. You've got to get him out of here quickly. Sabrina's nearly finished. She'll be coming out any minute. Tyson mustn't see her!"

Rocky looked at me suspiciously. "Why? I thought it was only unlucky for them to see each other on the day of the wedding? We've got three days to go."

He was right, but I wasn't going to tell him that. I wanted to get rid of him, so I gave him another push. I could see the girls on the bench watching us. "It's only half as unlucky, but it's still bad enough! And she doesn't want him to see her new nails."

No one likes to risk bad luck, not even bad boys like Rocky. He gave me a cheeky salute. "Are you going to meet me later? People are talking about you, Sammy-Jo, and I want to know what it's all about."

I shooed him off. "No, I'll see you at the wedding."

He shrugged his shoulders, and, with only the quickest

glance at the girls on the bench, he hurried away to meet Tyson. I watched them walk down the high street, and wondered about Rocky calling me Gypsy Girl. Somehow he'd heard whispers about me, which was dangerous. I'd have to avoid him and his questions, but it was going to be difficult. I was chief bridesmaid, and he was the best man.

By the time they were out of sight, Sabrina still hadn't finished, so I decided to go and get her earrings. I knew what she wanted and which shop sold them. I started walking past the hooded, feral boys by the clock tower. I knew they were watching me. The feeling of danger had faded as I talked to Rocky, but now it came back and I got that fizz of adrenaline again. I ignored it and them and sailed past. I had better things to do than waste my energy on thugs like them.

Just off the high street there's a tangle of little streets called the Lanes. I headed there and found the jewellery shop where Sabrina had spotted her expensive wedding earrings. They were in the window: two sparkling cascades of crystals, like miniature chandeliers. I got my phone out, and I was texting Sabrina to meet me here when goosebumps broke out all over my arms and my skin began to tingle.

Something was going to happen.

Running feet pounded the pavement behind me. I spun round. One of the feral boys from the clock tower was running straight at me, his arms outstretched like battering rams, his hands in fists. He hit me hard in the chest, flinging me back against the shop window, his foot coming up and smacking into my ribs. My phone sailed out of my hands, and in one quick move he picked it up and disappeared down the alley at the side of the shop.

Three seconds and it was all over. I'd been phone-mugged.

Did he really think I was going to let him get away with it?

6

I was wrong. It wasn't a phone-mugging.

That was just to get me to run down the alley after the thief. As I chased him to the dead end at the bottom, I heard footsteps behind me. I glanced back. Blocking the entrance to the alley were his two mates, heads shaved, fists up, faces leering. They were older than me. They'd taken off their hoodies and were wearing tight black T-shirts that showed off their biceps. I'd had trouble with boys like this before, the ones who wore their shaven heads and black clothes like a hate uniform.

I made a quick check back to the phone-mugger. He was coming up the alley towards me, laughing. There were high walls on either side. They knew I was trapped, so their eyes were gloating. Three against one – the sort of odds they'd like.

I backed against one wall, so I could keep them all in my sight. I'd been stupid. I shouldn't have gone running down an alley full of empty cans and bottles wearing me high-heeled ankle boots. I can fight in heels, but it's not easy. I couldn't even kick them off, because there was broken glass everywhere.

"Wait," I said, holding my hands out, as though appealing to them. "You can keep the phone."

They liked that. Thugs always like to see fear in their victims' faces. They were stalking closer, as dangerous as bombs ready to go off. I could hear their excited breathing. Their faces were as pale as boiled potatoes. They saw my long, dark hair with the new highlights of copper, honey and toffee I'd had done for the wedding. They saw my little cut-off top that stopped a long way from the waist of my tight jeans, showing off my tanned belly. They saw my heels. Their faces were cruel and excited, their eyes going hot as they imagined what they could do to me.

They thought they knew what I was like, but they didn't.

"We don't want the phone," sniggered the phone-snatcher. He was the tallest, and the other two kept looking at him, so he must have been the leader. Maybe it was the haircuts, but they all looked similar, like they were brothers.

"What do you want, then?" I said as they surrounded me.

The leader spat on the ground, his eyes burning with hate. "We want you gone. Out of this town. Bitch."

"You don't even know me."

"You're one of the Travellers."

"So?"

"So you don't belong here."

"Says who?"

"Says us."

I got in a stance, one foot forward, one foot back,

balancing myself, moving from the wall, spinning round slowly, keeping them all in sight. I raised my clenched hands. They glanced at each other, grinning, and came at me, hands reaching, grabbing, snatching at my clothes and hair.

Bad move.

They were rubbish. They might have been able to bounce round on their toes and throw a few kicks, but they had no fight skills, except for a bit of basic tae kwon do. They'd probably had two or three lessons and decided they knew it all. A few seconds into their attack, I got a kick in that hit the leader in the face and knocked him back. He roared like an animal as he staggered and held his face.

"Bitch! Get her!"

The other two came at me, vicious as pit bulls. I danced back, keeping them at bay, waiting for my chance. One of them grabbed for my hair. And missed. *Bam bam*. I gave him a kick to his chin and another where it hurts most. He rolled into a screeching ball. No time for cheering because the second one was in my face, his hands clawing at me. *Bam*. He went down to my strikes as well, shaking his head. He tried to get back up, so I clapped him hard on both ears with cupped hands and he fell back, dizzy and deafened.

Now it was just me and the leader. Me bouncing on my toes, even in heels, and the leader swaying, snarling, his chin dribbling blood where I'd kicked him. He'd seen his two mates floored, and he'd lost it, all caution had gone. He just wanted to beat me up.

He came at me fast and tried a kick to my face. Wrong.

57

Fast as lightning, I grabbed his foot, yanked it up and twisted. It was all over in a split second. His feet left the ground, he yelped and went down hard on his back, knocking the wind out of him. He lay gasping, his eyes confused. This wasn't supposed to happen. I'd turned his little world upside down. He should've looked at my eyes before he decided to attack me. They're dark grey, and when I'm angry they go as cold as the North Sea.

I rested my spiky heel on his chest and felt in his pocket for my phone. Something moved at the extreme of my vision. More of them?

"Sammy-Jo!"

My heart still sank. Sabrina was standing at the top of the alley.

"What?"

"Come on!"

I kept my heel pressed down. "But these boys—"

"Leave them be! You know Daddy told you not to cause trouble for us."

True. He'd never let me fight outside the gym, even if it was for all the right reasons. He avoided using his own fists, even though he could beat most men he met. He would go crazy if he ever found out that I fought in places much more dangerous than this.

I looked down at the boy beneath my foot. "He told me to get out of town. I was showing him I didn't want to."

"Who cares what he thinks? I want to get me earrings!" said Sabrina.

I stepped back, and the boy scrambled to his feet, hatred on his face now.

"Hope you learned your lesson," I said. "Don't ever attack a girl again."

"You wish." He spat out a bubble of blood. "Later."

"If you like." I dusted the grime of the alley from my jeans. "I won't forget your face."

The other two were trying to get to their feet, holding their jaws, gasping for breath. I pocketed my phone, turned my back on them and walked away.

7

Gypsy's Acre should've been quiet and peaceful, but it wasn't.

The noise from International Express floated through the trees – truck engines idling, the whine of the forklift, the banging and clanging of lorries being loaded, even though it was now night. Over the top of that I could hear the faint sound of country-and-western songs coming from the Mitsubishi Warrior parked by the gate, where me daddy was sitting and thinking.

Granny Kate was in her trailer doing something with the blackberries to turn them into her special wine. Me and Sabrina were in our trailer. It was small but neat, with comfy cushioned seats at one end, next to the little kitchen, and a tiny bedroom with twin beds at the other end. At least that was how it usually looked. Now it had been taken over by dresses. The bridesmaids' dresses were hanging in a line above the seats, so that ever time we sat down we were suffocated by net underskirts. And the wedding dress was hanging between our beds, taking up all the space. I had to fight through layers of net to see Sabrina asleep in her bed, wrapped in her Disney Princess quilt cover that she'd had since she was little. I wished I could fall asleep so easily. I lay back on my bed, but I couldn't relax. I kept going over the fight with the feral boys who'd jumped me. They didn't know me, but they wanted me to leave their town. And Mr McCloud was the same.

Earlier, I'd gone over to the hedgerows near International Express to check on the wild roses for Sabrina's bouquet. The place was busy – a lorry was being loaded – but there were no mistakes by the forklift driver this time and no split sacks lying on the ground. The silver Range Rover was parked in front of one of the buildings, which meant McCloud was around somewhere. The red, boy-racer Subaru with the HUD18 number plates was next to it. I wondered who it belonged to, because I bet none of the lorry drivers or packers could afford that kind of car.

I didn't get to find out because the ponytailed man had noticed me. Straightaway he called out to someone in one of the offices, McCloud probably. He must've answered because the man nodded and came swaggering menacingly over to the fence. I waited until he got close and then walked off. As if I'd want to hang around near their stupid property.

Not him nor anyone else would guess it from my face, but McCloud and the feral boys had disturbed me. Even lying on my bed, far away from International Express, I couldn't stop thinking about them. I don't like people hating us – we've never done anything except live a bit differently to most, that's all. Jeez, as if that's a crime. So I was glad when my phone beeped. It was a text from Kimmy. *Bored. There's a fight tonight. Big money. Let's go to it. Pleeeeeeeeeeeease. x*

Kimmy's the sister I should've had, but instead I got Sabrina. Kimmy's my soulmate, the kind who you can look at in a certain way, without saying a word, and they'll know exactly what you're thinking. She isn't a Gypsy girl, but we've been training and fighting together since we were both four years old. She's small and fair-haired, with freckles all over her face, like she's been splattered with fawn paint drops. Her skills are in Muay Thai and tae kwon do, but she can't fight in Maltese Joey's fights because there's not enough women fighters her weight and size. She doesn't have my strength. It doesn't matter too much what size my opponents are. I can fight boys who are heavy and taller than me, no problem. When we go off into the back streets, she's always there with me, watching my back, collecting my prize money, making sure we don't get ripped off.

I messaged her back straightaway. *No. I told you. No more before the wedding.*

This was the sensible thing to do, but I still couldn't relax. I tried to banish McCloud and the boys from my mind and turned over, so my back was to Sabrina. But that meant I was looking out of the little window right next to my bed. And in the distance across the fields I could see the lit windows of Langton House. I found myself wondering which one was Gregory's room.

And why did that bother me?

In the end I got up and pulled on my cheetah-print Lycra

fight shorts, my tight, matching crop top, and a hoodie over the top. I shoved my fingerless padded gloves in the pockets. I rang Kimmy.

"OK. Come and get me."

She gave a yelp of delight. "Yes! On my way!"

Most people will never see the places where I'm called Gypsy Girl. They're tucked away among dark streets, hidden from sight, staying open all through the night. If people wanted to find me, they'd have to knock at a door on a deserted estate, or ring the bell of a gym on the outskirts of a town somewhere. Maltese Joey has lots of clubs in different places.

They'd have to squeeze in through the crowd of fighters, their trainers and their supporters, some with girlfriends hanging on their arms. They'd place their bets and head for the cage in the middle, where lights blaze down, and wait to hear the loudspeakers hollering my name.

Then they'd learn about my secret.

Usually I worried that my father would find out about the fights. But that night all I could think about was Gregory Langton. If he knew that I fought like this, he'd be so shocked he'd never want to see my face again. He'd be wishing we'd leave town as well.

Those thoughts didn't stop me beating my opponent, an eighteen-year-old Irish boy with as many freckles as Kimmy and no technique at all. No wonder he ended up fighting in these places. Kimmy held up my hand as the crowd roared, and then she counted out my winnings as

I nursed my aching ribs. She got her split. I pocketed the rest. The wedding was costing more and more, but me daddy would never know. I'd made sure he let me take care of the bills.

Two hours later, I crept back through the trailers, the grass soaking wet with dew. I was exhausted, but I didn't mind. No one was about, just a lone fox sniffing around the place and giving me a sly look before heading off across the fields. And two magpies sitting on top of one of the trailers. Two for mirth, according to Granny Kate. Except there was no mirth about Sabrina today. As I tiptoed into our trailer, she was already awake, cross-legged on her bed, wrapped in the princess quilt and stressing out about something.

"Where have you been?" she said.

"I got up early to go running," I lied. I shook my damp hair. "Look at me, I'm covered in dew."

She wasn't interested. She was holding one of her wedding brochures, screwing it up in her hands. "That stupid manageress woman! She never told me, and now the marquee's all wrong!" A tear ran down her cheek. "She said the white satin roof drapes were the best. But I've seen something much better. I can't believe she never showed them to us."

We were holding the reception at the best hotel in Langton, the White Swan. There were too many guests coming to fit into their function room, so we were having a huge marquee on the lawn.

"Stop crying and show me."

She held out a brochure. "Look! They do starlight roof

drapes. We should've had those. Ivory and gold silk with lights, Sammy-Jo! Little twinkling lights, like stars." Her eyes went diamond shaped, and she gave a shuddering breath. "Imagine me and Tyson doing our first dance and little stars twinkling above us!"

She looked at me, pleadingly.

I looked at the brochure. They were in the deluxe section. Maybe the manageress didn't show them to Sabrina because they were so expensive. As if that would mean anything to my sister. "OK. I'll sort it. Just shut up and get dressed."

By the time we were ready, my father was outside enjoying the sunshine and shaving at the same time, the mirror balanced on the bonnet of his Mitsubishi, his face covered in foam.

"We're off to the White Swan. More changes," I shouted to him as Sabrina hurried me along. We were dressed for the summer weather, Sabrina in short shorts and me in pedal pushers – to cover any bruises – and a tiny gingham shirt tied in a knot at my waist.

He looked up. "Behave," he said, but only to me.

"As if I've got the chance to do anything else!" I said. "Sabrina's wearing me out."

"Just keep her calm." He glanced nervously at her as she backed the car over the grass towards us at speed. "Don't set her off."

I'm the youngest in the family, but you'd never know it. Sabrina was always our mother's favourite, her baby girl. She suffered the most when our mother died. Planning this big, fat wedding was the one thing that kept her going. She's been mad about Tyson since she was little, and she's always been dying to marry him. That's why I wanted to make her wedding the best ever.

And to shut her up, of course.

8

Thursday morning. *Only two more days to go,* I told myself, as I trailed round after Sabrina and the manageress.

The White Swan is in the centre of town, but at the back it has a lawn as big as a park. Our marquee was already set up in the middle of it. Sabrina was spending ages discussing the roof drapes. Even the manageress looked like she wanted to make a run for it. And when my phone rang I found out it wasn't just us being driven mad by the wedding.

"Hey, gorgeous," said Rocky. "Big panic. Alert BBC news. Tyson's lost the receipt for his suit."

"He hasn't. We've got it here. It's in Sabrina's car. What's he want it for?"

"He needs it. He's changed his mind again, and wants a different one. He's driving me insane."

"Join the club. You'll have to come and get it. Sabrina's changed her mind about the drapes for the marquee, so we're at the hotel."

"Jesus. Can't me and you just run away together and leave them all to it?"

"Tempting."

He sighed. "Wait there. I'll come and get it."

By the time I got off the phone, Sabrina and the manageress had agreed that twinkling lights and ivory and gold silk would look much classier than plain white.

"We'll go back to my office, and I'll ring the hire company up and get it changed for you," the manageress said.

Her office was at the front of the hotel, overlooking the road. She checked the price of the starlight drapes. "It's quite expensive, plus the fitting costs," she said, looking at me.

"How much all together?"

She told me. I swallowed. "That's fine." I got out my winnings, a big, fat roll of notes, and handed over the cash.

"Shall I give a receipt to your father?"

"No. To me," I said, quickly. "I'm dealing with the money."

She began going through the arrangements for Saturday, but I'd stopped listening. I don't believe in coincidences, but one was happening in the window right behind her head.

One of the feral boys, the leader, was looking in at us, his hands cupped round his face, his nose touching the glass. When he'd said "later", I'd thought he was saving face, but it seemed not. Soon as he saw me looking, he gave me the finger.

Sabrina glanced up and noticed him as well. "Jeez, look at that ugly mug!"

The manageress turned round. "Damn." She banged on the window and shouted, "Clear off!"

He gave her the finger as well and called us a few names through the glass before strutting away.

Sabrina grabbed my arm. "That's the boy you were fighting yesterday."

"I know."

"Why's he here?"

That's what I wanted to know. The whole town to roam in, and suddenly he's outside the hotel at the same time we're inside. Maybe Sabrina shouldn't have said out loud that she recognized him, because the manageress was staring at us in horror.

"I hope you're joking about fighting," she said. "That's Milo Scarret. He's always hanging round the town centre with his two brothers, looking for trouble. If I were you, I'd keep away from them." She lowered her voice. "Their father's in prison for murder. It was all over the papers."

"What did he do?" said Sabrina, who liked all the bloodthirsty TV programmes, like *Criminal Minds* and *CSI*.

"Hate crime. Attacked a foreign student."

Seemed he'd passed the hate on to his sons. I rubbed my arms – they were covered in goosebumps. Danger was back again. I squeezed past the desk and looked out of the window. So his name was Milo Scarret. He was strutting down the road with the other two. I was right about them being brothers. They must've followed us, but from where? We'd arrived in Sabrina's car.

"Have they gone?" said the manageress.

"Yeah."

But they hadn't. As I watched, all three of them turned off the street and into the entrance to the hotel's car park at the side.

"My sister will go through everything with you," I said, quickly, pushing Sabrina into a chair and backing towards the door. "I've got to get something for Rocky from our car."

And I wanted to see what Milo and his brothers were up to. I had visions of them slashing our tyres, or running a key along the paintwork and spraying "bitch" all over it. I was out of there before Sabrina could moan and heading towards a door that looked like it might lead to the car park.

I didn't reach it. All thoughts of protecting our car flew out of my head because coming towards me was Gregory Langton. My heart – which hadn't speeded up when facing Milo's threats – began thumping.

He'd seen me.

He was smiling at me.

He was going sweetly pink in the cheeks.

He was doing his golden-eyed stare.

I stopped dead in his path. I didn't get it. What was fate up to? Why make two people, me and him, so different and then decide to throw them together again? He came to a halt. We were inches away from each other. He was wearing a black T-shirt and trousers, with a black apron tied around his waist. His hair was moussed back to make it less unruly.

I gave a pretend sigh. "Are you stalking me?"

He laughed. "You wish. Where're you heading?"

"Outside. Me sister's driving me mad. I have to get away." I wasn't going to tell him about Milo. That wasn't his world at all.

"This way's quicker." He beckoned for me to follow him, then rushed forward and held a door marked STAFF ONLY open for me.

"I thought I might see you around," he said as we cut through a storeroom. "Everyone's talking about the big wedding on Saturday, and I realized it was your sister's."

He opened another door, and this one led us straight out to a car park crowded with cars and delivery lorries. We both stopped and faced each other. The sun was blazing down. I shaded my eyes.

"I didn't know you worked here."

"In the holidays. Me and Cooper – you know, the mate you saw me with yesterday." He meant the dark-haired one who fancied himself. "It's just while we're at college." He pointed over to the marquee in the middle of the lawn. "I'll be waiting on you at the wedding reception."

I liked the sound of that. "So I can order you to get me drink and food, like I'm a princess's sister at a royal wedding?"

He grinned. "I suppose."

He was shading his eyes, too, and gazing at me, like he was trying to figure me out. Maybe I should've walked off and played it cool. I didn't. I decided to forget about Milo for now. I wanted to make the moment last. I liked talking to Gregory. I liked the way he was running his fingers through his hair with his hand, messing it up again. I liked the way he scuffed his feet about because he wasn't sure what to say.

"So what're you doing now?" he said, eventually.

"I've got to get something from our car. Sabrina and Tyson keep altering their wedding plans," I said. "Are you on your break?"

I don't know what I was hoping. That we'd go and get a coffee and sit on the back of a bench like we were two normal people?

He pulled a sorry face. "No. I'm on kitchen duty today. I'm the dish pig."

"Huh, what's that?"

"It's my job. Washing dishes. Scrubbing the grills." He held out his hands. They looked red raw. I don't know why I did it, but I took hold of one of them, pretending to examine it.

"You need some of me granny's homemade balm."

"Ouch. Yes, please. Is it some wise old herbal remedy?"

I pasted an innocent look onto my face. "Yep. She makes it from boiled roadkill hedgehogs."

That made him laugh. "You are kidding, right?"

"What do you think?"

From behind him came the sound of something smashing and then a man's voice swearing and cursing. Gregory's grin faded. "Oops. That's our chef. He'll start shouting if he sees I'm not there. Worse luck."

I let go of his hand – which I still seemed to be holding – and stepped back.

"Ah. Right. OK."

My brain is always teeming with thoughts, but now I couldn't think of a single interesting thing to say. He broke the silence.

"So. See you around." He would've walked away, but something caught his eye in the car park. "Oh God, not him."

I followed his gaze. It was Milo, alone, leaning on a delivery van and watching us. All of a sudden my arms were covered in goosebumps again, my skin was tingling and my hair was rising from my neck and doing its wolf-hackles trick. I'd forgotten about the danger while talking to Gregory. Now it was back. Milo must've been there all the time, and I hadn't noticed. I was getting careless.

"You know him?" I asked.

"Everyone does. But I've never spoken to him. And I don't want to. He's a dick."

"Yeah."

He looked surprised. "You know him?"

I shrugged. "Just heard about him." I wasn't going to tell him about the fight. Now it was my turn to back away. "I better go. Before Sabrina finds something else to change about her wedding."

He nodded, but he looked worried. "Where's your car?"

"The far corner."

"Keep away from Milo. Ignore him if he says anything."

"I will. Boys like him don't bother me."

More shouting issued from the kitchen, along with

someone hollering Gregory's name. He glanced round. "Oops, sounds like I'm in trouble. Gotta go."

He gave a wave and a last glance and hurried towards a half-open door further away, where the clattering of pots and pans and the ranting of the chef floated out on a cloud of steam. I watched him go – I couldn't help myself – until he got swallowed up by the kitchen. When I turned back to the car park, Milo had disappeared into the maze of cars and delivery lorries. I wound my way through them and found him at the back, leaning on Sabrina's car, his hands stuffed in his hoodie pockets.

I walked over to him, checking his brothers weren't creeping up behind me. "Why are you following me?" I asked, making sure I was balanced and ready for him.

He really wanted to fight me: his feral face was sneering, his eyes hot with the need for violence. But he stayed where he was, and I knew why. Yesterday had shaken his little world. Girls should be easy to beat. They were weaker. They weren't meant to fight back. And win.

He looked me up and down. "Unfinished business."

"Really? You'd dare try and touch me again?"

"I wouldn't dirty my hands on you."

I did the same to him – looked him up and down, at his grubby jeans, his sweaty T-shirt. "Look who's talking."

His lip curled, showing his gappy, dingy teeth. "I don't need to touch you." He pulled his hand out of his pocket, and for a brief second I saw a glint of something metal. I caught my breath. Was it a knife, or was he just trying to

74

scare me? Knives changed everything.

I held my own hands out, showing him they were empty, showing him I wasn't going to do anything. "Look, I don't know you. You don't know me. So why not just go away and leave us alone? We're not doing you any harm."

He stared at me. "Don't care. I hate ya."

There was a yell of "Milo, quick!" and then footsteps approached rapidly through the crowded cars. It was one of his brothers, hyped and excited about something. He went over to Milo. "Leave the slag. We've got something better."

"What?"

He mumbled something. Whatever it was, it fired Milo up. He stopped leaning on our car. His pasty face split into a leering grin. "See you around, bitch."

He walked off after his brother, threading between a couple of lorries. I didn't get it. Boys like them didn't normally give up so easily. Maybe they were heading for the marquee, to destroy it in some way.

"Go anywhere near our marquee and you'll regret it," I shouted.

The brother ignored me, but Milo turned round. "Wouldn't dream of it." He grinned and gave me the finger again. "More interested in your boyfriend."

I thought he meant he'd seen me with Rocky yesterday, in the high street. I even laughed. "Seriously, you're going to get Rocky? He'll flatten you."

But he'd gone, bouncing on his toes like a fighter before a fight. Good riddance to bad rubbish, as my mother used to say. He was bluffing, talking big to save face. Even with a knife he wouldn't dare do anything to Rocky. It didn't sink in until I'd opened the car and was scrabbling about, looking for the receipt.

He didn't mean Rocky.

My arms goosebumped as the danger came back. I ran back through the cars. The kitchen door was still open. I looked round wildly, hoping to see his fair hair over by the sink as he scrubbed pots. Everything was hectic in there, chefs were pushing past me, shouting, "Hot! Mind your back!", pans clattered, waves of heat hit me, but I couldn't see him anywhere. I grabbed one of the chefs as he hurried by.

"Where's Gregory?"

He glared at me. "Oi, you're not supposed to be in here."

"Never mind. Where is he?"

He took one look at my furious face and said, "I don't know. He was looking out the window and suddenly he shot outside. He said he wouldn't be a sec. He wanted to check on someone."

On me? Had he seen me from the window walking over to Milo? No, no, no, please not that. I pushed past the chef and ran. I should've known it wasn't over. Scumbags like Milo never just walked off. Something bad was going to happen.

I slammed through the door and ran back to the car park, weaving my way through the lorries and vans jammed in between the cars. Something yowled to my left. Big wheelie bins were lined up along one wall, and a cat was standing on the furthest bin with its back arched, its fur sticking out like it had got a fright. It was staring at something I couldn't see because it was hidden behind two big delivery lorries. My heart began to thump.

"Hey, Gregory – where are you?" I called.

No answer.

I sped past the first lorry, checking every shadow. I still couldn't see anything. But I heard something, a faint groan from behind a lorry, and a burst of footsteps, fleeing. I ran. The car park ended in a head-high wall with a street on the other side. I saw a blur as Milo and his brothers disappeared over the top of it.

But I didn't care about them. I didn't care about anything except the huddled figure lying too still on the tarmac. And, next to him, the little puddle of crimson blood that was spreading out, inch by inch.

9

I ran to Gregory. I couldn't take my eyes from the blood.

Milo's knifed him! That's what it looked like.

I fell to my knees beside him. He was curled on his side, his legs drawn up, his hands hugging his ribs. His face was splattered with blood. His shirt was ripped and flapping in the breeze blowing through the car park.

I leaned over him, dreading to see a knife wound. "Hey, Gregory?"

I could smell the metallic tang of his blood. For a moment, he didn't move. And then suddenly he was coughing, spraying red droplets into the air as he pushed himself over onto his back, the breath hissing through his teeth.

He was alive, at least. I put my hands on his shoulders, but he thought I was one of the bad boys and tried to push me away. I had to grab his hands and make him lay back.

Straightaway there was a click from above us. "Aw, did your boyfriend get hurt?"

Milo was perched on the wall like a monkey, phone in his hand, taking photos.

"Why did you do this?" I shouted, my voice breaking.

He laughed. "To teach you a lesson. Next time it'll be your sister – if you don't leave town."

He gave me the finger again and disappeared over the wall, like a rat. I would've loved to follow him. My blood was boiling. But it could wait. I had to see to Gregory.

"It's Sammy-Jo. Just lay still. Let me check you over."

His eyes flicked open. He squinted at me, and then he relaxed back onto the tarmac. I pulled his shirt back, fumbling with the buttons. One was stuck. I ripped it away. He was skinny, his bones showing under pale skin that looked as new and tender as a baby's. I almost fainted with relief when I saw his ribs.

He hadn't been stabbed.

There was no wound, but he was a mess. There were bruises, already going purple and black, down both sides of his ribs. Milo and his brothers must have taken turns to kick him as he lay sprawled on the ground. A pain shot through my heart as I imagined Gregory trying to curl himself up as the blows rained down.

The cat miaowed and came rubbing round my feet, but I had to push it away, and it paddled off through the blood, shaking its feet. The puddle of crimson blood was coming from a gash in Gregory's head. It ran straight across his eyebrow and over to his temple. It would need stitches. I'd been trained to do the first aid at the gym because fighters are always getting cuts, especially on their eyebrows, where the skin is thin and hard bone lies just beneath. But this was the worst I'd seen. It hadn't been caused by a punch.

The cowards had jumped him from behind as he came looking for me. He'd fallen forwards and smashed his head against the kerb. I scrabbled in my pocket and found a paper napkin. I pushed his blood-soaked hair back, then folded the paper napkin and put it over the wound. Immediately it was patterned with crimson.

"Can you hold it there?" I asked him.

"Uh-huh. What happened?" He put his hand up. The knuckles were split and scuffed. He managed to push himself up.

"Never mind for now. Don't move. Lay still. You might have broken ribs. Does it hurt when you breathe?" I pushed him gently back down again, and he flopped back onto the ground. "I'm going to ring for an ambulance."

"No. I'm OK." He had a small cut on his lip, but it wasn't bleeding too badly. He'd bitten it when he fell.

"You're not OK."

But he was determined to sit up, and I really didn't think that was a good idea, so I got hold of him even more firmly and insisted he lay back, even though he tried to struggle.

"Oi! Stop!"

There were hurrying footsteps behind me, and a man grabbed me around the waist and hoisted me up off my feet and dragged me away from Gregory. I smacked my fist on his clasped hands, and when he swore and let go I whirled round, my own fists coming up. It was the chef from the kitchen.

"Get away from him," he shouted as I tried to head back

to Gregory. "I've called 999. The police'll be here as well as the ambulance."

"No, you don't understand," I said. "I'm trying to help him. He's been beaten up."

"I saw you. Didn't look like you were helping him to me."

Someone else was running towards us, one of the waitresses, her eyes wide with fear. "I've stopped a patrol car. An officer's coming!"

The policeman was right behind her. He barged straight by us and knelt down beside Gregory. "Just stay still, lad. Help's on its way. Whoa! Stay lying down," he said as Gregory tried to sit up again. "We don't know what damage you've got yet."

"It's his head, and maybe his ribs," I said, trying to get back to Gregory's side, but the policeman shoved me away.

"Someone keep her back!" he ordered.

I think the chef was pleased about that. Straightaway he came up behind me and grabbed my arms again, his fingers digging into my skin. I could've broken his hold in seconds, but I stopped myself. They already thought I'd got something to do with Gregory's attack. I wasn't going to show them how strong I was. So I watched as the policeman checked Gregory. His head had started to bleed again, and he was looking confused and trying to hold the napkin on to it, even though it was soaked in blood. The policeman came to the same conclusion as me. Gregory was going to live. No stab wounds.

His radio started squawking, and he began relaying Gregory's injuries. "Bruising, head wound, trauma. Not life-threatening." He patted Gregory's shoulder. "You're not too bad. But we've got paramedics coming for you."

I tried to move closer. "I know who did it. It was—" I began, but the chef dragged me back.

"You heard the policeman," he hissed in my ear. "Stay away from him or you're going to be in even more trouble."

I wanted to kick my foot back at his shin and drag my heel down it. That would have made him let me go.

"Don't you listen?" I said. "I was helping him, that's all!"

The policeman looked up. "Save it for later. For now, just keep out of the way." He was trying to keep Gregory still.

"I don't need an ambulance," he was insisting. He'd got himself up onto his elbow, and he was looking at me.

I forced a smile. "It's OK. You've got to get checked out," I told him. "You hit your head." I wanted to crouch by him and hold his hand, but I couldn't.

There was a crowd gathering at the entrance to the car park, both customers and staff. They kept creeping nearer, trying to find out what was happening. Until they heard the sirens. The ambulance must've been near by because it had taken only a few minutes for it to make its way here. The crowd moved back as its flashing blue lights reflected in the windows of the hotel and it came slowly towards us, manoeuvring between the lorries and the wheelie bins.

A couple of paramedics jumped out and rushed over to Gregory. They started by asking him if he knew what day it was and his name. They held a wad of bandage to his head wound and checked out his ribs, before trying to move him. Now that help was here and he could see that Gregory wasn't stabbed or bleeding to death, the policeman turned his attention to me. He signalled for the chef to let go of me. But only so that he could grab hold of my arm and pull me to one side.

"OK. Tell me what happened?"

"It was a boy called Milo Scarret. I had an argument with him yesterday. He followed me here today."

He frowned. "So if he was after you, why did he beat up this lad?"

Why couldn't he understand? "To get at me. To make me and my family move. He was too scared to fight me again."

I could tell by his face that he didn't believe me. No way would he think that Milo was scared of a girl. But I didn't care right now. I couldn't stop watching the paramedics as they checked Gregory over.

"So you know Gregory? He's a friend?"

"No. Yes." *He'd come out to check if I was OK. He'd done that, and now look at him.*

"Make up your mind."

"No, he's not a friend, not really."

The policeman was getting fed up. "So why would Milo Scarret think hitting Gregory Langton would make you leave town?"

I shrugged. How could I explain that he must've seen me

holding Gregory's hand, that he thought we were together, but we weren't and never would be? "Maybe you should be rounding up Milo and asking him."

That got me a blank stare. I'd annoyed him. "We don't need you telling us what to do." His radio squawked. "Shut up and stay still while I get this, or you'll be in trouble."

He turned away from me and began talking into his radio. I stayed where I was. The crowd had grown bigger. Two waitresses about my age, in black and white uniforms, were creeping forwards, trying to see what was going on, their eyes wide.

"Aw no! It's Gregory!" I heard one of them say. "Does Alice know?"

"Someone tell her. She's in the bar. No, wait! Here she is! Oh, poor Alice."

The girl with the fair, shiny hair and the kitten face came running towards us, pushing through the watchers.

"Alice! Quick. It's Gregory!" they shouted.

She was frowning. "What's happened?"

When she saw him and the pool of blood, her hand went to her mouth. She ran up to the paramedics, her blonde hair swinging from side to side. "Oh my God. Let me speak to him."

They ignored her. The policeman put his free hand out to stop her. "Hold on, miss. Let them do their job."

She saw me and frowned, probably trying to remember where she'd seen me before. "Do you know what happened?"

I didn't have time to answer her. She saw the policeman's

hand around my arm and her mouth dropped open. I could read her mind. She thought I was being arrested. Her perfect face crinkled up. Her eyes narrowed, her voice became all trembly. "You know something about this. What did you do to him?"

Stupid girl. I wanted to shout at her, tell her I would never attack anyone. But I didn't. "Nothing. I was helping him."

She came closer, her eyes going sparkly as well as narrow. "Helping him! You—"

But the policeman pushed her away. "Please, stand back. We'll find out all the facts soon."

One of the waitresses was tugging on her arm. "He's right, Alice, get away from her!" she whispered, in a voice loud enough for me and everyone else to hear. "It's her. Cooper told us about her."

"Does it matter who I am?" I said, glaring from one to the other. "Gregory's hurt. Shouldn't you be worrying about that?"

That shut them up. Alice gave me one last glittery look and hurried over to the paramedics, who were helping Gregory into the back of the ambulance.

"Can I go with him," she pleaded. "I'm his girlfriend!"

His girlfriend? My heart missed a beat. Miss Kitten Face, with the delicate ballet shoes and the perfect, shiny blonde hair, was his girlfriend. I watched as she climbed into the ambulance with him. And I listened to the whispers starting up close by. It seemed as though all the teenagers in town

85

had jobs at the hotel. I recognized Gregory's dark-haired friend, Cooper. He was standing with one of the waitresses.

"That's her. The girl from Gypsy's Acre!" he hissed. "What's she got to do with it?"

"Chef says she attacked him!"

"What? Like a mugging? No way. Her sister's wedding's costing a fortune. They don't need to mug people."

"Not a mugging. She just attacked him."

Another girl joined in. "I love her look."

"What? Slutty tart?" *Thanks, Cooper.*

"Shut up. She can hear. She says Milo did it."

"He's a dick, but why would he attack Greg?"

"I don't know. Why would she attack him?"

"She was giving him these looks yesterday..." Cooper again. "Maybe they got it together, and then he dumped her..."

"No. He wouldn't do that to Alice."

"You didn't see them together, the way she was looking—"

I swung round as best as I could with the policeman still holding me. Soon as they saw me looking, they shut up. It didn't sound like any of them were on my side, but I wasn't going to explain to them. Let them think the worst of me. I knew the truth. If I hadn't searched for him, Gregory would've lain there for longer and the crimson pool that still glistened on the tarmac would be bigger.

But he'd only been attacked because he'd come out to check on me.

86

A moment later, the whispering started up again, but that was because Rocky was pushing his way through, shouting, "What's going on? Someone said there'd been a fight."

Rocky is like me, he gets pulled towards danger. Most of the whisperers would know him. He'd probably been at school with some of them. And once you met Rocky, you never forgot him.

No one answered. Everyone looked at me.

"Gregory Langton got beat up," I said.

"Langton? Why would anyone fight with him?" asked Rocky as the doors closed and the ambulance eased its way out of the car park, taking Gregory and Alice off to the hospital.

I shrugged. "I found him. They think I did it, but it was Milo Scarret." I watched the ambulance disappear down the street. "Him and his brothers attacked me yesterday."

The policeman heard this. He raised his eyebrows. "You don't look like someone who's been attacked."

"I beat them," I said.

Rocky groaned and made faces at me, trying to get me to shut the hell up. People didn't understand about the Smith strength. The policeman definitely didn't. "You're saying you fought the three Scarret brothers? On your own?"

I looked him straight in the eyes, my chin up. I let him see I was telling the truth. "Yes. I had to defend myself. No one else was there to help me. The next time I saw them was this morning."

I told him everything, how Milo had pulled faces at us

through the hotel window, and how I'd seen him and his brothers go into the staff car park.

"Hmmm." The policeman didn't look totally convinced. "You're the family stopping on Langton's land, aren't you?"

"What's that got to do with it?" I asked.

Before he could answer, a voice shrieked, "Leave her alone!" It was Sabrina, blazing towards us. "She never did anything! Let her go."

She was in full princess mode, long, dark hair billowing, high heels tapping, her eyes blazing. She glared at the whispering waitresses as she pushed her way through them. "I can hear you! I can hear what you're saying about me sister! You should be ashamed of yourselves."

They backed away from her and looked helplessly at the manageress, who was hurrying along behind Sabrina.

"Go!" the woman told them. "Get back to work." She bustled forward. "Now, what's going on out here? What's happened to Gregory?"

I expect she was hoping that her bride's chief bridesmaid wasn't about to get arrested before the big wedding on Saturday, especially as I was the one who paid all the bills. The chef, who was still hanging around enjoying himself, told her all that had happened, and in the end the policeman let go of me and put his notebook away. I rubbed the finger marks on my arm.

"So I'm not a suspect?"

He cleared his throat. "For now, no. I'll go and talk to Gregory, hear his side of the story. But I might have to ask you some more questions. So go home and stay out of trouble."

"But what about Milo—"

Sabrina pushed me and gave me a warning look. "Sammy-Jo, leave it." For once she was taking control. She turned on the policeman, who took a hasty step back, away from her. "You better secure the crime scene." She poked him in the chest. "And get forensics onto this. Sammy-Jo never did nothing." Then she spun round to me. "Wait here. I'll go and get the car."

She stomped off through the thinning crowd, as everyone slowly drifted back into the hotel. In the end there was just me, Rocky and the policeman, who was waiting for support officers to arrive.

"So tell me all," said Rocky, quietly. "How come you were with Gregory Langton?"

I shrugged. "He works at the hotel."

He didn't look convinced.

"I didn't know he worked here," I insisted. "I'm not guilty."

"Never thought you were." He grinned. "You'd never beat anyone up. But I think you're guilty of something. I told you. I hear rumours."

"Right back at ya. I hear them about you."

He shook his head. "No, don't try to deflect me. You've got secrets, Sammy-Jo. You're up to something. Something dangerous. Something that gives you the name Gypsy Girl."

"I told you. It's not me. It must be someone else."

He gave me this long look. "I don't think so."

Luckily I was saved by Sabrina. There was a loud revving of an engine, and her car shot round the back of the lorry and screeched to a halt in front of us. Sabrina's idea of slowing down is to jam her foot on the brake as hard as she can. I threw myself gratefully into the passenger seat.

Rocky stood back, still watching me. "I'll find out if it kills me," he said.

"Don't bother."

Before I could shut the door, Sabrina leaned over me. "What're you doing here anyway, Rocky?"

"He wants a receipt, that's all." I rummaged about in the glove compartment. "Here it is."

I handed it to Rocky and slammed the door without another word to him, and sank back in my seat.

"Thanks for coming to the rescue," I said as we set off.

But she was back on planet Sabrina. She was glancing at her reflection in the rearview mirror as she drove. I could tell she was worrying about something.

"What's up?"

"My eyelashes aren't long enough. I need extensions."

"No, you don't."

"Yes, I do. I can't believe you'd let me go to me own wedding with short eyelashes."

It wasn't true. All the Smith sisters have got long eyelashes, but that wasn't good enough for Sabrina. She couldn't get married without them being super-long and studded with tiny little diamonds to make them glitter.

So back we went to the Paradise Beauty Bar. She had her eyelashes fitted, and I sat and fretted.

This was all my fault.

10

"Kings, that's what they were! Kings of the Gypsies."

Granny Kate's eyes were sparkling.

"More kingly than royal kings. In fact, royal kings were nothing compared to them – they only sat on a throne. Any old fool can do that. But the kings of the Smiths, our Samsons, they could've lifted the throne above their heads and thrown it across the palace!"

She paused from stirring the blackberry wine and leaned on the counter, looking into the distance, remembering far back in time. It was late afternoon, and we were in her trailer, listening to the history of the Smith fighters.

"The first of them all was old Samson Absalom Smith, three hundred years ago. He had the blackest hair and pearly skin, like a Greek statue. They called him Samson because he was so strong. Remember in the Bible – that strong fella who pulled down the temple, until Delilah cut his hair off? Well, our Samson was just as strong as that, and had hair to match. He wouldn't have put up with that Delilah, though. He wouldn't have cut his hair and been tricked. The Smiths were wily, even back then."

Granny Kate's trailer is an old one, with beautiful engraved mirrors on all the cupboard doors, lace curtains at the window and a tiny Queen Anne wood stove to keep her warm at night. But she likes her mod cons as well. In the corner, a little flatscreen TV was burbling quietly, showing one of her favourite black-and-white films. Today the whole place was steamy and smelled sweetly of blackberries.

"The housed folk were in awe of us back then," she carried on as she cooked. "They could tell we were special as we came rolling into villages and towns. They could see we were different, not heavy and stuck in the mud like them, but here today and gone tomorrow."

If you never learned to read and write, like travelling people back then, you had to remember your histories like this, as a story. Granny Kate had a good audience. My aunts and my sisters were squashed onto the green leather seats fitted in a U-shape at one end of the trailer. They'd come down to Gypsy's Acre to help Sabrina get ready for her hen night. Even my two sisters who lived down south, Suzie and Sylvia, had arrived an hour or two ago. The only one missing was the bride-to-be herself. She was in the little bedroom behind me, going through a whole pile of dresses that she'd thrown onto Granny's lace bedspread. She'd picked a dress for her hen party months ago, but now she said it wasn't right. And the one I'd picked out for her was the wrong colour. She'd started cursing and yelling at me for not being a proper bridesmaid and choosing the right dress for her, so I'd left her in there to make her own mind up.

Everyone was in their best dresses. It looked like a bunch of celebrities had descended on Granny's trailer. Bare, suntanned legs and high heels meant that you couldn't walk anywhere without getting tripped up. And there was a war going on in the air between their perfume and the blackberries. We'd all heard Granny's stories before, but it didn't matter. Everyone was spellbound. Except me. I should've been squashed on the seats with them, laughing and enjoying myself like always. But something inside me had changed. Now all I could see in my mind was a pool of crimson blood. And all I could think about was a boy who lived in the big house not far from here. A house that might as well have been a million miles away, it was so different from our life here in this little trailer.

As Granny paused in her storytelling to add a pinch of something to the saucepan full of blackberries, Beryl took the opportunity to produce a box of biscuits.

"Snack break," she announced, passing the box around.

"Don't let me near them," said Queenie, passing them straight to Sadie-May. "I'll have something else. I'll have cheese!" She waved at me. I was standing next to Granny in the little kitchen area. "Pass me one of those little Babybels, Sammy babe. No, just pass me the whole bag. Cheese is low-fat, isn't it?"

"Oh my God, it isn't, Queenie, it really isn't," said Star, through a mouthful of crumbs.

"Don't do it, Sammy-Jo," shouted Savannah. "Pass her an apple, quickly."

I reached into a net bag hanging next to the little sink unit and tossed her an apple Granny had picked from the trees growing along the lane earlier.

"Hmmm. Thanks," said Queenie, not very enthusiastically. Then she frowned at me. "What are you doing lurking over there?"

"Yes, come and sit down, we've hardly seen you," said Sylvia, looking up from her sewing. She's the practical one out of us – she can take up hems and alter the shape of any clothes we buy and don't like. Now she was trying to finish an outfit for one of her little girls in time for Saturday.

"I'm fine here. I'm helping with the blackberries," I said. And before Granny could deny this, I added quickly, "Anyway, shush, the story's not finished yet." I turned to Granny, anything to get away from Queenie and Beryl's keen eyes. "Tell us what happened next."

"Well – after Samson Absalom came Samson Shadrack Smith," said Granny, stirring her potion. "His nickname was Mad Dog, so you can tell what his fighting style was like. He fought in tavern yards, his toe against the line drawn in the dust, his fists like sledgehammers – until the king sent for him…"

"Ha, can't see that happening today," said Star. She put on a posh voice. "'Starlena Smith, international singing star, is invited to Buckingham Palace.'"

"You wouldn't be allowed in wearing that dress," said Beryl, eyeing Star's micro skirt and her long, suntanned legs.

Granny banged her wooden spoon on the counter,

silencing us. "Ah yes, but in them days being noticed by royalty could be a good thing or a bad thing. The king at the time was mad, you see, and sometimes he liked people and sometimes he'd have the same people clapped in irons for doing nothing. But our Samson went. He weren't afraid of anything. Smiths are never afraid. And do you know what happened?"

"No, tell us, Granny!" chorused Sylvia and Suzie, who hadn't heard Granny's tales as often as we had since they'd moved away.

"Samson was showing off his strength by fighting all the king's guards, one after the other, and beating 'em. But the king didn't know that because he'd nodded off. Nodded off when one of the best fighters in the country was showing off his talents! That was rude, even if he was a king. Well, Samson Shadrack Mad Dog Smith weren't standing for it. All the court people might tippy-toe round and try not to wake the king, but our Samson does the opposite. He goes over and claps his hands like thunder and wakes him up!

"Everybody thought he'd be swinging from a rope, but the king stares at our Samson, stares and stares, and the whole crowd goes as silent as the grave – until the king bursts out laughing. Samson were the king's fighter from that day onwards. He got given lots of gold, too, and built himself a big house with his fight winnings, but he couldn't stand all those doors and walls, and he soon returned to his vardo. It didn't matter. Everyone loved him. He could talk to high and low, just like we can now. It didn't matter who they were, we were Smiths, and everyone knew that we put the magic and excitement into their lives."

Granny elbowed me out of her way, rummaged in a cupboard, pulled out a bottle and emptied the contents into the blackberries.

"Wow, that's smells good and strong, Granny," shouted Beryl. "Let's have a taste."

"No, not one sip till the wedding," said Granny, firmly.

And then everyone was shouting for a sip of it, until Sabrina's huffy voice blasted from the bedroom behind me. "Can't you all shut up! You're giving me a headache. It's my special night, and none of you care!"

I knew how she felt. For the first time in my life, I wanted to get away from them all as well. But everyone just burst out laughing and shouted at Sabrina to stop being so miserable.

"Although maybe we should keep it down a bit," said Queenie, the peacemaker.

"I wouldn't worry," I said. "Sabrina complained her Coco Pops were too loud this morning." That got a laugh. Behind me the door rattled, as Sabrina had thrown something at it.

"Can we all shut up now?" said Beryl. "Let Granny finish. Who came next?"

Granny got that distant look again and licked her fingers where the juice had stained them deep purple. "That would be Fairground Sammy, who worked the booths and sideshows, fighting for prize money and winning against all comers. That was Victorian times. That's when we travelled with the fairs." Her eyes sparkled. "We were like a tidal wave, sweeping across the country, brightening up the world. Where would we be if we were all the same, eh? We breathe different air to other people, we make the most of everything. We know secrets that others don't. We see things others don't. It's a wonder our footsteps don't glow as we move around."

"Tell that to the idiot next door," said Sadie-May, suddenly. "When me and Savannah pulled into his lorry yard instead of the field by accident, he got some ugly man with a ponytail to come out and yell at us."

"That's right. Gave us dirty looks, and watched until we'd reversed and driven off," agreed Savannah. "As if we'd want to go near their place."

"Never mind. Just ignore people like that. Now let Granny finish," said Queenie.

As the history of the Smiths carried on, I sneaked a look out of the window towards International Express. McCloud had threatened to have us moved, but nothing had happened yet. Queenie was right. We would just have to ignore him. I turned my back, but this left me staring out of the little kitchen window towards Langton House. I knew Gregory was back from the hospital because earlier I'd seen his father's Audi come by with him in it. But that wasn't enough for me. What I really wanted to do was go and see him for myself. I had to explain.

As me sisters and aunts listened and laughed and enjoyed themselves, I hugged my arms around myself, images of blood and hatred circling through my mind, Milo's hate-filled face, McCloud's cold eyes staring as if we were trash. And Gregory, bloodied and battered, because he'd come and checked up on me. Danger was closing in around me. In the end I turned from the window and tried to concentrate on Granny's story. She was still talking about Fairground Sammy.

"… and when he died they burned his wagon as they always did in them days," she was saying. "And thousands turned up to see his soul being set free to roam for ever."

Beryl was nodding in approval. "They never burn wagons nowadays."

"Too expensive."

"Trust you to think of the money, Sadie-May."

"But," said Granny, giving them both a look to shut them up. "It didn't take long for another Samson to come along. He was born on the day old Samson's wagon was burned. Sammy Smith, the Gypsy King they called him. The first Smith to fight in a proper ring."

She smiled to herself, remembering him. "He was handsome, a real pretty boy. The only time he stopped fighting was to go and fight in the war. But he came back to us. Even when the world became a dark place, it destroyed others but never the Smiths. Not while we'd got our Samsons. If the world ever ends, the Smiths will be the last ones standing." She turned the stove off under the bubbling mixture in the saucepan. A bottle and a cork were standing ready. She was coming to the end of our history now. She glanced at me.

"And last of all was your daddy, Samson Smith. The first to win medals, and not bronze or silver, but gold! The world championships and Olympic glory were in his grasp. Samson Smith, King of the Gypsies, that's what we embroidered on the back of his dressing gown. He would've been the best of them all…" She gave a sigh. "Until he got hurt."

There were sighs from all around, and the shaking of heads.

"Poor Sam. It was a tragedy," murmured Queenie.

They were right. I've seen videos of my father fighting. He would've been champion of the world, but he had a car crash, not something the other Samsons had to worry about. It injured his back, and he had pins in it, so it wasn't safe for him to fight any more. That was why he ran the gym and taught others.

"We should add you on the end of the fighters," said Beryl, suddenly, looking at me. "You're the first female Samson."

That made me smile for the first time that day. I've seen pictures, old and tattered and done in that sort of brown ink that they used to use, showing Fairground Sammy striking a pose. He looked like all the Smith fighters, with great, bulging biceps and a barrel chest and massive thighs. All I can say is that I might have inherited the skills, but I don't look anything like the men fighters in the family. Thank the Lord on that one.

"And we mustn't forget Bartley in America," said Sadie-May. "He makes his living as a fighter. Everyone knows him."

"He's not a Samson," said Granny, as she inspected her brew. "Anyway, he only fights on telly."

Uncle Bartley had gone to America years ago. There's a whole branch of the family tree over there now. He works on a TV programme that we all watch on satellite. It's called *CAGED*.

"Quick, put it on," said Star. "Let's watch him. Last week's show's on catch-up."

She loved Uncle Bartley. She loved reality shows like *Big Brother* and *Strictly Come Dancing*. And Bartley's show was reality with fighting. There was a delay while everyone half stood up to see who was sitting on the remote. It was Beryl. She aimed and clicked, sorting through the recorded shows until she found *CAGED*. Granny Kate might talk about the old days, but she liked her satellite TV.

The picture changed to an MMA fight, the hexagonal cage holding a couple of rough-looking boys doing amateurish kicks. And then it cut to the presenters.

"There he is, there's our Bartley," said Queenie.

All my sisters leaned forward.

"Aw, look at him. Handsome."

"I love Bartley."

"Everyone loves our Bartley."

"Outta the way, Star. Let us all see."

He was the trainer on the programme. They would go and find street kids who were getting in trouble, and they'd teach them MMA skills. It means mixed martial arts, and you can use kick-boxing and tae kwon do and karate moves as well as wrestling and grappling. It might seem stupid to make rough kids even rougher, but they taught them discipline and survival skills as well. They taught them to respect others. They changed their lives. We all loved watching Uncle Bartley. He was a celebrity over there.

The camera cut to a close-up of his face. He was big and handsome, and wore his dark hair short and spiked. He'd got a couple of the fighters with him, and he was explaining some of the moves they'd be using that week. The boys looked like hard-as-nails street boys, but beside Bartley's big frame and fists they looked puny.

"He still wants Sammy-Jo to go over," said Star, enviously.

Bartley started asking me to go and stay with them last year. He'd seen me fighting at the gym, and he said he might be able to get me some work helping out with the training for the contestants.

All eyes turned to look at me.

"So are you going to go?" asked Queenie, with a glance at Beryl. Star, Savannah and Sadie-May gave one another sidelong looks as well. I had the feeling everyone had been talking about me, but hopefully not about Milo and Gregory. I'd warned Sabrina not to mention it to them, but I didn't think she'd even heard me. I was banking on the fact that she only had thoughts for herself at the moment.

I shrugged. "I don't know."

"Bartley's wife's strict," said Queenie. "She'd look after you. She'd stop you getting into trouble." As if that would make my mind up! But she and Beryl liked that idea and nodded to each other. Strict was good.

"I wouldn't get into trouble," I said. "I don't need anyone telling me what to do."

They all exchanged a few more glances. They'd definitely been talking behind my back.

"Yes. But there's lots of ways of getting into trouble," said Beryl. "Like you forgetting you're a Smith girl. Forgetting how we live. You might start to run wild."

She meant I might go running off with an American boy. Or any boy who wasn't a Gypsy boy. Or even one of those, if we weren't married first.

"But what would our daddy do without Sammy-Jo?" said Savannah.

That made them all look thoughtful. Since our mother died, he'd been having bouts of deep sadness. I was the one who took control when they overwhelmed him. What with the wedding and the gym and caring for our father, I'd hardly had time to have my own life.

The truth was I would've loved to go over to America. Me and Kimmy talked about it all the time. She would come with me. We'd see the world. We'd see something different. Don't get me wrong, I loved my life, but I wanted more than Sabrina, more than just a boy and a wedding and having babies.

"Is Bartley coming over for the wedding?" asked Savannah, changing the subject, thank goodness.

"Yes. Tomorrow." Beryl raised her voice. "Did you hear

that, Sabrina? Bartley's on his way over for your wedding!"

No reply. But there were no screams, either. Granny nudged me and shoved a strainer in my hands. "Hold it above the bottle, so I don't get any pips in the brew," she ordered. "And pay attention, or you'll get splashes down your best outfit."

Even though I wasn't in the mood, I'd got my new dress on, ready for the hen party. It was tight and strappy and very short, and in a colour that was halfway between pink and orange. The girl in the shop had told me it was called mango. It glowed against my tan and my dark hair. I'd got a pair of spiky heels to go with it, and I'd done my eyes with eyeliner, a smudgy pencil and lots of mascara, till I looked like the actress on Granny's most favourite old film, *Cleopatra*.

"There. Finished."

Granny put the saucepan back on the stove, took the sieve and funnel off me and put the stopper in the bottle. The blackberry wine and the history of the Smiths were done. So was Sabrina's anguish about her dress. The bedroom door banged open.

"What about this one?" she said, coming through at last. She was wearing a tight white dress and holding a pair of sky-high heels in her hand. Her lashes were so long now they looked as though two spiders had crash-landed on her eyes.

There was a chorus of "Yes, that's the one!" from us all. Anything to shut her up.

"I'm not sure," she said, and we groaned. But luckily she caught sight of herself in one of Granny's mirrors and stopped to check that everything about her outfit was perfect. She posed and twisted in front of it, and her moaning stopped.

I stayed where I was, by the little sink, staring out of the window and down through the trees to the big house again. A new thought came into my head to torture me some more. Gregory's girlfriend – her with the perfect shiny hair and the narrow suspicious eyes – was she there with him, holding his hand?

"Sammy!" It was Beryl. "Are you even listening to me?"

I turned round and found a circle of mascara-ed eyes staring at me.

"What?"

"Sabrina's got her dress sorted. So let's ring for taxis for us all."

I stared at her. I'd been looking forward to the hen party. We all had. This is what the Smiths did, we enjoyed ourselves together. But I couldn't do it. I couldn't go out for the night without seeing Gregory. I had to find out how he was. He'd only been attacked because he'd come out to see if I was OK.

"You go on ahead. I've got to go somewhere first. I won't be long." I gave Beryl a bright smile and hurried to the door as fast as I could. It didn't work.

"But we can't leave you behind. We're ready!" said Star. "Where you going?"

"She's probably going to see the boy in the big house," said Sabrina, still staring at herself in the mirror. I could've killed her.

"Why?" Beryl's like a heat-seeking missile when it comes to gossip.

"I reckon he fancies her," said Sabrina, twirling back and forth.

I froze in the doorway. "No, he doesn't. I was wondering if he was OK, that's all. He got attacked in town. I was the one who found him. It looks rude if I don't go and ask if he's OK." I looked at Beryl. "Sabrina's joking about him liking me. Honest."

"I should hope she is," said Beryl. She sniffed and smoothed her tight dress. "You'd never shame us like that."

No. Of course I wouldn't. I jumped down off the step and hurried away.

11

This is what Langton House looks like:

There's lots of windows in two rows, and then a few more above that, poking out from under the roof. Half of the bricks are covered in ivy. And there's a big front door with columns either side and a tiny roof, so that if it's raining you can leave the house and step into a car without getting too wet. Stretching away from the house is a big curved gravel drive.

It made me feel breathless just looking at the house. Not because I was envious. The place meant nothing to me. Maybe Rocky's family liked living in a house, but I couldn't do it. I liked our big mobile homes behind our gym. Houses made me feel closed in, like I was suffocating.

Today I was making an exception.

The front door had lilac round it, smelling sweet and strong in the evening sun. Below was a big stone step with a welcome mat on it, and a brass knocker on the oak door in the shape of a lion's head with a ring through its teeth.

I stepped on the mat and knocked. The door was flung open straightaway. I think someone had seen me walking up the drive. I'm not surprised. I'd taken my time, changing my mind every other step and telling myself I was being stupid. But I'd made it in the end. And now here was Mr Langton framed in the doorway, peering at me. Gregory must've taken after his mama because Mr Langton was a big man, his belly hanging over his jeans. He got his fair hair from his daddy, though.

"Yes?"

That's when I found out that the sweet lilac and the welcome mat weren't meant for everyone, and definitely not for me, because it wasn't a friendly greeting. But I'd never go anywhere or say anything if I always waited for people to be friendly. I flicked my hair back and gave him my best smile.

"Hello, Mr Langton." I waved my hand back towards the trailers. "I'm from over there."

His face went a bit more thunderous. "I know who you are. What do you want?"

He kept looking me up and down. He was probably wondering why I was all dressed up in my little mango dress with my Cleopatra eyes.

"I've come to see Gregory, please."

His fingers tightened on the edge of the door. "Well, you can't. Now go."

"But I'm worried about him. Please."

I was trying to look over his shoulder, trying to see if Gregory was near by. Mr Langton didn't want me to, and kept closing the door little by little to block my view, but I was managing to stand on tiptoe and see over his shoulder. I could see the hall and, at the far side, an open door into one of the rooms. There was a TV on the wall above a fireplace, and the channels were flicking over quickly as though someone was bored and aiming a remote at the screen.

Mr Langton put an arm out to the doorpost, blocking my way. "You don't have to worry. He's got us and his girlfriend to do that." He said the word "girlfriend" extra loud, like I wouldn't hear it otherwise. "So off you go."

He flicked a finger towards the driveway, as though I was some tiny child who could be dismissed. That got me annoyed. Politeness doesn't cost anything. He went to shut the door, but I stepped forward so he'd have to sandwich me, my mango dress and my new shoes between the door and the frame if he carried on shutting it.

"Please. I'll only be a minute. Honest."

A voice shouted from the room behind him. "Dad! Is that Sammy-Jo? Let her in!"

When Mr Langton heard that, he looked ready to explode. He stood there taking deep breaths for a while, like a kettle letting off steam, but eventually he swung the door wide open and moved aside.

I walked into the hall. Nothing much had changed in two years. I swear there was the same vase standing on the same old, scratched cupboard, exactly where it had been when I'd taken the money from under it. This time, instead of creeping through the house like a burglar, I stuck my chin in the air, gave Mr Langton another smile and walked across the polished floorboards with my heels tiptapping. The room at the back was huge. It was a wonder it didn't echo. There were three squashy sofas with covers thrown over them. A couple of coffee tables. A grand piano standing in the corner. And a fireplace with logs in a basket. The walls were full of gloomy paintings that looked like they needed a good scrub.

To tell you the truth, I didn't think much of the furnishings around me. Star, who thinks she knows everything about everything, says that old and shabby things are fashionable with some people, but they don't appeal to me. You should see Tyson and Rocky's house, if you want shiny, new and expensive. It's got marble and leather and chrome everywhere, and their TV was twice the size of this one.

But I wasn't here to like the furnishings. I took a deep breath and actually looked at Gregory. He was lying on one of the sofas. A great shaft of evening sunlight was streaming in through one of the long windows, with little specks of dust dancing in it. It was shining right on him and lighting up his fair hair and leaving other bits in shadow, like one of the old paintings on the wall. It wiped the image of him curled up and bleeding from my mind at last, and a little wave of happiness stole through me. He gave me a smile like he was really pleased to see me, but as I walked over to him it faded away and he did a double take at my dress. I think the sun had caught it, and the colour was glowing. Judging by his expression, he seemed to like my mango dress better than his father did.

"Hey," I said.

His poor cut lip curled into a smile. He put his head on one side and surveyed me again. "Do you always visit sick people dressed like that? You'll give them a heart attack."

I looked down at myself. "This old thing? This is what I do the cleaning in."

His face creased up and his eyes crinkled and he laughed silently and gently, his hand going to his ribs. He'd got a clean shirt on, and it was hanging undone. The skin of his chest still looked as tender as a baby's, but it was spoiled by the bruises at the sides, which had begun to turn yellow, green and purple now, like the colours of petrol in a dirty puddle.

The wound on his head, which went from his temple, straight across his eyebrow, had been stitched. His hair was brushed back away from it and still sticky with dried blood. He tried to sit up, so I'd have room on the sofa, pushing himself with his grazed hands. But he didn't get far before he winced.

"Stay still," I said.

There was a little footstool by the fireplace, so I went and fetched it and put it next to him. It wasn't a good move because when I sat down on it, I found myself so close to him that a terrible thought came into my head. I couldn't stop looking at the cut on his head and thinking how painful it must be, and I found myself wanting to lean over and kiss the corner of the wound, where it was jagged and sore. So I blinked and glanced away from his eyebrow and the stitches, but then I found myself looking at his mouth. His cut lip was healing well. I found myself wanting to kiss that too.

My brain wouldn't stop.

"How are you feeling?" I managed to say.

"I was lucky," he said. "My ribs weren't broken, just kicked and stomped."

"Oh. Good."

A silence fell and stretched out. I could hear the old grandfather clock in the corner ticking away and the birds having their evening squawk in the garden beyond the windows. I suppose for all its oldness and scruffiness, this was a peaceful room to be in. Or maybe Gregory was a peaceful person to sit with. He was so different to Rocky.

"What's up?" he asked, eventually.

"Nothing. Why?"

"You're staring."

I blinked. "So are you. You're always staring at things."

That got me another smile. "I know. I'm curious about the world. I like solving mysteries." He tried to sit up again, and managed by holding onto his side and moving gently. "You're a mystery. One minute you're here, and then you're gone. And now you're here again."

I thought of Granny Kate's story about our family tree. "We're the secret people. No one knows us."

He grinned. "I do. I can see Gypsy's Acre from my bedroom."

"The window on the end?"

"Yes."

So that was his bedroom. I could see it from my trailer

112

window. For some reason that gave me a shiver of delight.

"After I met you in the hall that first time, I used to wake up in the mornings and check whether you'd come back," he said.

I could see a picture so clear in my head, of him looking out of his window to our little camp. Our eyes met, and he smiled. All this smiling had made his lip bleed a little again. I had to clasp my hands together to stop myself getting a tissue from the box on the coffee table and dabbing it for him.

I tried to make myself think of something else, something far away from Gregory. Like my other life, the one where I fought in backstreet gyms, where I was Gypsy Girl, and where the crowd watched me through the bars of the cage, and gambled on me winning or getting hurt – either seemed to please them. It was a million miles from this comfy room with its squashy sofas and the long shadows of evening settling over it.

I was an imposter. And it was my fault he was in pain.

His phone beeped, disturbing the silence. He looked down at it. "More texts. And they're all about you."

"Is that good?" My heart gave a thump. Being talked about usually spelled trouble for me.

He held up his phone and showed me. "They've been coming in ever since I got out of the hospital. Everyone's texting about you."

"Saying what?" I knew it wasn't going to be good.

I got a blast of his amber eyes. "That you're this dangerous fighter girl."

He waited for me to answer. I wasn't going to lie to him.

"It's true I'm a fighter," I said. "It's my life. But I don't jump on people in the street. I fight in the gym."

He nodded. "Yes. But the texts say you had a fight with a girl in your town, and she's in hospital in a coma. That's why you came here, to get away from the police. And that's why you won't go back home."

When I heard that, my heart began to pound.

I knew he was watching me, giving me that deep deep stare, trying to work out the truth. I knew he was waiting for me to tell him it was a lie, but I couldn't do that. I shouldn't have been bothering about what a gorjer boy thought of me. But I was. I met his gaze.

"Do *you* believe it?" I sez. I threw it at him like I didn't care.

For a moment, the rest of the room faded away, so did the ticking of the clock and the birds outside. My focus was only on Gregory.

He continued to meet my eyes. "I make my own mind up. I don't listen to gossip and texts."

I heard his words, but my heart just wouldn't slow down.

"Why're you staring at me, then?" I said. "Like you're trying to read the truth from off the inside of me head?"

He blinked, but he never looked away. "Everyone looks at you, and you know it." There was a pause. "Even me."

Sabrina says when I'm walking through the town I flaunt along, like I'm a celebrity on a red carpet. But that was no excuse.

"You shouldn't. You've got a girlfriend."

Suddenly he wasn't looking at me any more. He bit his lip, which made it bleed a bit more. His hands began playing with a loose thread on his shirt. "It's tricky. Things haven't been right – but that's nothing to do with this…" He stopped. "My head's confused about my life at the moment. And that's before I hit the tarmac."

And because he hadn't asked to know the truth about the girl in the coma, I broke my rule and explained myself.

"There's a girl gang in our town. Five girls who think they're great because they copy the stupid boys who think they're gangsters. They pick on other girls, follow them, get them in a corner and then steal their phones, or their trainers. They picked on a girl in my class. She's not tough. They picked her because she's got no one to stick up for her. No brothers and no dad. So me and Kimmy went to help her. The leader of the gang came at me punching and kicking, so I pushed her. I didn't realize how strong I was. She flew back and hit her head on a wall and knocked herself out. She's OK now. It scared me when she got knocked out, but I wasn't sorry. She's a bully, and I hate bullies."

I sat back. Another silence fell. Gregory was watching me, his head on one side, licking his split lip.

"What?" I asked.

He smiled. "I'm glad it's that. I somehow knew it would be."

It made my heart swell to hear that, but now he could do some explaining. "Why is everybody texting about me?"

That stopped him smiling.

"You don't want to know."

"I do."

He sighed. "It's stupid. It's because you found me, and you were there with me when everyone else turned up, and rumours got started. And because of this." He held out his phone again. "Everyone's seen it."

I knew what it was straightaway. It was the photo Milo had taken as I tried to help Gregory. Only it didn't look like I was helping him. It showed me bending over him as he lay on the ground, and my arms were holding him down. It looked like he was fighting me off. The chef had thought the same when he saw me. The image must've gone round the town fast. It didn't matter that Gregory's crowd weren't friends with Milo – photos like this spread far and fast, like a disease.

My face went icy cold.

Milo was spreading it round that I attacked Gregory. Milo wanted me to get the blame. And if I got the blame, then Mr Langton would throw us off Gypsy's Acre.

The doorbell rang again, but neither of us were taking much notice. I could hear talking in the hallway. I suspected someone else had come to see Gregory.

"I told the police I saw Milo hanging around before I got attacked, but there's no proof he was responsible, and they've all got an alibi from one of their friends. False, obviously." He stared off into the distance. "And I couldn't explain to the police why they'd picked on me. I've seen them around town, that's all. Maybe they thought I was an easy target – even though they sneaked up behind me." His eyes narrowed. "They should've come at me from the front. Things might've been different."

I smiled at him. "I don't have you down as a tough guy."

He gave a rueful laugh. "I'm not. But I'm not a pushover, either." He flexed one arm, like a bodybuilder. "I never took fight classes, but I work on my dad's farms when they're busy. Throwing haybales around makes you tough. Tougher than a few karate classes." He rested his elbow on the sofa. He raised an eyebrow. "Try me."

I placed my elbow down and we grasped hands. He tensed his muscles and we pushed against each other, neither of us trying hard. He wasn't bragging and making himself bigger than he was. I could feel his strength. But I could also feel his breath on my cheek as we leaned in towards each other, and the closeness of him, and the warmth of his hand in mine. In the end I relaxed, and he could've pushed my arm down and won, but he didn't. He didn't let go of my hand, either.

"Milo shouldn't underestimate me," he said, quietly, and I could see that under all his smiles the attack had wounded him deeply. "Nor should anyone else. I would fight and I'd win if someone I loved was being hurt."

I had to torture myself. "You mean someone like your girlfriend, Angela?"

"Alice," he corrected me. I knew her name. I'd got it wrong on purpose to try and make her seem unimportant to me. "And not just her. I would fight for anyone that I loved or cared about." His lip curled, his hand squeezed mine. "They don't know me. They thought I was an easy target. But they shouldn't have picked on me."

"Ouch," I said with a smile.

He blinked and realized we were still holding hands, and that he was squeezing the life out of mine. He let go. "Sorry." He ran a hand through his hair. "You come round to visit and I end up challenging you to an arm wrestle."

"It's OK."

More than OK. I could've sat there all day holding his hand. But I had to tell him something. A confession. I took a deep breath."

"They attacked you because of me. I had a fight with Milo earlier. He wanted me and my family to leave Langton. When he saw us talking outside the hotel, he must've thought you and me were together. So he attacked you and took the photo. And suddenly everyone thinks I'm bad."

I never let it show, but it hurt that people were thinking badly of me and my family. We're proud of the fact that people usually like us. When we travel and take the horses with us, we always make friends with the locals. They bring their children down to see the horses and chat to me daddy. I didn't want to be hated.

Gregory thought about it, but shook his head. "No. I think that's a coincidence. He saw me out there, looking for you, and lashed out at me instead."

He didn't think the two attacks were linked. I knew they were. "They wanted to get me into trouble so we would be moved on."

"You're wrong. Don't try to understand why Milo does stuff. He's a dick. So are his brothers. They're screwed up. They hate anyone who's different. Asians. Black people. You. Anyone that's not them."

He still didn't get it. "Listen to me," I said. "You don't understand because everyone likes you, and you live in a big house, and you're kind of cute." He laughed. I didn't. This was serious. "But not everyone likes me. So if it looks like I attacked you, they'll hate me and we'll get moved."

"No way. No one's that desperate to get rid of you," he said.

"McCloud is."

"Don't worry about him," he said. "He can't do anything to make you move. He only owns the land around his business. You're camped on our land."

"Greg?" said a girl's voice from the doorway behind us.

My heart sank. It was Alice, with her perfect, shiny hair and her cute kitten face. I didn't know how long she'd been standing there. She was still wearing her white shirt, black skirt and flat shoes. She'd been warned I was there, because she glanced at Gregory and then her eyes fixed on me. She looked at my dress. It had started off short, but now that I was perching on the tiny stool I realized it had gone very, very short. I stood up, pulling it down.

"What're you doing here?" she said, her eyes glittering

again. Not with tears this time, but with anger.

"I wanted to see if he's OK."

"You complete bitch," she said, and she stormed over to me.

"Whoa, wait a minute." Gregory sat right up, holding his side. "You've got it wrong, Alice. All those texts – they aren't true."

She swung round at him. She hadn't yet asked how he was, or stroked his hair, or kissed his cheek. I would've done that. "Don't let her fool you!"

"I'm not. Just listen to me! It wasn't her. She found me. I might've laid there bleeding for much longer if she hadn't."

I touched her sleeve. I only wanted to get her attention, to tell her that I would never hurt anyone. She acted like I'd chopped her arm off.

"Don't you dare touch me!" she snapped. She squeezed herself next to Gregory, turning her back on me. She lowered her voice. "Haven't you seen the photo?"

"Yes. Of course I have. It's not what you think." He frowned. "You didn't show it to my dad, did you?"

She stuck her chin in the air. "Yes. Yes, I did. He should see it." I got another killer look.

Gregory groaned. "No. Why did you do that? Now he's going to go crazy."

He wasn't joking. I could hear raised voices in the hall, and a woman, probably Gregory's mother, saying, "Wait! You can't believe everything that gets passed around on phones!"

I turned to Alice. "Don't you see? It was Milo and his two brothers. Milo took that photo."

A crease appeared between her perfect eyebrows. "Well, you would say that, wouldn't you?"

"I don't lie."

She smiled, sarkily. "Of course. You're Snow White."

"Excuse me..." Mr Langton was in the doorway. His face was red with anger. He pointed a finger at me.

"A word, please, outside." He glanced at his son. "And no arguments. You should've shown me that photo." He turned to Alice. "Stay and cheer him up."

She got a smile from him, one that faded as soon as he escorted me into the hall. Gregory's mother was waiting out there, too. Gregory took after her, the same cheekbones, the same chin, the same straight eyebrows and golden eyes. She gave me a hurt and embarrassed look as Mr Langton flung open the front door.

"Out."

"Wait," I said. "I never hurt your son. I helped him."

"Out. And don't come back. And tell your father he can't stop here. You all have to leave."

"Why? You never complained about any Travellers stopping here before."

He poked a finger at me again. "There's no smoke without fire. I was suspicious when they said that you'd found him. And now Alice has shown us the photo." The finger jabbed towards me. "The police say it proves nothing. But I know girls like you – you're nothing but trouble, fighting in the streets, hitting other girls – yes, I saw the texts as well as the photo!"

Half of my brain was thinking that if I raised my hand and hit a certain point on his jaw he would fall at my feet, out cold. That would shut him up. The other half of my brain wanted to cry. I know I'm strong and fast, but I would never attack anyone. I only fight to stick up for my friends and family and anyone who's getting picked on, because I hate unfairness.

There was a movement in the doorway of the sitting room, and Gregory was standing there, holding onto the wall and leaning to the right to ease his ribs.

"Dad. Leave her alone. It's not her fault."

"You've been fooled. Now let me handle this."

Alice was fussing at Gregory's side and looking daggers at me. "Leave it, babe. You'll hurt your ribs even more. Sit down."

He shrugged away from her. "No. I don't like rumours. I don't like people being picked on." She didn't like him sticking up for me. She went red in the face and flounced off back into the room.

His father turned on him. "You can go and sit down as well!"

Gregory didn't move. There was an awful pause as we stood in our positions in the hallway. Mr Langton glared at his son. Gregory stared back. Neither would give way. All because of me. His mother broke the silence. Her hand went up to her mouth, her eyes fixed on me.

"See what you've caused. I didn't want to believe it, but it's true – you're nothing but trouble!"

I had to get out of there. None of them except Gregory would ever believe me. I stalked to the door and nearly ran into an old man who was pottering in, his walking stick tapping on the floor.

"What's all this shouting?" he said. He saw me and gave me a gappy smile. "Ah, you're one of the Travellers, aren't you? From Gypsy's Acre." He patted my arm. "Travellers have always stopped here since I was a boy. Lots of different families. Now, let me think, what were their names…?"

"It doesn't matter what their names are, Pops," said Mr Langton, barely able to speak to the old fella he was so angry. "She's leaving. It's different these days."

I don't think his pops was listening, because he smiled at me as he shuffled by. "I don't mind you being here," he said. "I always liked it when you came fruit picking."

He shuffled off, humming to himself. When he'd gone, Mr Langton swung round at me. He was in a towering rage. His face was deep maroon red now.

"I've got no problem with Travellers, none at all. It's you." He jabbed a finger at me again. "Stay away from my son. And I want you gone by morning. Off my land. All of you."

I never flinched. "No. Get a court order if you want us to move. Or wait till Sunday, we'll be gone by then."

"I don't think so." He moved closer, trying to make me back away. "If you haven't moved by tomorrow morning,

I'll get my farm workers to tow your caravans off with the tractors. Tell your father that. I mean it. It's my land."

"All right." I gave him a smile and walked out without a glance at Gregory. I slammed the door behind me.

We'd see about that.

12

Night had fallen, and the only light in Gypsy's Acre came from the windows of our three trailers and the yellow glow of the streetlights on the road and the bright white of the security lights at International Express. McCloud had his men working day and night it seemed.

As usual, my father was sitting in his Mitsubishi, listening to sorrowful country-and-western songs that reminded him of our mama. Ever since she died, he'd been spending too much time sitting in his motor with the windows down, his arm resting on the sill, staring out of the windscreen and listening to sad music about people dying and hearts being broken. He said he was remembering Maggie, because it was her favourite music, too.

Sometimes I leave him to get on with it, and I go and run the gym for him, or take some of the junior classes. Sometimes I hide his CDs and the keys to the Mitsubishi and try to make him get on with his life.

I think he was asleep as I opened the door.

"Come on, we've got to go somewhere," I told him.

He sat up. "I thought you were going to the hen party."

I'd thought that, too, but I'd changed my plans. I could hear my aunts and sisters laughing in Granny's trailer. They were getting ready to leave, but I wouldn't be going with them. A moment later there was a hoot from the road. Their taxis were here. A huge cloud of perfume wafted across the field as Granny's door flew open and out they all came – a whole flock of Smiths done up in their best dresses, looking like parakeets and sounding like them as well. Sabrina had stuck with the white dress, and looked like a true princess, only much prettier than most of the ones you see in magazines. Granny Kate had changed into a glittering gold top from about fifty years ago that had come back in fashion, so she looked like she'd just bought it from some expensive shop.

"Just in time, Sammy-Jo," said Beryl, giving me a very keen look. Probably checking that I hadn't been kissing a gorjer boy, or sitting too close to one. "Let's go."

"I've got something to do first," I told her. "With Daddy. You carry on."

That stopped Beryl in her tracks. "What have you got to do?" Her eyes narrowed. "Is it something to do with that boy?" she said, as though I was going to race back up to Langton House the moment they left and jump into bed with Gregory.

"It's a secret," I said. "So don't start on me, Beryl. I've had enough of people getting on at me today. It's a surprise for Sabrina."

That shut her up. She pursed her bright-red lips and

carried on after the others. Nobody else seemed to mind that I wasn't going. They all tiptoed off to the taxis, trying not to let their heels sink in the grass. When they'd gone, I got in the Mitsubishi.

My father yawned and got the engine going. "Where to, princess?"

"Tyson and Rocky's house. We're going visiting."

As we drove over the grass to the road, I looked back at our three trailers, all alone in the middle. Tomorrow morning Mr Langton would order his men to come and tow us off. Well, that's what he thought.

"I think we need company," I said.

"Hello, Sam." James Quinn shook hands with my father before he noticed me. "And Sammy-Jo!"

He swung the door wide and we walked into his house.

"If you're looking for Rocky, he's not here," he said to me. "You know Rocky. He's always out doing something."

I shook my head. "No. We came to see you."

His house was all marble floors, long cream leather sofas and curtains with swoops and tassels. Around the walls were glass cabinets that held all their Crown Derby china. Above the fireplace there was a huge flat-screen TV on a music channel. But it wasn't the house that I was interested in. Out of the back window we could see the stables and the yard. It was block-paved and neat, with two beautiful American Airstream trailers in polished chrome standing there.

"Ah, I love your trailers," I said.

"Pity he don't use them any more," said me daddy. Which was what I wanted him to say.

James scratched his head. "One day we'll go off along the roads again, Sam, you wait and see."

Quick as a flash I said, "Maybe you should do it now."

They both stared at me.

"I've got an idea," I said. "It's for Sabrina. She'll love it."

Half an hour later we were back in the Mitsubishi, leaving Rocky's parents scurrying round getting things ready.

"Where to?" said my father. He was beginning to enjoy himself. He knew what I was up to now.

"Down to the site."

The Traveller site in Langton is tucked away between a railway line and the motorway, which makes it noisy and dangerous in both directions. It's divided up into little plots, each with a small building that houses a kitchen and a bathroom. The site was crowded as we drove in. All the women had gone to the hen party, but the men were there. They were sitting outside, talking as usual, and the children were out playing. You can come down here on the coldest day, when the frost is thick, and they'll still be playing out. And at night they have to be persuaded to come back into the trailers and sit down, for once. That's why we're tough. We grow up outside. But it gets us into trouble at school. We don't like being inside when we can be outside, or sitting still when we can be running around.

Little boys were riding their ponies up and down or

cleaning the reins and harnesses that went with the racing sulkies – little carts that stood at the side of the trailers, each just two spoke wheels and a tiny seat. One of the boys came over and trotted his pony beside us. He was Thomas Hamilton, and he was going to be a page boy. He was covered in grass stains and grime, probably from falling off his wild little black-and-white mount. He was the scruffiest child alive. Any speck of dirt lying around would stick to him. But Sabrina had insisted that he wear a small white suit on her wedding day. He was going to need plenty of scrubbing before Saturday.

We parked up, and a little girl ran over to me as I got out. Her name was Whitney Jade, and she was going to be the flower girl at the wedding. She was so cute all you wanted to do was pick her up and kiss her. She had long dark curling hair and big brown eyes like chocolate buttons. It's a wonder she ever learned to walk because everyone wanted her to sit on their laps.

"Sammy-Jo! I'm going to die, I'm so excited," she squealed, clinging onto my hand as I walked towards the men. "I can't wait to wear me dress!"

Her dress was a tiny replica of Sabrina's, but with a ring of white flowers for her hair instead of a tiara. "It's beautiful, and it's waiting for you in our trailer," I said. "Not long now." But it wasn't Whitney Jade I'd come to see. "Run along and play, because I've got something to discuss with the men."

"What's up?" said one of my uncles as I walked over to them.

I told them my idea but not the reason for it. I didn't mention Mr Langton's threat. They listened. They raised their eyebrows. They nodded. My job here was done.

The hen party was in the White Swan Hotel. I could hear the music from outside in the street. We'd booked their biggest party room. If the cloud of perfume didn't knock you over as you walked through the door, then the dresses would. The DJ had set up flashing lights, and he'd turned the music up to full volume. Everybody was dancing.

I put Milo and his brothers out of my mind. And I put Gregory out of my mind as well. I got myself on the dance floor with everyone else, and I danced without stopping. The girls from the nail bar were there, and some of me sisters' friends, who live in houses near them. Everyone knows that if you want a good evening out and lots of dancing, you should come to a party held by the Smiths.

Sabrina and Star borrowed the DJ's mike and gave us a couple of songs, and then Star insisted that all the sisters get up and sing like we used to. Afterwards, we did all the old dances that my aunties are fond of, like the "Macarena" and "The Loco-Motion". We did funny ones, like "Gangnam Style". We did rock and roll because we all love jiving. We danced all night, but I hadn't shut Gregory out entirely, because every so often I would remember the wound on his head and the bruises on his ribs, and how I wished I could get hold of Milo and his brothers and do the same to them.

I made sure that I kept away from my aunties. There were a lot of whispers and glances being cast in my direction during the evening. But at some point Queenie and Beryl managed to corner me with a pincer movement, each of them coming from a different direction.

"So where did you go?" said Beryl, her hand on the wall to stop me slipping away.

I told them my idea, and they both looked relieved that it had nothing to do with Gregory Langton.

"Ah, that's a good idea!" said Queenie. "Sabrina will love it. And I bet if Maggie was still alive she'd love it, too."

So when we drove back in a fleet of taxis, I covered Sabrina's eyes and then whipped my hands away as we pulled up.

"Surprise!" I said.

Because there weren't three trailers on Gypsy's Acre any more. There were twenty or more. Rocky's parents were there, and a couple of his sisters and their families, along with uncles and brothers-in-law. There wasn't a spare inch of grass.

Sabrina looked and laughed, clapping her hands in delight as she scrambled out. I followed her.

"You did this for me!" she said, and hugged me, all trace of Bridezilla gone.

"I did. Aren't I the best bridesmaid ever?"

"You are." Then she had one of her freaky flashes of wisdom. "Did something happen? Did that stupid man from the barn tell you he was going to get his men to tow us off the field?"

"No. He isn't going to throw us off here before your wedding, I promise you." It was the truth. Mr Langton was the problem now. Not McCloud.

I thought I'd got away with it, but Sabrina nodded and said, casually, "I bet it was Mr Langton, then. I bet he was going to chuck us off, because of his son getting beaten up and everyone thinking it was you."

When Sabrina got her insights, it was no use lying to her. "Not any more he isn't. I've seen to that. But don't tell anyone else that's the reason. We don't want any trouble."

We stood in the middle of the field, surrounded by all our folk, and we looked through the darkness to Langton House. The windows were blazing.

"There you go, Mr Langton, don't try and bully me sister," said Sabrina, shaking her fist at the house.

"Yeah, try and get your tractors to come and drag us all away now," I added.

I thought I was the cleverest girl on the planet. But I wasn't. I didn't realize what I'd done. And what it would end up costing me.

-13-

It was well past midnight, but no one was sleeping. It was like our own little Appleby Fair, just a load of people sitting round talking and laughing and singing.

I couldn't relax, though, as I walked among Smiths and Quinns. We'd set up a square of four big canvas gazebos in the middle of the grass to make a covered area, with everyone dragging their sun chairs and patio tables under it. What with my aunties and sisters being in their brightest clothes for the hen party, it looked like we had our own outdoor nightclub here in the field.

Solar lamps were giving out tiny sparkling lights, like fireflies, but someone had rigged up proper lights as well, and a generator was fut-fut-futting away to one side. None of the children were in bed. They were running round everywhere, or falling asleep on someone's knee. Music was playing, competing with a babble of happy voices laughing and shouting to one another.

Even my father was happy and relaxed. He loved it when all the families got together. I knew this wedding was getting him down, because it reminded him that it should be Maggie who was organizing everything, not me. But Gypsy's Acre was full to bursting now, and he was moving around shaking hands and talking. I hadn't seen him this cheerful for a long time.

Granny Kate was right in the middle of everything – centre spot in the gazebos – sitting in the best chair because she was the head of the Smith family. Everyone else was squashed in around her. There were calls for her to open the blackberry wine, but she refused, saying it was for Sabrina's wedding and not before.

Sabrina was somewhere in the darkness talking to Tyson. He shouldn't have been there at all, because they weren't supposed to be seeing each other before the wedding, but he'd snuck in a few minutes before with Rocky.

While everybody enjoyed themselves, I found myself walking up and down the edge of the field. Something was bugging me. The lights were still on at the big house. And the International Express security lights were blazing. As I passed the entrance to the field, I noticed a group of people standing watching us. I quickly moved back into the deep shadow of the two horse-chestnut trees that stood to one side. From here I could see and hear them, but they couldn't see me.

There was Mr Langton and a couple of men I'd never seen before, probably some of the farm men who were going to get their tractors to pull us off the field. Parked beside them was the silver Range Rover, its headlights lighting up the road. Mr McCloud and Pony were standing in the beam of light, their shadows stretching almost to the horse-chestnut trees and my feet.

Pony was in shorts and a vest, his straggly white hair scraped back, his beefy arms folded. He stood there glaring at all the trailers. McCloud looked like the perfect businessman as usual.

"It's the security aspect that worries me," he was saying. "I know it's your land, Langton, but it affects us as well."

"You want me to get our men together?" I heard Pony mutter.

"No." That was Mr Langton. He sounded nervous. He'd realized there were too many of us to boss around. "It won't be necessary. This is annoying, but we don't want trouble."

That made Pony laugh. "I'd give them trouble. Especially that girl. She's a—" He called me a name that made Mr Langton wince. Me and Sabrina can swear when we get going, but we never use that word. Me daddy would go crazy to hear me called that.

Pony spat on the ground. He was a real charmer, spitting and swearing. "She deserves everything she gets."

Mr Langton and McCloud nodded.

I felt the anger start to sing in my veins like it does before a fight. They had no right to hate me. They didn't know me. I was doing no harm being there, but they wanted me gone. I knew I shouldn't retaliate, but I couldn't help myself. I tossed my hair back and started to walk towards them. I wanted to face them all, not hide in the shadows. I didn't get further than a step or two before a hand clamped over my

135

mouth and an arm curled around my neck and dragged me back into the horse-chestnuts' shadow.

"Leave it," whispered Rocky in my ear as he pulled me back into the field. "Don't rattle their cage."

His arm was tight around my neck. His hand was clamped over my mouth. I still managed to bite him. He swore softly and pulled his hand away. He didn't let go of my neck, though, and his grip tightened into a stranglehold. I got both my hands up and tried to loosen it, but he wasn't joking around. He wasn't letting me go.

"Keep out of this," I gasped, digging my nails into his bicep, but he wasn't budging. "This is my fight."

He was holding me tightly against him, his face pressed against the side of mine. "No," he whispered. "No fighting."

He dragged me further back towards the gazebos and the party, keeping hold of my throat, until we were away from McCloud and the others.

"When they leave, I'll let you go," he murmured in my ear. "Not before. And if you bite me again, I'll bite you back."

I didn't risk it. I could imagine Rocky biting someone. He had perfect teeth. He held me tightly until we saw Mr Langton and his men walk back towards the big house and Pony and McCloud getting into the Range Rover and driving the short distance to International Express. Even this late, I could hear one of the International Express lorries idling in the yard as it got filled with boxes and crates.

I thought Rocky was annoyed with me for trying to get

in a fight with Pony. But instead I could feel him start to laugh as he loosened his grip on me.

"What's so funny?" I demanded.

"How do you do it?"

"What?"

"Irritate everyone!"

"It's a gift."

He let go of my neck, but he didn't release me. He spun me round so we were facing each other. He kept a hold of my arms. "So that's what this is all about. Langton was threatening to evict you, and you thought you'd invite us all round. So there would be too many of us to be towed away."

"Maybe."

"Did you tell anyone else?"

"No. Sabrina guessed, that's all."

I thought he'd laugh some more at my trick. He didn't. He'd gone serious. That was a rare thing for Rocky. The only other time I'd seen him being serious was with the spiky-haired older woman in the leather jacket.

"Why didn't you just move?" he said. "You could've pulled onto our land."

"No. Sabrina wanted to be here. This is where our mother stopped before she was married. We've got to pick the wild roses."

He looked at me blankly. "Why?"

"They're for Sabrina's bouquet." He didn't get how something that little could be so important to us. I tried again. "Moving would upset Sabrina, and that would set

Tyson off. He'd probably go up to Mr Langton and argue with him. Or go to International Express and rattle the gates and demand to know why they wanted to move his bride before her wedding. Then it would all go wrong. Tyson would get in a fight and lose his boxing licence ... and—"

Rocky shook me to shut me up. "OK. I get it." He nodded towards the barn. "Who owns the business?"

"A guy called McCloud. The one standing next to Mr Langton. He started all this. He wanted us gone soon as we got here."

Rocky went all thoughtful. "Who's the other one?"

"The dirty-mouthed white-haired pig-troll?" I said. "Security, I suppose. Why?"

"I don't like the look of him. I want you to promise to keep away from him." He looked dead straight at me. "In fact, I don't like the look of him or his boss. So leave them alone. And don't go near their business again."

I stared over at a lorry leaving the place. "Maybe McCloud's up to something," I said. "Why would he need security men just to protect a load of crates and boxes waiting to be shipped abroad? 'Import and export,' it sez. Not precious jewels."

Rocky rolled his eyes, like I was some silly girl. "There must be tens of thousands of pounds' worth of goods stored in those buildings, waiting to be loaded. It must be tempting for thieves. It makes sense to have security." His hands gripped my arms. "So keep away. I don't care what they're doing. Neither should you."

"But—"

His hands got tighter. "I said leave it, Sammy. Do you hear me?" He shook me. "McCloud's a businessman. He's got a business to run. It looks like he's all matey with Langton. So keep your head down. And on Sunday, drive away and forget him."

He was right. Forget McCloud and Pony and that thug Milo. Enjoy the wedding and leave. But behind Rocky I could see the lights of Langton House. The end window was lit. Gregory's room. When we left on Sunday I'd be leaving him as well. Was he in there? Was he looking out? Had he got his girlfriend with him? Maybe Alice was sitting on the bed, watching him as he stood at the window, her eyes going all narrow again as she said, "What are you looking at, hon? Hope it's not that girl. Come here and lie with me..."

Before I could stop myself, I started thinking about his split lip and how I'd wanted to kiss it better. And I began to imagine what it would be like to kiss Gregory properly, even though that was never going to happen. I'm not saying it doesn't happen sometimes, Gypsies and housed people marrying, because it does, but if you've got aunties like mine who think it's shameful to hang around with gorjer boys, then you'd probably get shouted at for even thinking about kissing one.

Rocky shook me again, gently this time. "I'd love to know what you're thinking."

A confession. I was sixteen, and I'd never kissed a boy. Kimmy thought that was hysterically funny. She'd had three boyfriends, and she'd slept with all of them. I forced myself to look away from Gregory's window and made myself look at Rocky instead. He was the one I should be thinking about kissing, even though he was too old for me. The moonlight suited him. It outlined him in silver. Three years ago, when I thought I was madly in love with Rocky, I would've loved to be here with him holding my arms and looking down at me.

I don't know why I said it, but I did. "So do you want to kiss me?"

He raised his eyebrows and laughed. "What?"

Suddenly I was desperate to find out what it felt like.

"I know you're not interested in me," I said. "Not like Beryl and Queenie think you are. But it doesn't matter."

He let go of my arms and put his hands either side of my face and tilted it up. For a moment, I thought he was actually going to kiss me. He didn't. He gave me a puzzled smile. "What's wrong, Sammy-Jo?"

"Nothing. I want to know what it feels like, that's all."

"Hmmm." He didn't look convinced. "You don't want to kiss me. Who do you want to kiss?"

I couldn't help it. My eyes flicked towards Langton House. Rocky glanced over his shoulder to see what I was looking at. He gave a groan. "That place? Jeez, don't tell me you've fallen for that boy. Not Gregory Langton." He shook his head. "Forget him. Seriously."

I broke his grip on my arms and pushed him away. "No, I won't."

I walked off, but he pulled me back. "You really want a broken heart?"

I peeled his fingers from my arm. "Mind your own business. You should look after your own love life."

"What's that supposed to mean?"

"Who are you saving your kisses for? Your probation officer?"

"Miss Stroud?" He gave a smug smile. "You have no idea."

Maybe I didn't, but I had eyes. I'd seen him. But I couldn't be bothered to argue with him any more. I left him there and walked off back to the crowd under the gazebos. One of me uncles was strumming a guitar, and Star was singing a Dolly Parton song, with Beryl and Queenie acting as the backing.

Above us the stars were bright. I found myself a sunlounger on the edge of the group and threw myself down on it. Whitney Jade came over and snuggled up beside me, and started sucking her thumb. She smelled of chocolate and cherry cola. I hugged her, and lay back and listened to me aunties singing along to the guitar. I didn't see Rocky again. I thought he'd gone back to his own home. We stayed up for hours, no one wanting to go to bed and end the night. Sabrina was the only one who wasn't enjoying herself any more. She stumbled past my lounger, sniffing and dabbing at her eyes.

"What's up?"

She stopped and did a few more sniffs, wringing a

shredded tissue between her hands. "Nothing. Saying goodbye to Tyson."

"Heaven's sake, Sabrina, you'll be seeing him again soon."

"Suppose so." She stared across to the dark road beyond the exit. "He got a lift from someone."

"Who?"

She shrugged. "Don't know. What do I know about his life?"

"I thought you knew everything. You're getting married to him, so you should."

The sniffs stopped. She stamped her foot. "Don't keep going on about the wedding. Just leave me!" And she stormed off.

I thought it was wedding nerves, so I let her go.

Eventually everyone began to get sleepy, and started to go back to their trailers. When Star came and took Whitney Jade, I stayed where I was. I listened to the sounds of everyone settling down, shouting to one another, saying good night, telling the children to go to sleep, until little by little everything went quiet. It was still warm. Something was rustling and snorting in the bushes near by, probably a hedgehog. I could smell the green scent of the leaves on the trees around us, and the stink of exhausts as the lorries came and went from the place next door.

There wasn't only darkness around me, there was darkness inside me as well. My family were all here. Some friends, some relatives. This was where I belonged. But it was never enough. If you live in a house, you probably think trying to exist in a trailer in the dead of winter, on the side of a road, is hard. Not if you're born to it. It wasn't enough for me. I had to have danger as well.

I made sure no one was watching and I walked across the field and down over the next one, until I could see Langton House clearly. Gregory's bedroom light was still on. I didn't walk any closer, or I'd have been on their drive. I perched myself on the gate. A moment later, he looked out. Maybe he'd seen a movement in the darkness. Or maybe he'd sensed me coming closer. He stayed and stared out of the window, leaning to one side, one hand holding his ribs. Soon as I saw him I got the same tingle running through me that I got before a fight. Only it wasn't fighting I was dreaming about doing with him.

There was only a patch of grass between us, but it might as well have been the width of the whole world. After a while I jumped down off the gate and went back to my trailer.

Rocky was right. I should forget him. But I couldn't.

14

Friday, and I woke with my heart beating fast, as a scream filled our trailer. It was Sabrina. I wanted to put a sock in her mouth. I wanted to go back to sleep, but she wouldn't shut up. In the end I sat up and fought my way through the frothy wedding dress until I could see her.

"WHAT?"

She was sitting on her bed, staring into a little mirror. She blinked tearfully at me, her trembling hand pointing to her face.

"Look!"

I squinted at her. Something was wrong, but I couldn't figure out what. Suddenly her mouth went all trembly.

"Can't you see? It's me eyelashes, Sammy-Jo!"

"What about them?"

"I can't get married like this!"

I wanted to strangle her. "Like what?"

"They've fell out!"

I managed to get round the wedding dress and have a closer look. She was right. So they had.

★ ★ ★

It wasn't just the extension lashes, it was her own as well.

Rocky drove us into Langton. Sabrina was crying too much to see the road. He seemed to have made himself our official driver for the day. He'd turned up while everyone else was having breakfast together under the gazebos, the smell of sizzling bacon scenting the air. I was trying to ignore him, because he kept giving me curious looks, and I didn't want him to start going on about Gregory again. Nor remind me that I'd asked him for a kiss, which he'd refused.

We went straight into Paradise, and the girl who'd spent all the time fixing the extensions on yesterday took a horrified look and tried to remedy the situation with more false lashes.

"What's going on?" I said to Sabrina, as the girl tutted and fussed. "Why did you sit and pick at your eyelashes?"

Sabrina definitely looked like a sulky princess today. "I just did, all right?"

"You only do that when you're fretting."

"Of course I'm fretting! I'm getting married tomorrow."

She didn't need to tell me that. I'd spent the last few weeks fighting to pay for it.

"Is it Tyson? Did you argue?"

"No. I love him."

"What, then?"

"Maybe I'm scared of leaving home!" she said. "And I don't know how to cook."

She was lying. Since when did Sabrina worry about things like cooking?

"So what? You'll learn. That's not the reason."

"OK, then. It's because I never lived on my own before. His father's giving us a bungalow for our wedding present. It's lovely, but I'll be on my own."

"Rubbish. You know you'll see us all the time."

It was true. The Smiths are a big family. No one ever really leaves. Sabrina knew that. We were always seeing our sisters – they'd come for a day with all their children and end up stopping a week. "What's really the matter?"

I couldn't see Sabrina's face because she was leaning back in the chair as the girl worked on her eyelashes, but she was swivelling her engagement ring round and round her thin finger. And her bottom lip was beginning to stick out like Whitney Jade's when she gets told off.

"It's Tyson!" she burst out at last.

"What about him?"

She would've been in floods of tears, but she couldn't because the girl was sticking new lashes on in place of her own. Instead, her mouth opened and a long, tragic wail came out, all mixed up with some words.

"What? Stop crying and speak properly."

"I think he's seeing another woman!"

Me and the eyelash girl looked at each other. I'd heard boys talking down the gym. Some of them had girlfriends they were cheating on. The other boys thought it was funny. I didn't. I told them off when I heard about it. But Tyson? He was an amazing boxer and heading for glory, but he wasn't that bright. I could've sworn he hadn't got the brains or the cunning to cheat on Sabrina.

"Are you sure?"

She nodded, miserably. "Yes! I saw her outside their house. And last week after his stag night I turned up early the next morning, and I saw her outside again. He was talking to her. I drove past. He never noticed me."

"You sure it wasn't someone from his boxing agents?"

"No! I know all of them! I asked him about her the first time I saw them. He pretended he didn't know what I was talking about. And last night she was outside Gypsy's Acre waiting for him! He looked around, seeing if anyone was watching, and then got into her BMW and they drove off fast."

"BMW?" said the eyelash girl. "So she's got some money, then."

That made Sabrina wail again. "I know!"

"What does she look like?" I asked, even though I knew the answer.

Sabrina's lip curled. "A dirty, slutty tramp in a leather jacket, and she's got spiky, bleached-blonde hair like a punk, and she's too old for him. Why would he want her and not me?"

"She doesn't want Tyson. She's Rocky's mystery woman, but you can't tell anyone."

That stopped her. "Why?"

"He says she's his probation officer."

Even Sabrina didn't believe that. "Since when do they turn up after midnight?"

"Exactly. I expect he's keeping it secret from his daddy because she's not a Traveller girl and because she's older than him. Now stop fretting about it."

She gave a sniff. "You sure? Or are you just trying to make me feel better?"

"Honest. Cross me heart. Tyson's had a lucky escape. If he had been seeing another woman, I'd have had to fight him."

Sabrina's face broke into a sheepish grin. "Did you hear that?" she said to the girl. "See how me sister looks after me!"

I patted her shoulder. "Now get your eyelashes fixed, and I'll see you later."

I got out of that place as quick as I could, ignoring Milo Scarret, who was sitting across the road, hood shading his face, hands in his pockets. I had no idea how he'd found us – he'd arrived half an hour ago and sat himself down so he could watch the doorway. As I walked off, I saw him get up and start to follow, but I didn't show him that I'd noticed. He was too scared to come near me. I busied myself ringing Rocky.

"You nearly caused the wedding to be cancelled," I said when he answered.

"How?"

"Tyson got a lift from Miss Stroud. Sabrina was convinced he was having an affair with her."

Rocky gave a hoot. "Tyson and Miss Stroud! Now that would be a marriage made in hell."

"So who is she, and what was she doing hanging around our field last night?"

There was a pause. "She came looking for me, but I'd left already."

"Why did she come looking for you?"

Another pause. "None of your business."

He rang off before I could question him any more. But at least the wedding was safe and Sabrina's lashes were being fixed. Now I only had a million more wedding things to do before tomorrow. And one of them was to go to the hotel to make sure the cakes had arrived and that they were in the marquee, ready to be displayed. After that I had to go home and decorate a plastic garden arch with silk flowers for the bride to walk through as she left the trailers, and trim the patio chairs with white satin bows.

The manageress took me over to the huge marquee, which was now standing on the lawn. We went inside and she showed me the brand-new ivory-and-gold roof drapes, with the tiny little lights twinkling like stars. It did look amazing, like a fairy-tale palace. Sabrina would love it.

The cakes had been delivered and were stored in boxes on the wedding table. There were three of them: one traditional fruit cake, one sponge and one chocolate. Which doesn't sound much until you realized that each cake had seven tiers. Twenty-one cakes in all. I hoped all the wedding guests would be hungry. There were three big stands to display the cakes, beside the wedding table. The marquee was already set out with the chairs and tables which would be filled tomorrow by the wedding guests. There were Smiths coming from all over the country to see Sabrina married.

As we left, the manageress said, "It was such a shame about poor Gregory, wasn't it?"

"Uh-huh." I didn't want to talk about it. She did. I think she'd got it on her mind. One of her staff was injured, and the girl paying for the huge wedding was rumoured to be involved.

"I've had a word with all my girls. They know they were wrong to gossip. It was silly of them."

"Don't worry about it," I said. "It was nothing."

It only got me thrown out of the Langtons' house, and nearly got us thrown off the field.

"I wanted to let you know that we're all on your side. We're looking forward to the wedding," she said. "She's going to be beautiful bride."

I smiled and smiled and told her what a good job she'd done organizing everything for us, and how I was sure everything was going to go fine, and that all the staff were being very nice to us. Only to find five minutes later that I was wrong. There was one member of staff who wasn't going to let me forget.

We had one of the best rooms booked for tomorrow, where Sabrina and I would have our hair done, rather than down at Gypsy's Acre. I got the key and checked it out. It had a big four-poster bed with white silk hangings, and, unlike our trailer, it had enough room for us and the two hairdressers and all their equipment to fit in. Everything was going well. Too well. Just when I thought it was all sorted and I could go and get Sabrina, I walked out of the room –

and ran into Alice standing at the top of the stairs, pale as a vengeful ghost.

At first I thought she was just going to stare at me as I went by, but she didn't move aside. She stood there, blocking my path. Her eyes were red-rimmed. I had a feeling I was going to get the blame for that.

"'Scuse."

She didn't move. She kept her hand on the rail, blocking me. "What's going on?"

"About what?"

Her face screwed up. "You chasing after Gregory. Going up to the house to visit him, like he's a friend or something."

"I'm not chasing after him. I'm not trying to take him from you."

"As if you could." She laughed, but there was no humour in it. "Do you really think I'm jealous of you?"

"Maybe," I said. "But I don't hang around with gorjer boys. And that's what Gregory is. So don't worry." Even as I spoke the words, I knew it wasn't true.

"I'm not. I think you're making a fool of yourself. Everybody's laughing about it."

I shrugged. "Let them. I don't care."

She gave a little cry of rage, and then the truth came out. "Me and Gregory have been going out since Year Eight, and suddenly you come along and ruin it."

I tried to push past her again, but she wasn't budging. "I didn't do anything."

"Yes, you did! Last night we had a big row. It was all

151

because of you. He had a go at me, because I showed his dad the photo."

That stopped me. "The photo was wrong."

She rolled her eyes. "Yes. I *know.* He told me over and over. Big deal. You just happened to be there – rescuing my boyfriend, who was only out there because he was checking on you! And then there you are at his house, sitting right next to him, practically on his lap, in your stupid slutty dress. Making out that you're sorry he got beaten up."

"I was sorry."

"Yeah, right. I've heard all about you. You're always getting into trouble."

She hadn't heard *all* about me. She had no idea what I was up to at night. I tried to imagine her going to a no-rules fight. But things like that didn't exist in her world, or Gregory's. She would never have a sister who wanted the biggest, most expensive wedding in the universe. It was no use talking to her.

"Yeah, whatever. Now 'scuse."

She wouldn't let me get by. She kept her arm blocking the stairs. Her face crumpled. "Everyone's right. You are a bitch."

I was tempted to show her that I was. One quick strike with my hand, and I could knock her down before she blinked her red-rimmed eyes again. I was tempted, but I met her eyes instead. "I'm not. I'm a good person. I want everything to be fair. I don't want to fight with anyone. Not even you."

It was true. I couldn't be bothered to argue. She didn't mean anything to me. After tomorrow I would never see her again. I would never be her friend. But she still didn't move out of my way.

"He's not speaking to me. We're over. All that time together!"

I'd had enough. Sabrina's eyelashes, Rocky's mystery woman and now this. I tossed my hair back.

"Maybe it's time you had a change, then. Maybe he was fed up with you anyway. I would be. Don't you do anything but moan, moan, moan?"

Her mouth dropped open, her eyes brimmed with tears. I went to push past her, but she did the pushing. She gave an annoyed squeal and shoved me hard. I went down the first three steps and grabbed for the first thing to stop myself. It happened to be her arm. We half slid down the rest of the stairs and landed at the bottom.

"You nearly killed me!" she cried as she got to her feet.

"No, she didn't," boomed someone, before I could speak. "It was your fault. You pushed her."

Someone sticking up for me. That was a novelty. I turned round and there was the beaming handsome face of Uncle Bartley from America. It was a wonderful sight, but that's where the wonderfulness ended. Standing next to him was Beryl, glaring at me in horror. And following behind was Rocky, wheeling Bartley's suitcase, with Sabrina bringing up the rear. Rocky was grinning. Sabrina was staring at me and Alice, open-mouthed. There was no doubt about it. They'd all heard the argument.

I was in trouble now.

15

We were in Bartley's room. He'd booked in at the White Swan. He was perched on the windowsill, dividing his time between looking at me and staring out of the window.

He's the youngest of all my aunts and uncles and hasn't got any children of his own yet. He went over to America ten years ago, and he soon got a name for himself as a fighter on the Ultimate Fighting Championship circuit. After every contest he'd give a speech, telling everyone he was one of the fighting Smiths. It didn't matter if he won or lost, he'd still take the mike off the host and address the crowd. They loved him. So when they started the *CAGED* programmes, they went straight to him to present it. It had made him loads of money, as Sabrina was finding out.

She was happily unwrapping a whole suitcase-full of presents he'd brought from America for her. Her eyes were looking luscious again. The Paradise girl had done a good job on her.

Beryl was pacing up and down. "I can't believe you'd do this to us, Sammy," she said.

"What?"

She stopped and stood in front of me with her hands on her hips. "We all heard. You've been hanging around with that Langton boy. And he's got a girlfriend!"

"Had a girlfriend," I said. "He fell out with her, if you'd listened. It's not my fault. I never asked him to."

Beryl began pacing up and down again. "That's not what we heard. She says you're after him. I wanted to go up to her and tell her that no way would you shame us by going near him. But I can't, can I?"

I had to get out of there – they were driving me crazy – but Rocky was leaning on the door, his arms folded. I was stuck.

"I told you. I went to his house because I was worried about him. That's all. She got jealous. She saw us talking. People are spreading rumours about me to cause trouble."

I don't know why I bothered. Beryl wasn't listening to a word I said. She'd made her mind up.

"Tyson's cousin Scarlet married a man from a house near the site," she said. "You go and ask them how that worked out! She hated living in a house. He hated living in a trailer on the site. It doesn't work."

"I know."

"All right, leave her now, Beryl," said Bartley. "Maybe we won't have to worry about her and this boy. Not if she comes back with me. Your aunt Crystal would love to see you over in California." He smiled at me. "I've been hearing good things about your fighting, Sammy. You've got the strength and the speed. You've won everything going."

155

"I have."

He nodded. "Good. Me and you will have to talk after the wedding. I reckon I can get you some work behind the scenes, helping with the training. How about it?"

"Maybe," I said. "But I've got things to do. I'll have to see."

"She needs a holiday," said Beryl. "She needs to get away from Sam's gym."

"Yes," said Rocky. "Take her back with you."

"No!" I headed for the door. I'd had enough. "I can run my own life. I don't need everyone telling me what to do." Rocky didn't move. He leaned back on the door, watching me. "And why are you following me around?"

"You've got yourself into trouble."

Bartley was looking out of the window. "She certainly has. There's a skinhead boy in a hoodie who's been watching this window since we brought Sammy up here." He looked over at me. "Who is he?"

"Milo Scarret. He's nobody."

He'd followed me from the nail bar. I was hoping no one else had noticed.

"Doesn't look like nobody to me," said Bartley. "He looks like trouble. What's going on?"

"Nothing, Uncle Bartley. Nothing I can't handle. He tried to pick a fight with me, and I beat him, that's all."

He didn't look convinced. "I get to choose the lost boys that go on *CAGED*. I go into the streets. I judge them with one look. I know who can be saved. Who can learn to

156

control themselves. All I need to do is look at their faces." He stood up and came over to me, and grabbed my shoulders with his big fighter's hands. "He's not saveable. Keep away from him."

I shrugged him off. "Thanks for the advice. But I don't need it. I don't need anyone's advice." I turned on my heel and looked Rocky in the eye. "'Scuse."

He moved out of my way at last. I stormed out without another word.

There was definitely something wrong with my brain because after all that shouting and upset and everyone getting mad at me, all I could think about was this: *Gregory had fallen out with his girlfriend!*

But as I walked outside, even that fact went out of my head. Milo had moved. He was in the street outside now, and he wasn't alone. A car had just pulled up in front of him, a battered old Jeep. I skipped back into the doorway, because I'd seen that Jeep before, parked in between McCloud's Range Rover and the red Subaru in the yard of International Express. And the driver was none other than Pony. He'd got the window down, and he was talking to Milo like they were good mates. And they were definitely discussing me because Milo kept looking back at the hotel as he spoke. In the end, Pony said something to him and he got in the car and they drove off.

I left it a few minutes and then strolled away. Here was me thinking that Milo and McCloud both wanting me to move was a coincidence. It wasn't. McCloud must've set

Milo onto me, to keep himself away from any rough stuff.

He was cleverer than I thought.

Night fell. The clock headed towards midnight. Sabrina was curled up in her princess quilt beneath the skirts of her wedding dress, fast asleep. I wished I could do the same, but I couldn't relax again. Outside, under the gazebos, I could hear Bartley telling everyone tales of America, CAGED and the boot-camp training that he ran for the fighter boys on the show. Even more of our friends and relatives had come down to see him. Motors and lorries were parked all the way along the road because the field was so full now.

Everyone was having a good time except me. I wasn't speaking to anyone. I was angry at them all. I was angry at myself, and at Alice and Gregory. The whole world was getting me in a rage. I rang Kimmy.

"Find me a fight. Then come and get me."

She gave a whoop. "On my way."

I changed into my favourite coral-pink Lycra shorts trimmed in black, and a matching tight crop top with a zip-up sweater over it. I squeezed out past the dresses. No one saw me leave. Everyone thought I was sulking in my bed. I walked to the road, and began marching along it towards town, watching out for Kimmy's Golf.

Someone started following me straightaway. I was hoping it was Milo or Pony, so I carried on walking. I made sure I was balanced on my toes, my ears wolf-sharp and directed back to the footsteps, which were getting closer. I hoped

158

they'd come near me. Please let them start something. My hands were already in fists. Please let them want to fight me.

The road was dark, but every so often there was a street light. As I approached the first light, I slowed. I wanted to get a look at them. Let them come closer. They were being too slow to attack. The footsteps were hurrying to catch me now, so I spun on my heel, my hands coming up. I was hoping for Milo. He deserved another beating.

It wasn't Milo.

It was Gregory. He walked into the circle of light and stopped quickly. He held up his hands. "Whoa. Wait. It's me."

I could see that. What the hell was he doing out here? And why did he have to look so cute in an old jumper and a pair of crumpled jeans? I could feel my heart start to beat faster. Too much adrenaline was flooding like fire through my veins, ready to take on a fight. But there was no fight, just me and him staring at each other again. Half of me was overjoyed to see his face. The other half carried on being angry. What was the use of being glad to see him?

"What do you want?" I asked.

I think the same fire was running through his veins.

"I'm sick of everyone telling me what to do," he said. "I wanted to see you."

16

"Sorry. I didn't mean to scare you."

"You didn't. I nearly kicked you in the head." I was walking fast down the road towards town. "You shouldn't be here. Go home."

He was keeping up with me. "No."

Fine. He wanted to walk with me. I let him, for now.

"I can't sleep," he said. "I can't think straight."

Me neither. But I didn't tell him that. A car approached, its headlights sweeping over us, and carried on by. It wasn't Kimmy. I kept walking.

"You should keep away from me," I said.

"Why?"

"I'll get you hurt again. Milo's mad at me, and he is going to use you to hurt me if he can. There's something going on. I can't figure out what it is yet, but Milo's at International Express now. He's with Mr McCloud. They're connected."

That surprised him. "Connected? How?"

I shrugged. "Working for him, I suppose. I can't see them being big mates."

"Why would Mr McCloud hire a dick like Milo?"

He'd missed the point. I stopped and turned to him. "Don't you get it? That means it *was* my fault you got beat up. McCloud must've told Milo to beat me up and scare me away. But he daren't, so he got you instead. He knew if he made it look like I'd hurt you, it'd get us thrown off the field."

He still wasn't convinced. "Seriously? Mr McCloud? He's a big businessman. There's a chain of International Express companies, not just this one. He's loaded. He's not a Bond villain. I don't know why he'd care that much about you."

"Just because he's a rich businessman, it doesn't make him an angel." I started walking again. Gregory could think what he liked. I knew the truth.

He caught me up. "Look, I still can't believe he'd order someone to beat you or me up." He grabbed my arm. "Can we stop, please?"

I shook him away and carried on. Another car went by without slowing. Half of me wanted Kimmy to get here quickly. The other half wanted to stay and argue with Gregory all night.

"You should go back. Me aunties would go mental if they knew I was out in the dark with you."

"Why? What's it got to do with them?"

"I'm a disgrace. My uncle wants to take me back to America with him."

The headlights of another car were approaching. It lit up the road sign that announced we were entering Langton. The town with the same name as the boy beside me. Maybe once upon a time they owned the whole place and were lords of the manor. I stopped by it. This was where I had to meet Kimmy.

Gregory stopped, facing me but keeping his distance. "It's the same at my house. My dad's watching me all the time. My mum thinks you've bewitched me or something."

I tossed my hair back. I tried to smile. "Maybe I have. I'm the seventh daughter of a seventh daughter, that makes me special. It means I can get boys in me power."

He didn't laugh. His mood changed suddenly. The anger went out of him, but his eyes were still blazing. "I half believe you. You look witchy tonight. Gorgeous and witchy."

He moved closer and held out his hands like we were going to grapple. He waited for me to make a move, his mouth curving into a small smile. I took his hands.

"More arm wrestling?" I said. I had to joke. His touch was electric. He shook his head.

"Does everything have to be about fighting for you?"

"Yes. Yes, it does." He really didn't know. He didn't know how the fire ran through my veins before a fight, like it was doing now. And how my nerves tingled and every part of me was too alive. I shouldn't be near Gregory when I felt like this. It made everything too intense.

He didn't realize. He looked entranced.

"You look like you're either going to strike me down or put some kind of spell on me. I can't decide which."

My heart had begun to beat too fast. The only thing

between us was our joined hands, as though any moment we might start to fight for real. One of us would twist and try to get a throw, or sweep with a foot and knock the other over.

But we both knew it wasn't fighting that we wanted to do to each other.

"I always remembered you," he said, softly. "But I didn't think I'd ever see you again. You were this mystery girl who I found in the hallway. And you dashed away. I went up to the site looking for you, but you'd gone. There was nothing left except flattened grass."

There was nothing left of the world now except this little patch of grass and the road sign and the dark road. And me and Gregory so close to each other.

"Did you want to see me again?" I said. My eyes were used to the darkness, and I could see his face more clearly.

"Yes. You're a mystery. I always want to solve mysteries."

"Have you solved me now you've met me again?"

He shook his head. "No. I can't figure you out at all."

We were so close together. I could feel his warm breath on my cheek. I had no idea how I was going to stop my heart aching when we left on Sunday. Because this little world of me and him was a false one.

"It'll be the same this time," I said. "In two days I'll be gone."

"So what am I going to do about the fact that I'm crazy about you?" he said.

There's always a tipping point in a fight, a tiny moment

when you suddenly know that you're going to win or lose. Was this the tipping point for me and Gregory? Win or lose, all I wanted was for him to kiss me.

It didn't happen. Another set of headlights approached. They swept over us. The car slowed to a stop. It was Kimmy's Golf. I let go of his hands and stood back. The spell broke. We weren't alone any more. The real world was back.

"I have to go," I said.

"Where?"

How could I tell him that I was going to make money fighting in a place where they called me Gypsy Girl, and where some of the boys were too scared to fight me? How could I say that the reason he thought I looked witchy and entrancing tonight was partly because I was ready to fight in a cage?

He didn't belong anywhere near Maltese Joey's clubs. He didn't even know they existed. What would he think of a girl who went to them willingly, even when she wasn't paying for her sister's wedding, who needed them to put danger and thrills into her life?

The car window slid down.

"What's up?" shouted Kimmy. "Are you getting in, or what?"

"Yes. Give me a moment."

I turned to Gregory. "You think you know me?"

"I do. I'm good at reading people. I watch them. I can tell what people are like."

"Not me."

He didn't believe me. He shook his head.

"Do you want to know the truth?" I opened the car door. "Dare you to come with me."

"Where to?"

"You'll see. I want to show you who I really am."

He looked at the car, he looked at Kimmy. He looked at me.

"Fine."

17

Kimmy was mad with me. She was ignoring Gregory.

We were cruising through a maze of dark streets, miles away from Langton, in the opposite direction to my home and the gym. We'd come straight down the M1, though, so it hadn't taken us long to get there.

We turned a corner.

"In fifty yards you have reached your destination," announced the satnav.

Our destination was a street lined with old warehouses and run-down businesses. Most of the businesses along here were cheap garages and workshops that resprayed hot cars, ready for resale to unsuspecting customers. Two of the streetlights were broken, and the third was a dull orange and flashing fitfully.

One place had been turned into a small nightclub with a bad reputation. Men paid money for girls to pretend to like them, and dance in front of them. It didn't seem to be doing too well because there weren't many cars parked in front of it. But further down there was a bigger building that had been turned into a gym, one that held fights at night.

Its car park was full of cars. They'd drawn a good crowd. That would mean more prize money, and more for Gregory to see.

He was sitting quietly in the back seat, watching everything, trying to work out what sort of place we were taking him to. Kimmy parked the Golf and led the way to the front door. She'd noticed all the cars, and knew we could make good money tonight. She'd almost forgotten about Gregory and began to look happier. Like me, she did this for the money and for the thrill of doing something edgy. It made us both feel alive.

There was always the scent of danger at these places. It sparkled in the air, hanging over the buildings and the fighters and their supporters. That's what drew them back, time and time again. We were like bees to a jar of honey. We needed the thrill of doing something that wasn't allowed, the tingle of not knowing whether the club would get raided and busted for gambling. No one could tell how the night would end. That was the draw.

Over the door, a CCTV camera blinked red, telling us that we were being videoed. Even from outside, we could hear the noise of the crowd, a continual, rumbling howl, the sound of people shouting for their favourite fighters. The door swung open. A bouncer stood there, an ex-fighter with a broken nose and the stunned look of someone who'd taken too many knocks to the head.

"Gypsy Girl to see Maltese Joey," said Kimmy.

He looked me over. "He's not here. He's busy."

"Yeah, I know." That was the story. Maltese Joey was never in his clubs. Some people thought he didn't exist at all. I knew differently, but I played along.

"You're late. They're waiting for you." The man waved us through. "Go to the main hall."

Kimmy was usually first in. She liked to get the money business over with at the start. She sorted out my fee and my winnings. She made sure I got well paid. But tonight, as I walked in with Gregory, she didn't follow us. She was looking back outside, as though she'd seen something worrying.

"What's wrong?"

She gave the street one last look and followed me and Gregory inside. "It's nothing. While I was driving I thought I saw someone."

"Who?"

"No one. Forget it."

I shouldn't have done, but I did. I was too busy watching Gregory. He'd gone very quiet. There was another set of doors to get through before we were in the main hall, but the cheers and boos were louder now.

"What is this place?" He frowned at me. "Is this a joke?"

I unzipped my sweatshirt so he could see my crop top with the name Gypsy Girl stencilled on it. "No joke. Welcome to Maltese Joey's world."

The bouncer threw open the inner doors, and a wave of heat and noise smacked into us. Me and Kimmy were used to it, but Gregory stepped back as though the bellowing of the crowd was a fist that had hit him hard. It was a savage, wild sound that rose and rose. One of the fighters had obviously hit the mats. This was the supporters shouting for their men to hit and kick and grapple harder. It was the sound of the cage fight.

In front of us the main hall opened out. It was a big space with a high ceiling. The edges were dark, but the centre was lit so brightly you'd think a UFO had landed. The light was coming from a big lighting rig high above the hexagonal cage. It was a million miles away from me daddy's gym. In our gym, the practise cage is brand-new and the bars shiny, the mats clean. Here the bars were rusted in places and bent in others where the supporters and trainers hooked their hands through and shook the bars if their fighters weren't fighting hard enough.

Gregory looked round silently, his eyes drinking everything in.

"I know what this is," he breathed. "It's a fight club. I didn't think they existed."

"Now you know they do," said Kimmy.

He swung round at me. He looked angry again. "You actually fight here?"

"Yes."

"I don't see any other girls. Tell me you don't fight against the boys."

"I do."

We were standing by the warm-up area, where men and boys were waiting for their fights. They were sitting

169

on benches or warming up, hitting punch bags, skipping, sparring with each other. Some were sitting nervously, loosening their shoulders or shaking out their calf muscles, while their trainers gave them last-minute instructions. Some of them looked like Milo and his brothers, with shaved heads and tattoos. Some were prettier, with styled hair and tanned muscles. Gregory looked at them, and then he looked at me, in my crop top and little pink shorts. "This is madness."

I couldn't read his face. He looked horrified, excited, disgusted and curious all at once.

"It's what I do," I said. "You thought you knew me. Now you'll see that you don't."

I walked away.

"Wait!" he shouted, angrily, but I didn't go back.

A man came over. He was one of the managers who were supposed to run things for Maltese Joey, and I didn't like him at all. Dark, greased hair, hands like bunches of sausages, eyes diamond hard. He had a scar running from the corner of his mouth in curve over his cheek, where in the past someone had put a Stanley knife in the corner of his mouth and pulled, so one side of his face always had a fake smile. He didn't look pleased to see me, but it wasn't always like that. When I first met him, he was all over me. Some of the men think girls are pushovers, but I can handle it. I smacked him in his scarred face and told him to back off. Since then he'd kept his distance.

"I've got a fight for you," he said. "A Jamaican boy. Euston."

He nodded over towards a black boy, probably a year or two older than me. He was taller but not heavily built. His dark hair had elaborate patterns shaved into it.

"What do you think?" said Kimmy.

She always left the final decision to me.

"OK."

Kimmy went over to Euston's trainer and began negotiating. Boy fighters either grinned at me, thinking they were going to knock me down in seconds, or they looked spooked because they'd heard about me. Euston looked spooked. I hadn't seen him before, but he must have heard something. No man or boy likes being beaten by a girl. If they did beat me, the rewards would be good, so they chanced it. But it made them edgy. When they got in the ring, they were determined to stop me as soon as possible. My reputation was spreading.

Most of the supporters were clustered around the cage, but a few were walking about in the less crowded areas, or talking in groups. There were a few women among them, staying close to their boyfriends. I was getting lots of attention. I always did. There was a buzz around me. The manager knew that I was a big draw. Even though I'd only decided to fight an hour ago, he would've been sending out messages to the regulars.

The noise rose again to a continual roar as the men gathered round the cage for the next bout. Two heavyweight fighters prowled around the ring, eyeing each other up like wolves. And that's how the crowd treated them, holding onto the bars, rattling them, yelling and shouting. Kimmy was pushing her way back to me. She organized my fights, took bets, got my winnings, made sure we were paid in full and most importantly she watched my back and got me away from there after I won, as quickly as she could. Sometimes the men didn't like paying out money because a girl had beaten their fighter.

"You're on next," she said. "Win and we'll make good money."

I took off my zip-up and began to jog on my toes, warming my muscles. Euston was still watching me. So was Gregory. He was standing all alone amidst the crowds, getting pushed this way and that. All they saw was a slender girl in Lycra shorts, black gloves and a crop top, with long hair in a plait that came to her waist. Once Euston saw how slight I was, he began to relax. He was wrong. He thought that strength only came with big muscles.

And Gregory? What did he think of me? I still couldn't read his face.

I waited, jogging and doing my stretches, Kimmy by my side and Gregory watching, as the two heavyweights finished their fight. As they were helped from the ring, one of them shaking drops of blood from a cut eyebrow, music began blaring from loudspeakers. It was telling everyone that a new fight was going to start.

"Make way for the next contestants!" bellowed the scar-faced manager.

A corridor opened up in the packed crowd, ending at the

door of the cage. Kimmy led me through, lashing out at the hands that reached out to touch me, yelling at the men to keep back, hitting them if they didn't move out of the way fast enough.

I didn't know where Gregory was. He wasn't following us. I thought for a moment that maybe he'd taken the opportunity to leave and forget he'd ever been brought to a place like this. I ducked into the cage and moved over to the middle. The lights blinded me, until my eyes got used to the brightness.

Gregory hadn't walked out. He'd made his way to the front. There he was, two metres from me, crushed in on all sides by supporters trying to get the best view of the fight. He was holding onto the bars. If he hated me, he didn't show it. If he liked the thought of watching me fight, he didn't show that, either. He looked like he was afraid for me. No one had ever been afraid for me before.

I jogged on the spot as I waited for my opponent to make his way into the cage. All around me the men shouted and howled at me. All except Gregory. He made no sound; he just watched. I breathed in the smell of sweat and the metallic tang of blood, mixed with the hundred different aftershaves and perfumes that wafted from the crowd surrounding the cage. I could see Kimmy pushing her way to Gregory's side and hanging onto the bars, so that she could shout instructions and encouragement to me during the fight.

All I needed now was Euston. The music kept playing, the crowd kept cheering, but a minute passed, which was a long time to be bouncing on your toes in a cage, waiting. The cheering changed to boos.

Something was wrong.

The manager was at the cage door, arguing with someone. It wasn't Euston. He wasn't the problem. I could see him near the door with his trainer, who was looking annoyed. I looked round for Kimmy, but she wasn't by the bars any more. She was fighting her way towards the manager. But it wasn't him she was aiming for. She was shouting at someone I couldn't see, telling them to go away, to get lost.

I gave up on the jogging and went over to Gregory. The crowd was turning round, looking at someone who was approaching the ring.

"What's happening?" I said to him.

"I don't know."

"New fighter coming," said a man, pushing his way to the front, beside Gregory. "He's paid to fight you!" He leered at me. "He must really want to beat you."

My hand was on the bars as I strained to see. Gregory slid his down and grasped mine. I think he'd seen the fighter.

"You're going to fight *him*? Are you crazy, or is this a fix?" he said, urgently.

I pulled my hand away. I didn't care who I fought. Gregory was scared for me, but I scare myself. I'm too good. Someone should stop me.

I could hear Kimmy above all the men, her higher voice carrying. She was still shouting at someone to go away – the new fighter, I supposed. Yelling at him that Sammy-Jo had an opponent, she didn't need another. Yelling at the manager that he should stick to the deal and not change sides just because he was offered lots of money.

But the crowd didn't seem to mind. They were urging the new fighter to get in the ring. All I could see was the top of the new fighter's head as he began to push his way through the crowd. I backed away, into the centre of the cage, my heart starting to pound. Gregory was right. Kimmy was right. Not him. He should go away. I didn't want to fight him. But it was too late. He was ducking through the door and strutting towards me.

I could hardly get me breath. I wanted the ground to swallow me whole.

"Looks like you're going to fight me," said Rocky.

No wonder Gregory knew him. Everyone in Langton knew the Quinn brothers. Rocky looked round and saw Gregory.

"You've got quite an audience."

And this time there was no rascally sparkle in his eyes.

"You fool," he said.

18

He was furious with me.

"This is stupid, even for you." He had on black-and-white shorts, low on his hips and tight fitting. He pulled on his fingerless gloves. The muscles of his chest and arms gleamed.

The sides of the cage were a mass of shouting faces, some shouting for Rocky, some for me. No one seemed to mind that I was fighting him instead of Euston. Rocky has the sort of swagger that fight fans love.

He paced around me. I stayed still in the centre. The noise was deafening, but it meant nothing to me. All I could see was Rocky, with Gregory's face in the background, watching.

"You followed us," I said. "Kimmy thought she saw something."

"Don't talk to me about Kimmy. She should be ashamed. Bringing you to something like this."

The crowd began to boo. They wanted us fighting, not talking to each other. Rocky carried on pacing around me. I let him. His hands were in fists. I kept my own down by my sides.

"So, aren't you gonna fight me?" he asked. "Are you just going to stand there in your little pink shorts, looking cute for all the punters who want to bet money that you're going to get beaten up?" His lip curled.

I twisted round on my heel, keeping him in sight. "No. I want you to go away and leave me alone. This is nothing to do with you."

"Sorry. That's not going to happen. You want to fight men? You can fight me."

He came straight at me, and the crowd roared. He was trying to take me down in the first few seconds, but even though he'd taken me by surprise, he wasn't going to succeed. I blocked him, knocking us both to our knees, but not for long. We both got back on our feet, circling each other. He wanted a fight, so I'd give him one. And he wasn't going to beat me. He wasn't going to get me on the floor and get a stranglehold on me, and then drag me from the club.

Why couldn't everyone let me live my life how I wanted?

I have a move, a signature move. It looks like nothing much. A foot sweep. As I bounce around the ring and they're still thinking I'm nothing more than a girl, I move fast and hook one of their feet delicately, and push them over. That's all it takes to get most fighters on the floor. A little distraction, a quick flick of my foot, and I catch them off balance. It comes out of nowhere, while they're still figuring out if I'm for real. It turns their momentum against them. Once they're on the mats, they're mine. I can get away with it because I'm fast and light, and men and boys can't move like me.

I forced a smile as I danced around him. "OK, Rocky. I'll fight you. Let's do this."

He wasn't even looking at my feet. He didn't notice my move until his legs went from under him and he was falling. I dropped down fast and trapped him on the mats. Half the crowd was screaming with delight, and the others were groaning and shouting that Rocky should get a grip and stop messing around.

I managed to hold him for a couple of seconds, but he was furious and he was strong. He threw me backwards into the air, and I bounced to my feet, but I was off balance, and I went stumbling back and hit the bars before I could slow myself. I glimpsed Gregory's face right there beside me. While Rocky was getting to his feet, I grasped the bars.

"I'm sorry. I shouldn't have brought you here."

The man beside Gregory shouted for me to go back and fight. We both ignored him.

"Why, Sammy?" he said.

"This is my life. My secret life."

"Don't do this." I saw fear in his eyes. Fear for me.

"I can beat him. Don't worry." The adrenaline had got to me. I blew Gregory a kiss, and the supporters around him howled. And then I hurled myself back at Rocky.

We fought. Oh, how we fought. I hardly ever used all my strength, all my speed, all my agility against an opponent. Tonight I did. I bounced off the bars, I somersaulted, I threw him and rolled. He tried to pin me, but I was as slippery as an eel. He got me down once, straddling me, sitting on me, trying to hold onto my hands, his face inches from mine. I'd never seen him so angry.

"You could get killed, or injured," he hissed. "Someone throws you hard and you never walk again. It's happened. Do you want that? Huh?"

"It won't happen to me. I can handle myself."

He gave a snort of pure anger. "Are you so short of money you have to do this?"

"No."

"Don't lie. We all wondered how Samson could afford Sabrina's wedding."

"Don't you dare tell him. Or I'll tell your daddy about Miss Stroud. She's not your probation officer. You're a liar. You're up to something."

I grabbed his hands as I bucked with my hips. It threw Rocky forward, but he couldn't land on his hands because I was grasping them now, pulling them down, so he tipped forward and hit the floor with his face. It was a beginner's move. He was off balance because he was so mad at me. But he was up onto his knees straightaway. So was I.

I hit him, and he reeled back. It meant nothing; the next second he jumped to his feet. I was right there, though, ready for anything. The crowd was going crazy. All except Gregory. I could see him behind Rocky's shoulder. His pale face among the screaming ones, watching me, drinking it all in, fingers hooked through the bars, trying to make sense of me and the fight.

"Sabrina's a fool. Three seven-tier cakes because she couldn't decide on sponge or fruit or chocolate," he said. "She doesn't know that you're doing this to pay for them."

"She'll never know. I swear, Rocky. You tell, and I'll tell on you."

I hit him again, but he was ready. He ducked to the side and came back at me faster than a snake. He came in close, in my face, grabbing hold of me, tripping me, but I had hold of him, too, and we were going down on our knees together. A wall of roaring faces upped the volume. I could hear Kimmy over all of them, screaming at me to get him on the mat.

Stranglehold, that was one of my strengths. Rocky knew it. All I wanted to do was get my arms around his neck and lock my fists together, cutting the blood to his brain and making him black out. We were wrapped around each other, closer than we'd ever been, our faces almost touching. The heat coming off his body was frying me.

"You could've asked me," he hissed in my ear. "I told you, I've got money."

I tried to get my arm around his neck, and failed. "No. We're proud."

"I would've kept it a secret. Chrissake, Sammy. I'm so angry with you." He tore my arm away and threw me down on my back, and he was on top of me straightaway, pinning me down. "Look at this place. No referee, no safeguards, no one to stop the fight if it goes too far."

I stopped trying to throw him off me. "It's sweet that you care. But you shouldn't. Imagine if Beryl got her way and we went out together. We'd destroy each other." I stopped struggling. I let him think just for a moment he'd worn me down.

He grinned, tightening his grip "Like I'm going to do now? Even though you're pretending to be beat."

He shouldn't talk during a fight. Boys can't do both. Girls can. Me sister Sadie-May says it's called multi-tasking. While he was ranting, I'd got in a position to knock him off me. I twisted and moved so fast that before he could do anything it was me on top, and he was beneath me.

"Give up now?" I said. "Before I destroy you."

There was no grin on his face now. "Maybe we should've hooked up together. Then I could've stopped you doing stupid, dangerous stuff like this."

"You don't want me. You want your secrets and your older woman."

"And you want rich boy over there. And that's cruel because he's fallen for you, and you're going to leave on Sunday and never see him again."

"That's why I brought him here. I wanted him to see what I was."

Rocky let his head fall back onto the mats, and laughed. "You thought that'd stop him wanting to jump your bones? You really don't know boys."

The crowd was getting restless. So was Scar-face. "Stop talking, and fight!" he bellowed. He wanted to see me get beaten.

Rocky smiled. "Let's do this."

He pushed me off him and leaped to his feet. We began circling each other. Kimmy was shouting through the bars, rattling them. Gregory was next to her. He looked so young and fair among the men, eyes locked on me, his hands holding the bars. Golden-brown eyes staring at me, trying to understand why I was doing this. Why I was in a cage with people shouting at me, betting on me.

Rocky tried every trick he knew to trip me, but I was too quick for him. In fact, he tripped himself, only for a second, but long enough for me to skip round and leap on his back like a monkey. He tried to tip me off, using his full strength now, but it made no difference. My arm was locked around his neck, pulling his chin back, destroying his breathing and his balance, until he sat down and I could squirm from behind him, still holding the lock.

It should've worked, but somehow he half-slithered free, and twisted, and then it was equal, deadlock. We both had a hold of each other, but neither of us had the upper hand. I'd used the last of my power, but so had he. We lay there, wrapped around each other, gasping for breath in the middle of the cage.

I tried to finish him off, but I couldn't. My grip on him slipped, until finally he broke free and reared up on his knees. I was undefended. All he had to do was pin me and get a stranglehold, and I was finished. He'd won.

I held my hand up in surrender. "Not my face," I said. "I'm a bridesmaid tomorrow." I couldn't be bruised. Sabrina would go crazy.

He groaned and sat back on his heels.

"Jeez, Sammy. What are you doing to yourself? What are you thinking? I'd never hit you."

He jumped to his feet and held out his hand.

"Come on. Let's go home."

I could've cheated and grabbed his hand, thrown him and won. I didn't.

The crowd booed. Kimmy looked spooked. Crowds are like wild beasts, they can turn on you at a moment's notice.

Rocky pulled me up, breathing in great gulps of air. Another few minutes and he would've had no strength left either.

"Run!" shouted Kimmy, throwing the cage door open. "They're mad at both of you!"

We pushed our way out of the cage, squeezing past the fighters waiting to come in. As Rocky passed Kimmy, he grabbed hold of her and hauled her along beside him. They were shouting at each other, but I couldn't hear what they were saying over the booing. I didn't care, because the crowd had parted to let me through and Gregory was there, waiting for me. If the fights were like a honey pot to me, so was Gregory. I'd shown him what I was. I should've walked away and left him. But I couldn't. I went up to him.

"You could've been injured," he said.

"That's my business."

He stumbled as he got pushed to one side by the crowd. I took his hand. "We have to get out of here. They're mad because I didn't finish the fight."

I thought he might push me away, but he didn't. He started shoving his way to the door, making a clear path for me, dragging me along, holding tight to my hand. I was glad of it. I had hardly any strength left. My blood sugar had dropped like a stone, my knees were shaking.

"Does your dad know what you do?" he said.

"No. No one does except Kimmy. And now you and Rocky. Don't ever say anything."

He looked around for the last time as we made it to the exit doors. "This place is the pits. It's horrible." He pulled me through the doors into the cold night air. My legs buckled, and I almost fell. No more adrenaline in my blood, no more energy in my muscles. He put his arm around me, holding me up. "But you were amazing. How can you fight like that?"

I shrugged. "I'm a Smith."

His arms were still around me. The car park was quiet. Rocky and Kimmy were still inside.

"Good job we won't be seeing each other again," I said. "You can forget that places like this even exist." My whole body ached after fighting Rocky, but it was my heart that ached the most. "This is goodbye. I bet you're glad, now you've seen what I do."

"No," he said.

I pushed his arms away from me, even though I wanted to stay wrapped in them for ever. "Go away. Go back to your girl. You fell out with her for no reason. I'll forget you by next week."

"I won't forget," he said. "I won't forget you."

A door slammed, and now Rocky was dragging Kimmy over to us.

"Get your hands off me!" She was thumping him and trying to kick him. He shoved her towards her motor.

"Get in and drive, and don't let me see you again."

I turned away from Gregory and shouted, "Leave her alone."

Rocky swung round at me. "She helps you go to these places. What sort of friend is she?"

"My best friend. She doesn't boss me around. She doesn't tell me I should be marrying this person or that person, like everybody else."

Kimmy bipped open the doors, fumbling the key in her haste to get away. I got in and lowered the window as Rocky came over. "Take Gregory home. I'm going with Kimmy."

He gripped the ledge, so I couldn't close the window. "Fine. But I tell your daddy the moment I get back."

My heart gave a thump. "You wouldn't."

"I would." He slammed a fist down on the window ledge. "You gonna tell me what's going on in your head, Sammy-Jo?"

"No. And you won't tell my father anything. You've got secrets as well."

"Not like yours."

"Right. A boy gets in trouble with the police, and they let him off. Something happened to you a year ago."

Everyone else was relieved he hadn't got sentenced. But

I noticed that he started disappearing off by himself, saying he was doing part-time jobs for someone or other.

"No mystery," he said. "I got into trouble and charmed me way out of it." He stopped and listened. In the distance, a siren was wailing. "You hang around in those places and *you're* going to get into trouble with the police. And then your daddy'll find out. And Beryl and Queenie."

He was trying to panic me. It didn't work.

"Before you got into trouble you stopped training and fighting," I said. "Why?"

He thumped his fist again. "I told you. I told everyone. Someone I knew got injured. Billy Lee, he's called. He broke his neck. He'll never walk again. It put me off, OK? That's why I don't want the same thing happening to you."

I wasn't going to back down. "So how come that crowd knew you?" I'd heard a few of them shouting out his name while we were fighting. "You didn't just follow us. You've been to these fights before. That's how you knew the name Gypsy Girl. So it's OK for you, but not for me?"

For the first time, he looked uncomfortable as well as angry. "What I do is none of your business."

"Why?"

"It just is. You'll have to take my word for it."

"I might start following you round as well."

"I wouldn't do that if I were you," he said.

I smacked my fist down on his hand to make him let go of the door. "Well, you're not me. And you're not my keeper."

Kimmy revved the car. "Police siren's getting nearer. They might be coming here. We've got to go."

She was right – it was louder now. "Drive," I said.

The Golf shot forwards, and Rocky, swearing and cursing, had to step back to avoid getting his foot run over. We left them in the car park, Gregory staring after us and Rocky kicking furiously at a piece of rubbish blowing across the ground, before storming off to his car.

I spent the rest of the journey in silence, while Kimmy chatted on and on. All I could think about was Gregory's arms around me and how safe and secure it had felt. And now it was over. It wouldn't happen again.

Gypsy's Acre was still except for the fox again. It was high-stepping around some black bags of rubbish we'd piled up to take to the dump, trotting up and down like a ghost creature in the darkness. I should've been tired but I wasn't. My heart was aching too much. And if I closed my eyes all I would see was Gregory's face watching me as I drove off with Kimmy.

I wandered through the trailers. A couple of dogs lying under Tyson's daddy's trailer lifted their heads and watched me go by, then went back to sleep. There was a light in the sky to one side, over Langton House. Dawn wasn't that far away. I was going to be a bridesmaid with bags under her eyes if I wasn't careful.

Everyone else was fast asleep. I was the only one who heard the lorry engine idling and the bumps and bangs coming from the International Express yard. I could see that all the lights were on over there. And I could see something else. There were two men in the driveway, given away by the glowing ends of their cigarettes. One was watching this field, one was turned towards the road. Did McCloud think that we were so desperate to come and rob him that we'd sneak over in the night, when they were still working? They seemed to do more loading at night than they did during the day. Suddenly I wanted to go and have a look, and show them that even with security all around, they couldn't stop me.

So I took the little overgrown path – which they hadn't thought to guard – safe under the cover of darkness, or so I thought. The lights in the yard were as bright as day, but the brambles and bushes were still in deep shadow. I picked my way through carefully and saw two more men standing guard by the closed gate. They should've been paying attention, but they were both leaning on the fence and playing with their phones. No one was looking my way. I supposed they never thought someone would creep through the brambles at night. I moved forward until I found a spot where I could see the yard and the two lorries, and crouched down to watch.

I should never have done that. I thought my life couldn't get any worse. I was wrong.

19

The yard was busy with people and vehicles. There were two lorries, both with their backs open. One was being loaded, the other was being emptied. McCloud's silver Range Rover was parked next to the red Subaru Impreza with the personalized HUD18 plates.

You'd think McCloud would leave all the night work to his staff, but he was standing watching them as they shifted crates in and out of the lorries. Beside him was a boy. He got my attention straightaway. I hadn't seen him before, but it seemed that the Subaru was his, because he was leaning on it, laughing at something someone had said. He looked older than Gregory, and he was dressed as though he'd been out clubbing before coming here – I even got a scent of aftershave on the breeze, Paco Rabanne. He was as sleek as the car, his dark hair all styled, his clothes expensive and his smile Hollywood–white. When you looked from him to McCloud, you could tell they were father and son, except McCloud never smiled and the boy never seemed to stop. I didn't know what his name was, but I bet it was something to do with the HUD18 number plate. The car had probably been a present for his eighteenth birthday.

Pony was there too. He jumped out of the back of the lorry that was being loaded and went over to McCloud. They were close enough for me to just about hear them.

"We're nearly ready for it, boss."

"Good. Our man's waiting at the docks..."

"We'll get it loaded and then block it in with the rest of the crates."

McCloud's son was more interested in the second lorry, the one that was being unloaded by a couple of men. When a wooden crate appeared, he called to the men, telling them to bring it over to him. He said something to McCloud, who nodded, and the boy levered the top off. Whatever was inside pleased him.

"Sweet!"

He pulled something out. When I saw what it was, my heart began to hammer. He was holding a rifle. I don't know much about guns and weapons, but it was the sort you see in films, the sort that shoots about a million bullets in a few seconds. Pony pulled another one out and examined it. The crate was full of them.

I sat back on my heels, stunned. Jeez, all that shouting at us, telling us to move as though *we* were the lawbreakers, and it turns out that McCloud was the crook. He was transporting weapons but pretending to be this lawful businessman. I should've scarpered right there and then. Gone back to the field, pretended I'd never seen anything, wiped it from my mind. But no, my heart was still aching, and I'd got a whole lot of anger simmering inside me after the fight with Rocky. I stayed where I was and watched. It was like a bad joke: McCloud, who looked down on us as if we were scum, was a criminal in a designer suit. I took out my phone and switched to the camera. If he or any of them got nasty with us again, I could wave a photo in their face and tell them to leave us alone.

It was the worst idea I've ever had.

No one was looking my way – they were too busy checking the crate of weapons – and even if they did, they wouldn't see me, because everything beyond the yard lights was pitch-black. I aimed just as the boy raised a gun and posed with it, laughing and larking about. There was only a very quiet click, but he must've had ears like a hare.

He looked over, straight at me.

I froze, crouching in the undergrowth, cursing myself for being so stupid. But after a few moments, he looked away and began talking to Pony and McCloud. I relaxed a little. No one else had taken any notice, but I had to get out of there as soon as I could. I stayed crouched, my calf muscles cramping, and waited for my moment. It wasn't going to be yet. There were too many people milling around. It seemed as though something was about to happen, as Pony swung the barn doors open.

"Hudson – catch." McCloud threw a bunch of keys to the boy. So I was right about the personalized number plates, HUD for Hudson. "Drive it out."

"I'm on to it!"

He disappeared inside the barn. There was the sound of

a motor revving and then settling to a purr. Then a sleek white Porsche shot out of the barn, slowed, and drove up the ramp and into the lorry. Immediately, the forklift started loading crates, blocking it in, hiding it from sight. All eyes were on the lorry. I should've taken my chance and run, but I didn't.

International Express had guns *and* stolen luxury cars.

Rocky was wrong. Gregory was wrong. McCloud wasn't this upstanding businessman with a string of sucessful export businesses across the country. McCloud was crooked, and so was his business. No wonder he tried to have me beaten up so we'd leave. No wonder they'd made sure none of us came close. I looked at the men doing the loading and unloading, and the ones on patrol at the gate. They were heavies – you only had to look at how they handled themselves. And Hudson McCloud was in on it as well. He was making his way out of the lorry, leaving the Porche inside. I couldn't see him, but I could hear his clanging footsteps.

"Hudson, we can get off home now," McCloud called.

"Hang on, Dad."

That shocked me. His voice sounded close, too close. I froze, but I was sure no one could see me here. I was in the deepest shadows. As I crouched and waited, a moth landed on my face. I don't like moths, and this one was enjoying itself, crawling round my nose and over my mouth. I desperately wanted to brush it off, but I daren't move. Very slowly, I tried to blow it away, but it wouldn't budge. I nearly raised my arm to brush it off. Thank God I didn't.

A footstep crunched on gravel. It was on the other side of the fence but only feet away. There was a blast of Paco Rabanne. I risked a glance. The boy was there. He was peering into the darkness. The moth began to crawl all over my face again. I wanted to sneeze. I needed to sneeze, but if I did, I was done for. Better to have alien antennae and horrible, freaky little feet tickling my face than be at the mercy of McCloud and his son.

"Hudson?" It was McCloud again. "Come on. Let's get moving."

"*Wait*. Pony – throw me the flashlight."

Jeez. No, no, no. I tried to slide farther into the undergrowth. It was too late. Suddenly a beam of white light blasted into my face, half blinding me. My heart nearly stopped. I thought he'd seen me, but it moved off and swept over the bushes either side.

"I'm sure there's someone out there, Dad."

Footsteps approached. At first I couldn't see a thing, just the dazzling light and shadows moving on either side. Then I saw McCloud.

"Fitz! Morgan!" he shouted. I saw more shadows as the two guards on the drive came running. "Check the bushes to the right of the gates."

Easy for him to say, but the tangle of shrubs, creepers and brambles was head-high and so thick with thorns and nettles they'd need a machete to get through it. I could hear them cursing as the brambles tripped and ripped at them.

"Pony. Get the gates open. Go and help them." McCloud

was staring this way. I held my breath.

"Yes, boss."

"And get more torches out there!"

For the first time in my life, I didn't know what to do. Should I run for it? They would see me, but the nearest men were trapped on the other side of the brambles and they'd never catch me. Or should I stay hidden and hope they didn't find me? A moment later I got the answer. Two more flashlights clicked on, coming from left and centre. This time I was spotlit in the middle, like a rabbit in headlights.

"Yes, I knew it. There she is!" It was Hudson, sounding like he'd won the lottery. He was standing behind the fence, fingers grasping the mesh, his father at his side.

"I knew I saw a face," he said, without taking his eyes off me. They were shark eyes, like his dad's, but the smile was all his own.

I stood up slowly, not taking my eyes off him. He was enjoying this, looking me up and down, his face full of glee.

"So this is the one who's been freaking you out? Seriously, Dad? I know she beat Milo up, but that's not difficult."

McCloud was standing very still. He really did look like a respectable businessman. Except that now he looked ready to murder someone. He glanced at his son. "Go and help with the loading. Leave this to me."

I thought Hudson would obey. Everyone else obeyed McCloud all the time. But he grinned and said, "Are you kidding? I want to see how this goes." And McCloud didn't say a thing. He just turned his attention to me.

"Have you heard the expression, curiosity killed the cat?"

I held his gaze. "Nope. Sounds stupid. I only came to see what the noise was about. And it's just you working through the night, packing stuff up. Big deal," I bluffed.

Hudson gave a delighted laugh. "She's lying. She's not stupid. She saw it all, Dad." He gave me a fake sorrowful look. "You're in trouble, girl."

McCloud signalled for him to shut up. "She knows. She's not like her ridiculous, screaming sister. She thinks she's fearless. But she has a weakness, and that's all we need." His eyes were fixed on me. "I warned you to leave, but you didn't. You came spying on us."

I backed away a few steps. The spotlights followed me. "It doesn't matter. We're going Sunday," I said. "I don't want to know anything about your stupid business. Do what you want."

Something moved to my left. Pony had managed to get through some of the brambles. He was within touching distance of me. I backed away some more, and he stumbled as a creeper wound itself around his ankle.

"He won't get me," I said. "None of you will catch me."

"We don't have to," said McCloud. "You're not going to say a word about what you saw tonight. Because bad things will happen if you tell tales or go to the police."

I was ready to run, but that stopped me. "What are you talking about?" It was the way he'd said *bad things*.

He leaned right up to the fence, gripping it with his

fingers. His knuckles were white. He was seething with anger.

"You think you're unbeatable, you're not. I will exploit your one weakness – your family. You've shown me there's no shortage of them. Maybe you aren't scared of me, but you should be scared for your father, your sisters, their children, your aunts and uncles. Do you understand?"

I could hardly get my breath. "Yes."

"One word to anyone…"

"I said yes. We don't talk to the police. And I don't care what you're doing. After the wedding, we move. You won't see us again."

He nodded and glanced at his son. "I want her watched every second of every minute until she leaves. But make it subtle. We don't want anyone noticing."

Hudson grinned. "It'll be my pleasure. Oh, by the way" – his grin disappeared, and he pulled a sorry face at me, like it couldn't be helped – "I think she's got a phone with her. I bet she took a picture. I would've done."

I backed away some more. "I didn't. I told you. I'm not interested in what you were doing."

"No matter. She wouldn't dare use it," said McCloud.

It didn't stop Hudson smirking at my little shorts and crop top.

"Damn. I would've enjoyed patting her down and checking." Did he never stop that creepy smile? "Ah well, at least I get to watch her." He wagged a finger at me. "Keep your mouth shut and you'll be safe. But if you don't – I've got to warn you – you'll make my father and me and everyone here very, very angry."

I couldn't stand it any longer, I turned and ran.

I'd been in some dangerous situations in the past, things that made most girls tremble, but I'd never been this scared. Speed and strength don't count when there are weapons around. I flew down the little path, leaping the creepers and crashing through the bushes, and dashed out into the safety of the trailers. I was back with my family, but that just made me feel worse. I was safe here, but I'd made it unsafe for everyone else. I'd brought danger to all of them – Sabrina, Granny Kate, everyone who knew me. And all because I was too proud. Too sick of people telling us to get off their land even though we weren't doing any harm.

As I walked through the trailers, I felt totally alone. A couple of lights were on, and one of the doors was open. I could hear a radio burbling. A baby was crying somewhere. Soon everyone would be awake. It was morning, and it was Sabrina's wedding day.

I pushed my way through the dresses and underskirts and sat on my bed, my mind racing. For the first time in my life, I couldn't stop shaking. I got my phone out and looked at the image of Hudson with the guns. It was proof, but I couldn't show anyone. I couldn't risk it. And the police – what use were they? They wouldn't believe me; they'd believe him. And they'd go and tell him, and he'd make sure we suffered.

I wrapped my arms around myself to try and stop the shivering. I'd been fighting in my daddy's gym since I was three. I know Muay Thai, Brazilian ju-jitsu, judo and karate. I have fighting in my genes, I have reflexes like lightning. I can beat most people, even the men – men might be stronger than me, but I'm faster, and when it comes to winning a fight, speed and fast thinking can triumph over strength. Until now I'd never seen a fighter that scared me, even in the back-street clubs, where there are no rules. But I was scared to death of McCloud. And his son.

I lay back and thought of Hudson's last words. All I had to do was not talk and leave after the wedding. But I didn't trust his smiling face one little bit. If he caught me on my own, I bet he'd make sure I never talked to anyone ever again. I hugged my phone to me.

Tomorrow I would stay surrounded by people at all times.

20

"It's going to be wonderful!" said the manageress.

Sabrina's wedding day had dawned sunny and warm, with just the right amount of magpies sitting on the marquee in the grounds of the White Swan Hotel.

One for sorrow, two for mirth, three for a wedding. Granny Kate would be pleased. I wasn't. I just wanted it to be over, so we could leave this place and never see McCloud and his creepy son again. The day might've been sunny, but my mind was dark with fear, my body was bruised from the fight with Rocky, and my heart was aching because of Gregory. No one would've guessed, though. You would've thought I was the perfect bridesmaid as I smiled at the manageress.

"Yes, it's a wonderful day."

"It's been a pleasure doing business with you," she said. "We're all excited. We can't wait to see the bride!"

The girl setting out rows of wine glasses on the buffet table behind her wasn't quite so excited, judging by her sulking face. It was Alice, and she was dividing her time between getting the marquee ready for the reception and giving me evil looks.

When the manageress left, I went over to her. At first she pretended not to see me, and carried on arranging a whole load of little liqueur glasses on the table.

"That's too many," I said. "The blackberry wine is just for our family. There's only one bottle. The other guests will have champagne, so you need more flutes."

She huffed and slammed a few of the glasses back on the tray and went to walk off.

"Maybe you shouldn't be here," I said to the back of her head. "I don't want any trouble."

She stopped. She turned round. I thought she was going to shout at me, or burst into tears, but she didn't. And it wasn't evil looks she was giving me any more. Now we were close I could see that she looked tired and sad. She nodded. "I know. I've tried to change shifts, but I can't. There's no one to take my place. You're stuck with me." She put her chin in the air. "I don't want to ruin the wedding. It's not Sabrina's fault. It's yours."

That didn't surprise me. Everything was my fault.

"So, I'll keep out of your way," she carried on. "You keep out of mine."

"Fine."

I pushed past her and made my way upstairs to Sabrina's room. The hairdressers were there to do our hair. One of the girls was already curling Sabrina's raven locks into long, long curls that would hang around her shoulders and down her back. The rest were twisted cleverly on top of her head, framing the Swarovski crystal crown. The girls kept saying how beautiful it was, and how it must've cost a fortune. Sabrina had no idea. Only I knew it had cost me one fight with a man who took great delight in hitting me as hard as he could. Me daddy thought it cost a quarter of its true price.

Every surface was covered in make-up, straighteners or tongs. I perched myself on a chair by the window so the other girl could get started on my hairstyle. While she sectioned my hair and started giving me the same long curls as Sabrina, I glanced outside. I knew what I'd see. Hudson was there. He'd been true to his word. He was going to watch me every second, but he was much better at it than Pony or Milo. He was in the Impreza, but he'd parked it where he could see both entrances, and I could only get a glimpse of him sitting behind the wheel, half watching me, half messing around on his phone.

"Where's your dress?" said my girl, bringing me back to earth as she clamped the tongs onto the last lock of hair. "I bet it's amazing, isn't it?"

"It is, but it's back at our trailers."

"You should've got changed here. We could've helped you. We're dying to see the dresses."

She was right – it would've been easier – but Sabrina had insisted on setting off from Gypsy's Acre.

"She wants it to be exactly like our mother's wedding," I explained. "The same field, the same flowers, the same church, the same hotel for the reception." That's why I'd been busy putting up the bower of roses by the trailer door and making sure everything was ready for the photographs. I looked at myself in the mirror as the girl arranged the long, shining curls. No one could tell that I hadn't slept and that someone had threatened the life of me and my family. Nor that a few hours ago I was fighting Rocky. My arms knew it, though.

By the time our hair was finished and our make-up was done, all the girls at the hotel – except for Alice – were crowding round the door telling Sabrina how beautiful she looked.

"Come on, time to go," I said to her, as she twirled in front of the mirror, in full make-up, false lashes and jammy-red lips, with her long curls swishing about her and the crown sparkling on her head. "Daddy's waiting in the car park. I'll call him to come round to the front door and meet us."

"Why bother? We can go to him in the car park," said Sabrina as we clattered downstairs, our hair and make-up perfect, our tiaras glittering, but still in our oldest jeans and tops.

I couldn't tell her that I didn't want just the two of us to get too close to Hudson.

"Nah, you're a bride, you have to have luxury." And I got my phone out.

Me daddy met us at the front door. That's when I spotted Milo sitting in a bus stop opposite, talking on his phone and watching us. I wanted to go up and hit him. I wanted to whirl through 360 degrees and bring my leg up and kick him in the chin and send him crashing to the floor. I wanted to go and tell the police and Mr Langton and everyone else that it wasn't us that they should be so worried about, but a respectable businessman. But I couldn't.

"Sammy!" Sabrina was already inside the car. "Stop daydreaming."

It wasn't a daydream I was having, it was a nightmare.

"Coming."

I thought I'd be able to relax on Gypsy's Acre, but even here among all my aunties and uncles and friends, all I could think about was the danger I'd put everyone in.

There were children running round everywhere, or riding their bikes and push-alongs. They weren't in their wedding clothes yet, because they'd only get them dirty. Some of my aunts had gone into town to the hairdresser's, some were hurrying between the trailers borrowing shoes or trying to find where they'd put their new fascinators.

"Look what we got, Sabrina!" shouted Star as we dodged between the children. She was waving a bunch of flowers.

Star, Suzie and Savannah had been collecting the wild roses to tuck into Sabrina's big bouquet, and came hurrying over to give them to her.

"The flower people delivered the rest of the bouquets as well," said Suzie. "Come and look."

They led her away, followed by an admiring crowd of little girls, including Whitney Jade, who'd spent the night with her hair in rags so that she could have ringlets as well.

When I was all on my own, I turned slowly round and round, listening and looking for any more of McCloud's men who might be watching.

Hudson's Subaru had followed us home. It was now parked on their driveway, so that it was in view of the field. He would be in there watching me. I turned my back. And came face to face with Beryl. She grabbed hold of me, her hair in big heated rollers. She looked stressed.

"Thank God you're back, Sammy-Jo. Don't tell Sabrina, but we've lost Granny Kate."

My first thought? McCloud had got hold of her.

21

Beryl pointed to the road. "I've got the men going along there in case she's decided to walk into town for some reason. And I've been searching the trailers, but she's nowhere. I'm at my wits' end. I didn't need this, not today. This is going to hold up all the arrangements."

"I'll go check the fields next to ours," I said.

She dashed off, but before I could move, Bartley appeared from nowhere and was standing in my way.

"'Scuse," I sez.

He didn't move, just carried on looking down at me like he was trying to read the thoughts in my head. I didn't like this.

"Outta my way, Bartley. I've got to find Granny."

Still he didn't move. Just nodded. "I think the poor old girl's losing it," he said. "She was talking about all sorts of weird things this morning. Going on about magpies. About there not being the right number."

"That's just an old superstition." I skipped round him and started walking. "She won't be far," I called back.

"Wait." He caught me up and gave me a sharp glance. "What's up with you?"

I kept going. "Nothing?" I summoned up a big smile. "I'm fine and dandy, thank you, Uncle Bartley."

"So why do you keep looking over there?" He pointed back to International Express.

"You're imagining it."

Bartley's not an easy man to fool. He grabbed me arm. "You haven't been irritating anybody there?"

"No. I don't care about them."

He frowned. "Not even that skinhead boy who tried to beat you up?"

"No. Now let's look for Granny."

He wouldn't be put off. "She's wandered off, that's all. Not like you to be worried."

That was because I suspected McCloud might've got hold of her. But I couldn't tell him that.

"Beryl's worried. And when she's worried, everyone suffers." As I got closer to the gap in the hedge that led to the next field, I saw a figure in the distance, leaning on a gate. A wave of relief swept over me. "Oh, there she is!"

Before he could question me any more, I trotted thankfully away. It didn't take me long to reach her. She was enjoying the sunshine and leaning on the gate that led down towards Langton House. She wasn't alone. On the other side of the gate was the old fella, Gregory's great-grandfather. His scrawny neck stuck out of his collar and tie like a turtle's out of its shell. He'd stuck his walking sticks in the ground and was leaning on the gate as well. It seemed Gregory's dad had been looking for him too, because he was walking towards them from the other direction. He didn't look happy, unlike Granny Kate. She'd got her precious bottle of blackberry wine with her, and there were two little glasses balanced on top of the gate.

"We were worried about you, Granny," I said as I reached her. I smiled at the old fella. "Nice to meet you again."

He chuckled. "Don't you look lovely! I've been telling this lady here how I remember when she looked like you, with all that long, dark hair!"

This made Granny Kate smirk like a cat. "Aye. Those were the days."

"See how we can all be friends," I said to Mr Langton as he walked up to us.

He ignored me. He wouldn't even meet me eyes. He held out his hand to the old man. "Come on, Pops, let's get you home. We didn't know where you'd got to."

"Stop fussing!" said the old fella, waving his hand away. "What sort of trouble could I get into at my age? I've been tasting this lady's special wine." He twinkled at Granny Kate. "A bit too sweet for me nowadays, a sip is enough. It's a long time since I first tasted it. During the war, wasn't it?"

Granny Kate nodded.

"So you remember each other?" I said, trying not to smile because Mr Langton looked horrified.

"We do!" he said.

I've seen a photo of Granny Kate when she was young. It was faded and crumpled, but you could tell she had the Smith looks back then, with her dark hair hanging down her back, big hoop earrings and long skirts. She was standing in front of a wooden vardo, just like the one she said would be coming to get her when she died.

I looked at them now, as they basked in the sunshine, on either side of the gate, not caring what me and Mr Langton thought of them. And I wondered if she and the old man had ever looked into each other's eyes like me and Gregory did. Would she ever have been allowed to hold hands with him, like I had with Gregory? My heart gave a few quick beats as I remembered the feel of his hands in mine, and later his arm around my shoulders holding me close as he helped me from the club. But that was over. It would never happen again. Not so much had changed in all those years.

Langton was scowling and still trying to persuade the old man to get hold of his sticks and come away. He must've been annoyed that his grandfather was being so friendly to the people who were making life hard for him. The old man wasn't bothered, though.

"Kate's family came round every year to help with the fruit picking on the farms. But during the war they stopped here and didn't move away. All the men were gone, you see. All the stopping places ploughed for food." He smiled at Granny. "That's why I remember the Smith girls."

"We over wintered on this piece of ground," said Granny. "We should've been travelling on, but the war changed everything." She gave Mr Langton a sharp look. "The farmers didn't mind us hanging round in them days."

Mr Langton had had his fill of their reminiscences.

"That's enough, Pops, let's get you home."

The old fella ignored him.

"I remember looking out of the window and seeing the wooden caravans—"

"Vardos," said Granny Kate.

"That's right. First there was the pea picking."

"Then it were the fruit – apples, pears, raspberries."

"And lastly the potatoes."

"Oh, I hated tater picking," said Granny Kate.

They both started laughing. I was wondering how much of Granny's potent wine they'd had. Mr Langton kept sneaking glances at me. I supposed he'd never seen a girl wearing a crystal tiara, with highly styled hair and a pair of ripped jeans.

"Come on, Granny, we've got to get ready for the wedding," I said. "And after that we'll be leaving here." I looked down at the old fella. "Sounds like it was nicer in your day. We're not so welcome now."

He patted Granny Kate's hand. "This lady's welcome any time."

You should've seen Mr Langton's face! But before I could get Granny moving, she insisted on pouring the old fella another small glass, and one for herself. He held up his glass.

"Here's to the bride."

He took a dainty sip compared to Granny, who swigged it back, and then they clinked glasses, an old gypsy woman and an old gorjer man. Maybe when you get that old you can't be bothered to worry about where people come from or how much money they've got. After that last toast I managed to get her moving. She was a bit wobbly. I suspected she'd had too much of her brew, even though there wasn't much missing from the bottle. As we walked back through the fields to Gypsy's Acre, she stumbled a couple of times. This wasn't like her at all. I linked my arm through hers and made sure she didn't fall again. She seemed fragile today, more like a little bird than her usual self.

"You all right?"

She clutched at my hand with her thin, knobbly one. "Bit dizzy. Nothing to worry about, chavvy."

Even the smell of the blackberry wine made my head spin. It was a good job that it would only be served in small glasses at the reception. I think Granny had made a potent brew.

Everyone was relieved to see her back, and Beryl took her off, still clutching her bottle, to get changed into her wedding outfit. There was no rest for me. I only had time to sneak a look at the red Subaru before Sabrina hollered from our trailer.

"Sammy-Jo, come on! It's time for me to get me dress on!"

I swear, we nearly needed a crane.

22

It took four of us, me, Sadie-May, Star and Queenie, to get Sabrina into her wedding dress.

First she had to stand on a chair in her pants and bra while we tied the big padded beanbags around her waist to make the dress stick out far and wide. That created the first panic, because Sabrina's got a tiny waist and the beanbags were too big. I was beginning to doubt that she would be able to walk down the aisle at all, but finally we got them pinned around her.

Next came three separate underskirts and the huge puffball skirt of the dress, glittering with Swarovski crystals, that had to be tied tightly. Last of all was the boned bodice, which we had to lace up at the back and pull so tight that Sabrina would have an even tinier waist by the time we'd finished. As we arranged the huge skirts, we looked like Victorian maid servants dressing her ladyship. And when we'd finished, Sabrina looked like the richest girl in the world. The only problem was that she couldn't sit down now, not without disappearing into a great cloud of silk and tulle.

Queenie told her to stand still and not move.

My dress was a lot easier to get on, and a lot more comfortable. I wriggled into it while no one was taking any notice of me. I didn't want anyone seeing my bruises from last night. Star laced it up the back for me and pulled it tight. I looked at myself in the long mirror on the back of the wardrobe door.

It was quite a transformation.

No more little lycra shorts and tiny crop top. No more half-gloves to protect my knuckles. I was head to toe white silk and crystals, tight all the way down from the boned strapless bodice to where the dress flared out into its froth of net skirts so that I could walk.

Think Pippa Middleton but with more swagger, more tulle and lots more crystals.

I looked very different to the girl Hudson had spotted crouching in the brambles. But all the dresses in the world couldn't change the state of my mind. I just wanted the wedding over and for us to go home. I'd left my phone in my jeans, but I went and got it. It wasn't going to leave my side today. There was only one problem: there was nowhere to put it, not in a dress this tight. In the end I breathed in deeply and managed to tuck it down the front of the bodice.

By now the photographer was here and wanting to take our pictures, so we squeezed Sabrina out of the door and through the rose bower. We posed beside the satin-trimmed patio table and chairs. The whole site had come to watch us, but I couldn't stop myself glancing over towards

Langton House. No one was watching from there. Gregory was nowhere in sight. Good, I told myself, as I smiled and smiled. I'd wanted to drive him away, and it looked like I'd succeeded.

When the photographer had taken about a hundred photos, I forced myself not to check on Hudson and got on with my chief-bridesmaid duties. These seemed to consist of keeping the little flower girl, Whitney Jade, from getting chocolate down her dress and getting Thomas Hamilton to stop riding on his quad bike, because he was getting oil all over his little pageboy suit. I bet Pippa Middleton didn't have to stop any of her pageboys riding a quad bike round and round a field.

There was a panic when we thought we'd lost my father, and my heart started beating fast in case McCloud had got *him* now. But everyone else was saying that perhaps the wedding had been too much for him and he'd gone down the pub. It turned out he hadn't. He was sitting quietly in his Mitsubishi, listening to music and staring out of the windscreen. When he saw Sabrina, he came out and hugged and kissed her, and said she looked wonderful, until she told him to stop because he was creasing her dress. As Sabrina moved away, I found him staring at me.

"What?"

"You worry me, Sammy. I keep catching you looking scared. You're never scared."

All of a sudden I wished I could tell him about McCloud's threats. He was still a powerful man. His fists were huge and could hit like sledgehammers. I wished he would go and beat McCloud in a fight, but I could never tell him what had happened. If I did, he'd go and get Bartley, Tyson and Rocky and all the other men, and they'd go storming over to International Express. I shivered, even though the sun was blazing down. We were stronger, but it would make no difference. It would end in disaster – for us.

So I gave him a hug instead. "Everything's fine, Daddy. Now go and get your suit on. The limo will be here soon. And the horse and carriage. It's Sabrina's big day. What could go wrong?"

I pointed to the nearest tree. Two magpies were sitting watching us all, or more likely they were watching the crisps and biscuits that my little cousins were spilling everywhere as they ran from their mamas, who were trying to force them into their best clothes.

"One for sorrow, two for mirth, that's what Granny Kate sez."

It seemed to be working, because Sabrina was looking happy and even Beryl had stopped shouting at everyone. She was dressed in her wedding outfit, with her new fascinator perched on the side of her head. It was a bright red flower made out of feathers, with a couple of extra long plumes like antennae.

The exception to all this happiness was Rocky. My heart sank as he pulled his Shogun onto the field. He was either going to have another go at me, or ignore me. So I was glad when he went straight over to Bartley and started talking.

My delight didn't last long, though, because they both turned and glared at me. I was the centre of more stares than Sabrina, as she posed for photos with our sisters and aunts.

I tried hard to keep out of Rocky's way as we waited for our transport to turn up, but in the end he came swaggering over, looking even more handsome in his best man's suit. It was grey with a white shirt and a skinny grey tie. He was on his way to pick up the groom, who was getting ready at their house.

"Aw," he said, clasping his hands like one of me sisters and putting on a soppy voice. "Look at you! Ain't you pretty!"

"Stop it."

He came closer. "Don't worry. I'm not going to mention last night. Not today, anyway. But we will talk about that soon, I promise."

I shrugged as though I didn't care. Behind him, I could see Queenie approaching.

"Doesn't she look gorgeous," she shouted as she hurried up to us.

He put a smile on his face. "Like a royal princess. No! Better than one of them."

Queenie was wearing a shining gold dress that was as tight as a sausage skin around her middle. "I hope she's more comfy than me. I can't breathe."

"I told you to stop eating chocolate," said Beryl, trotting up to join us. "And where's your fascinator?"

"Sat on it. It's crushed. I didn't like it anyway."

They went off, arguing. My sisters were all ready to go

as well. There was definitely a Smith sisters theme. Bright colours in all the shades of the rainbow, skyscraper heels, long dark hair up and twisted into curls, or hanging straight and glossy to their waists. I thought this was my opportunity to get away from Rocky, but he stood in my way.

"You're being watched again, by that red Impreza in McCloud's driveway," he said. "What have you been up to?"

"Nothing."

He sighed. "If you're not going to tell me, I'll have to go and ask him."

I put a hand on his chest. "No."

That got him scowling. "Why? Has something happened?"

First Bartley, then my father, now him. I had to think quickly. "They hate travelling people, that's all. They think we're all thieves and we're going to steal their stuff. Or poke our noses into their business. Just leave them. We're gone soon."

Before he could question me any more, I gave him a push towards his car.

"Now go and move your car, or the limo won't be able to get into the field and Sabrina will go crazy!"

By the look he gave me, I could tell he wasn't convinced, but there was nothing he could do. "Watch yourself, Sammy-Jo. Just keep to being a bridesmaid for today."

"Yes. Yes," I said. "Now go."

He was only just in time. As he drove away, our hired

stretch limo turned into the field. It was pure white, with satin ribbons tied along the bonnet. That got all the little children excited. Thomas Hamilton was racing alongside it, shouting to all the other children that he was going to ride to the church in it. So were my sisters and aunties. It had disco lights, a driver in a uniform and a cocktail bar. There were "oooh"s and "aaah"s from everyone as we peered inside.

Me and Sabrina had different transport, one that didn't have an engine, and it was on its way. We could hear the clip-clop of hooves on the road outside the field. The little girls forgot about the limo and went running to the entrance. Round the bend came two white horses with their manes plaited with satin ribbons, their dappled coats shining in the sun, their tails swishing. They were pulling the most romantic and handsome carriage in the world, with the leather top folded down like a pram hood and the coachwork sparkling. Steering it was my cousin Freddy and his wife, Mandy. Like all the Smiths, they loved their horses, but Freddy had turned his into a business.

My daddy shot straight over to inspect the horses, stroke their noses and talk to Fred. This was more his style than the limo. Sabrina was making her way over to it, a whole crowd of little girls holding her dress up off the ground for her. She had been smiling, but now the carriage had arrived, she looked ready to burst into tears.

"You sure you want to go through with this?" I said.

She nodded, but her eyes were sparkling like diamonds. "Course I do," she said. "And there's nothing wrong with me except that this dress is killing me. It weighs a ton. And my shoes are hurting already."

We'd both got new Jimmy Choo high-heeled silver sandals for the ceremony. But waiting back at the hotel room were some flats to change into later.

"Don't worry. It'll be over soon," I told her.

The church service would, but not her married life. I was glad it wasn't me. None of it – not the beautiful dress or the carriage and horses, or being given a bungalow as a wedding present – could make me want to get married. I looked around at Tyson's cousins and the other boys as they got in their motors to drive to the church. These were the boys I should've been dreaming about, but I wasn't. I looked over at Langton House. There was only one boy that made my heart beat quicker.

"Sammy!" said Sabrina. "I can't get up the step. I need help!"

It took three of us. Two pushing from behind and Freddy hauling her up from inside the carriage. He was used to it. No girl could move in such a huge dress.

I skipped up the steps easily enough, but Sabrina had disappeared. In her place was what looked like a puffball of netting and white satin taking up all of one seat of the carriage, with Sabrina's head almost buried in the middle of it. It turns out that not only was the dress too heavy, it nearly didn't fit inside the carriage, either. Somewhere underneath all the lace and netting was Whitney Jade.

We had a very squashed ride to the church. People

walking in the streets stopped and stared. Some came out of their houses to watch us go past. I didn't blame them. It wasn't every day you saw a horse and carriage, especially one carrying two girls and one little girl almost drowning in a sea of white net petticoats. But I relaxed a little.

No one could get near me now. The limo was behind us, crammed with aunties and sisters and me daddy. And behind it was a whole line of cars belonging to us. I could hear music playing as we made our way towards the town and through traffic lights and up the high street, past the hotel. The girls at the nail bar were standing in a row on the edge of the pavement, ready to wave at us. So were the hairdresser women and all the friends of my aunts and sisters.

I waved like a princess.

But I couldn't forget that somewhere far back, Hudson was following me.

23

Granny Kate says that in the old days Gypsies didn't get married in a church like St Stephen's, with its little steeple and stained-glass windows and the beautiful old churchyard out front, where the photographer was waiting to take our pictures. They didn't have balloons lining the aisles, and someone videoing it from the side, and a whole load of relatives dressed in their wedding finery, waiting to greet us as the horses trotted into the churchyard pulling the carriage, with the limo gliding in behind. They didn't need two strong men to help get the bride out of the carriage and standing on her own feet.

Instead they used to jump the broomstick.

That's what she told me. They actually used to jump over a broomstick. They would lie one on the ground. The girl and boy who were in love and wanting to get married would hold hands and jump over it, with everyone standing around to witness it. And when they landed on the other side, they were husband and wife.

Jumping the broomstick — I wish that's what we were doing today. I wish Sabrina and Tyson would jump the broomstick in five minutes, and then we would all go far away and never come back.

As I walked up the aisle behind Sabrina and our father, trying to keep Whitney Jade from running off, and trying to stop Thomas Hamilton from sticking his tongue out at the other children as he went past, I looked at the guests in their fine clothes, and the children dressed like little princes and princesses. I thought we looked like a fine people. A people who didn't do what everyone else did.

Rocky was standing at the front. He should've been concentrating on giving the wedding ring to Tyson. He wasn't. He kept glancing my way. I don't know what he was expecting me to be doing.

As the service began, and Tyson got his first look at his beautiful bride, I sat myself down next to Granny Kate on the front pew. Beryl had told me to keep an eye on her, because she'd had a couple of dizzy spells in the limo. She was wearing a handsome lace dress with a shawl around her shoulders and her long hair hanging in a plait down her back.

She leaned closer to me, as the vicar droned on and Sabrina and Tyson gazed happily at each other, and whispered, "I don't like this. My thumbs are prickling. That's always a bad omen."

"What's wrong now, Granny?"

"Didn't you see the magpie sitting all on his own on top of the steeple? One for sorrow."

"Don't worry, I bet there was another one close by,"

I said, but I felt a shiver run down me own spine. I didn't need magpies to tell me that there was danger around.

She took my hand, and I could feel her shaking. Now I was even more worried about her. Granny shouldn't be shaking. She was as steady as a rock.

"And that's not the worst of it, Sammy-Jo. There's a mullo here."

"A what?"

"A mullo, Sammy-Jo. One of the dead who are still walking."

Beryl was right. There was something the matter with Granny. First she goes wandering off with old Langton, and now she was talking about the walking dead.

"You sure, Granny?" I smiled and patted her hand. "There's a zombie in the church?"

"No! They don't go in churches. He's outside." Granny lowered her voice. "He's waiting for us. Someone should go and scare him away."

We were all getting up to sing the first hymn, so I turned and looked. The church door was half open and framed in it was Pony. Milo was next to him. Hudson was doing a good job of making sure I was watched the whole time.

"Him with the white hair. He's a mullo," Granny whispered. "You remember I used to tell you about them. The walking dead. People without souls, who can be ordered to go and kill."

Granny Kate knows all the old legends. She used to love telling us horror stories from those dark countries with high mountains far away in the eastern parts of Europe, where Gypsies first gathered hundreds of years ago. We came from India, that's what people say. We were thrown out, and we began travelling. We thought we'd soon find a new land to call our own, but we never did. So we're still travelling now. But some of us stopped on the way. There's scatterings of Gypsies in lots of countries. And in some they tell dark tales about Gypsy ghosts and Gypsy witches. But a Gypsy zombie?

It sounded about right for Pony, though. I knew Granny's talk of mullos and the walking dead couldn't be real, but at that moment, in the dark church with the organ playing and the stained-glass windows throwing splashes of crimson and green and blue over everyone, and the smell of incense, and the plaster saints staring sightlessly at us, I felt that evil things could be real.

And if mullos did exist, then they would look like Pony, with his white, stringy hair. He looked like he had no soul, like he could be ordered to go and do terrible things without worrying about it or feeling guilty.

"I think we call them psychos these days, Granny. They're not really dead, just dead inside, so they have no feelings."

She wasn't listening to me. "I've seen them before, when I was a girl. And during the war. Sometimes we'd stop in the country and a man would come by, and we'd know. He'd look at us, and he'd have no shadow and no reflection, and we'd know he was a mullo off to get revenge on the living."

She was still staring at the distant figures. "Dead eyes. Eyes without soul," she muttered. "That's how you can spot them. That and the white hair hanging down their backs, corpse hair." She clutched my hand again. "And if they come for you, then you're dead. Don't let him come for you, Sammy-Jo. I noticed him, but no one else did. He keeps looking at you with his dead man's eyes."

I squeezed her hand. "Don't worry. I can look after myself."

I wished she'd shut up about mullos. She was spooking me. But worrying me as well. What if she'd got dementia, after all this time? She was looking really scared and glassy-eyed. Granny Kate was never scared of anything. You don't get to ninety after a life lived mostly on the side of the road by being scared.

She wouldn't give up. "You can't kill a mullo, Sammy. You can fight them for ever and you wouldn't win. Listen." She grasped my arm and made me look at her. "Steel is the only thing that will kill them. You have to make them bite on steel. Or stab it through their hearts."

There was a sniffle at me side, and a little hand clutched mine. It was Whitney Jade, in her frilly white dress and her garland of white flowers in her hair.

"What's the matter with you?" I said.

"Is there really a mullo in here?" she whispered.

I picked her up and held her on my hip. "No. They're not real," I whispered back. "Granny Kate's only joking." And I began to sing the hymn. Anything to shut Granny up.

But the singing didn't stop the fear growing inside me. A fear that something bad was going to happen soon. I couldn't concentrate on the service, or the signing of the register, or Sabrina and Tyson, now husband and wife, walking down the aisle and out in the sunshine as the organ played the "Wedding March". Pony had disappeared, but I knew him and Milo wouldn't be far away.

As we milled around on the grass and the photographer took hundreds of pictures of us, I kept watching for them, but they were being very cautious – until I suddenly heard Pony's voice ranting and swearing. It was coming from behind all our cars, which were parked beside the church. Everyone else was busy with the photographer, so I walked carefully over, keeping a safe distance. Until Thomas Hamilton came running out from between the cars, his face full of mischief and glee. I knew that look.

I grabbed him as he ran by. "What have you done, Thomas Hamilton?" Pony was still cursing. "Did you go near that man?"

He squirmed, trying to get free. "I only letted his tyres down. Don't like him. He shouted at me."

Letting tyres down was Thomas's favourite trick, but I wished he hadn't done it to those two. I picked him up and made him look at me. "You don't go near those men ever again. Do you understand me? Nowhere near. They're bad men. Really bad men. They'll take you away and they won't bring you back." He wriggled and squirmed like a cat. "So stay away. OK?"

"'Kay. Let me go."

"Promise?"

"Yes. I said so, didn't I."

I put him down and ruffled his hair. "Good boy. Now go and have your picture taken and don't tell anyone about this."

He was gone in seconds, running over to ruin a few photographs by sticking his tongue out. I walked a little closer to the Jeep, but still keeping my distance. For the first time that day, I wanted to laugh. Pony was standing staring at the flat tyres on the Jeep. And Milo was shouting down the phone to someone. We'd be long gone before they got them pumped up again. When I turned back, I saw Granny Kate standing on her own, staring up at the church roof. I went over to her.

"It's still there, Sammy." She pointed to the single magpie.

I put my arm through hers and made her turn away. "Forget it. We've got to go to the hotel now."

I thought she'd be glad to sit down and have something to eat, but she sighed. "I'm tired today. Tired of everything, even this wedding."

"Sabrina should've jumped the broomstick," I said.

At least that got Granny laughing, quietly to herself. "It would've cost your daddy a lot less. And he's still got to pay for your wedding."

"I'm not going to get married, Granny. So that'll save him some money. Or we'll jump the broomstick, like in the old days."

226

No sooner had I said that than Gregory's blonde hair and brown eyes appeared in my mind. I pushed them away. As Sabrina and Tyson clip-clopped by us, together at last in their carriage, there was a flutter of wings above us. The magpie had flown away.

"There you go, Granny. The sorrow's gone. Let's go and ride in the limo!"

That's how I came to see Rocky. The car park had emptied fast as everyone raced to get to the hotel to greet the bride and groom. But we weren't the last to leave. Rocky's Shogun was still there. As we drove past, I saw that there was someone in the motor with him, sitting close. I saw a leather jacket and spiky blonde hair, one foot up on the dashboard. Miss Stroud. As far as I know you don't invite your probation worker to a wedding, so who was she?

Their heads were close together, and they were talking. Rocky noticed the limo gliding by and said something to her. A pair of cool eyes looked me over, before she turned back to Rocky and answered him. He smiled grimly.

It was interesting to know that Rocky's mystery woman was watching me as well.

I thought maybe I'd be free of watching eyes for a while, but as soon as we got to the hotel, I saw that Hudson was waiting for me. I'd wondered when he'd show up again. He was sitting outside the open French windows of the bar, sunglasses on, pretending to read a newspaper. No one would ever question why he was there, not even Bartley or Rocky. He was dressed in designer clothes and looked every inch the rich boy.

I let him see that I'd noticed him, then I turned me back on him and busied myself with helping to heave Sabrina out of the carriage and arranging her dress for her. When we'd finally got her upright, and stopped her snapping at her new husband for treading on the end of the dress and causing her to nearly lose the skirt in front of everyone, Beryl clapped her hands together.

"Now we can party!" she shouted.

Everyone knows about our weddings these days. The workers and guests at the hotel were out on the steps, in the sunshine, watching us. There was plenty to see. There were the dresses, for a start: not just my aunties' and sisters', but all the guests', and especially my girl cousins'. They were short, they were bright, they were extreme. Some were little more than bikinis with fringing.

A hog roast was set up beside the marquee for later tonight, in case any of the hundreds of guests who were starting to spread out across the lawn should feel faint with hunger after all the dancing. A bouncy castle was waving and jolting in one corner, so I suspected my older cousins were already throwing themselves around inside it. I could see Whitney Jade and Thomas Hamilton desperately trying to get away from their mamas, so they could go and jump around as well and ruin their wedding outfits, or get buried in the ball pit next to it. There was a worried-looking clown in the middle of the lawn, already surrounded by children as he blew up balloons and made animals out of them.

Inside the marquee, the tables were stacked high with food – sausage rolls, sandwiches, quiches, cakes and gateau. There was a chocolate fountain with fruit and marshmallows on sticks. That was before we got to the weddings cakes. Beryl and Star were arranging the three separate seven-tiered cakes on their stands behind the wedding table. Later on, when Sabrina and Tyson had finished greeting all their guests, they would sit there on the two white satin thrones for the feasting. A DJ was setting up in the corner. When we'd booked him, I'd told him to bring lots of music so that we could dance all night long, but now I was wishing for the day to be over. McCloud and his son had ruined everything.

I walked outside and looked round at everyone enjoying

themselves. I could see Smiths from all over the country, and Quinns, Wilshires, Lees and Gaskins. The sun was shining. Every face I saw belonged to a friend or a relative. All but one face – and I couldn't look away from this one.

It was Gregory. He was neither friend nor relative; he was heartache.

I couldn't work out what was he doing here. Hadn't he learned enough about me last night? Seems not, because he started to come over to me, which wasn't good, because Beryl, who was standing right next to me, had seen him, too. I got a dig in the ribs and a warning glance, and she dragged me off to have more photos taken with the bride and groom. It didn't stop me getting a few peeks at him, though, while I smiled. He wasn't in his waiter's uniform, and he wasn't standing anywhere near Alice. She was on the steps with the other waitresses and hotel staff, watching us with a tiny, tight mouth and narrowed eyes. Gregory was biting his lip, as though he was desperate to come and say something to me. But I turned away. I'd shown him my true self. There was nothing else to say. So I shook my hair out, and laughed and joked with my sisters and aunts like I hadn't got a care in the world, and tried to forget about him.

It wasn't until the photographer had finished and everyone was heading for the marquee to start the feasting that I spotted the Jeep. Pony must have called out the AA, or pumped up the tyres himself, because there it was, parked between the other cars in the car park, almost hidden. Pony was sitting in it. Milo was sitting near by on the low wall that divided the hotel grounds from the streets beyond. They were keeping far away from me, not like Hudson. I had to walk by him to go and get Granny Kate. She'd wandered off again, and Beryl said she'd seen her heading to the bar. I found her clinging onto the bottle of blackberry wine, and trying to organize glasses for the toast.

"It's all sorted," I told her. "Don't you remember? The glasses are already in the marquee."

As I led her outside, I could feel Hudson watching me.

"I don't like some of the people here," she said fretfully.

"Me neither. But as long as we all keep to our promises," I said, loudly, "we'll be fine."

Another glance. He'd heard. In some way, he was worse than his dad, Milo and Pony rolled into one. He looked handsome and well-dressed, but no one should smile as much as that. It made me shiver. Seemed Granny agreed.

"Don't like that chavvy over there, for a start," she said, nodding towards him. She might be confused today, but she was still sharp.

Maybe he heard, because he stood up as though he was about to come over to us. There were plenty of waitresses buzzing around collecting empty glasses, so it was safe. He wouldn't try anything here.

I sat Granny down in a chair. "Wait here for me."

I walked back, close enough to see myself reflected in his sunglasses. But not close enough to be in danger. He looked me up and down, and grinned. It made me want to bruise his handsome face right there and then.

"I don't run to the police," I said. "None of us do. So leave us alone."

His smile got wider. "I'm enjoying watching you."

That smile didn't last long, though, because there was a banshee howl from our left and a whole load of little boys ran screaming and hollering between us. One of them tripped and fell almost at Hudson's feet. It was Thomas Hamilton, overexcited and running round screaming with some of his cousins. Once upon a time they'd all been dressed beautifully, but that was before they got their hands on the chocolate fountain. They were now the stickiest children you could ever meet.

Hudson's face changed. "What the—?" His perfect jeans were smeared with chocolate. He swore and went to grab Thomas, but I moved like lightning and grabbed the little boy first. I swung him into my arms and backed away quickly.

"Don't even think about touching any of these children. You'd regret that."

Without the smile, Hudson looked a lot like his father, with his dead, cold eyes. "Are you threatening me?"

"No. Just telling you the truth of what will happen if you touch any of them. I'm keeping my word. You better keep yours and leave us alone."

He took a step towards me, but I moved quickly away, holding onto Thomas, who was trying to wriggle out of my grasp.

"If I let you go," I told Thomas, "you've got to promise

to keep away from him." I pointed at Hudson. "Don't go near him. Understand?" The rest of the little boys had clustered round him. "None of you."

Thomas stared back at me. "Why?"

I used to be like that. Scared of no one. I wish I still was. "Just do as I say. Or I'll make you go and sit with your mothers."

That did it. The whole gang ran off to find somewhere else to play. Granny was still waiting for me, so I took her arm and I led her into the marquee. As we left the bottle of blackberry wine on the table with the champagne, I could feel her shaking.

"I'm not feeling too good. I don't think I'll be dancing," she muttered.

"When I'm ninety, I won't dance either. Here." I found her a nice, comfy chair at the back, away from the shrieks and shouting as everyone greeted relatives and friends they hadn't seen for a while. "I'll go and get you something to eat."

Suddenly she grabbed my hand. "Be careful." She looked into my eyes. "You're special. That's going to get you in trouble all your life." If only she knew. "And remember, keep away from the mullo. He'll try to kill you."

So she was back to imagining that the dead walked. "OK, Granny. Will do."

I loaded a plate with little fairy cakes and a couple of ham sandwiches, and took them over to her.

"Come on, Sammy-Jo!"

It was Sabrina.

"What?"

"I'm going to throw me bouquet."

When Star got married a few years ago, it was Sabrina who caught the bouquet. On the dance floor there was already a cluster of my girl cousins and a few of the other girls and women.

"I don't want to catch it," I said. "Let someone else get it."

"No. You have to come and do it as well," insisted Beryl, who'd come over with Sabrina.

She tried to push me to the front of the girls, as Sabrina positioned herself at our head. Her bouquet was white roses and lily-of-the-valley, all mixed up with the wild roses, which were wilting a bit now. It seemed a shame to throw it, but everyone was shouting at her to do it. She turned her back so she couldn't see where she was aiming at and chucked it over her shoulder.

I was standing right at the back. Even Beryl couldn't persuade me to go forward. But it seemed Sabrina had some of the Smith strength, because she did a mighty throw, and I saw it heading towards me, far above the heads of my cousins and a couple of Quinn aunties who'd never married and would dearly love to. I wasn't even concentrating. I don't know why – it must have been a defensive move – but when I saw it heading towards me, I reached out and caught it.

"I don't want it," I said, and I threw it carefully back into the aunts. But they gave it back to me.

"It's the custom. You caught it," said one of the Quinn aunts sadly.

But I wasn't paying attention, because my bodice had started vibrating. Someone was ringing my phone. I quickly wriggled it out. I didn't recognize the number, so I should've ignored it, but I didn't. I answered it.

"Who is this?"

There was a pause. "Gregory."

My heart gave a thump. "Wait." I quickly walked outside so no one would overhear. "How did you get me number?"

"Sorry. It was on the wall of the office. In case you had to be contacted about the wedding."

"What do you want?"

"I have to talk to you. McCloud's been to the house to speak to my dad."

"I don't care about him. We'll be gone tomorrow."

"Please. It's important."

I glanced over to the bar. Hudson wasn't there any more. I didn't want him or anyone else seeing me talking to Gregory. "OK. But not out here."

"Where?"

"Wait for me upstairs, outside our room." I clicked the phone off and went to find Sabrina.

"Do you want your flat shoes?"

She gave a huge sigh. "Oh God, yes! These are killing me. They're in my case in the room."

As I walked out, I managed to avoid Beryl, who was giving the DJ instructions about the music for the first dance, but then I ran slap into Rocky. "And where are you going, Gypsy Girl? Not to make more trouble, I hope?"

"No. To get comfy shoes for the bride."

He didn't look as though he believed me.

"Not running after the Langton boy again?"

"No."

"Funny. I saw him going upstairs just now."

For a moment, I desperately wanted to tell him all about McCloud and his threats, but I couldn't. Rocky would start a fight, and that would be dangerous. "Please. Just leave it, Rocky. OK?"

He raised an eyebrow but let me go.

I marched across the lawn to the hotel doors and dashed up the stairs two at a time, my dress rustling. Gregory was waiting for me outside the room. I let him in and closed the door behind me and leaned on it.

"What?" I said. "This'll ruin me reputation. Spending time in a bedroom with a boy. Beryl will make you marry me, if she finds out."

He didn't laugh. His eyes moved over my hair and face and dress.

"I thought you'd got something to tell me," I said.

He nodded. "Yes, I have." He ran his fingers through his hair. "It's just that you look amazing. Like a film star or something. I've been trying to forget you, but I can't."

My heart sang, but I didn't let it show. "Is that what you wanted to tell me?"

"No." He blew out a breath. "Sorry. I can't think straight with you this close."

Him and me both, but I was hiding it better. "I thought

you'd hate me after last night."

"No. Never." He pulled a sorry face. "Even though Rocky drove off without me and I had to hitch home." He reached out and touched my arm with his fingertip and slid it down till he was holding my wrist. "I can't believe that tomorrow you'll be gone. I won't see you again."

Nor could I. His touch burned like fire. I wasn't thinking straight, either. We were never going to be together – I could never come back here – so why not make the most of these last few minutes? Why not have something amazing to remember?

"So you better kiss me now," I said.

25

He was so close, I could feel his breath on my face.

"No." It was more of a groan than a word. I hadn't expected that. First Rocky, and now Gregory. Did no one want to kiss me?

"Why not?" I said.

He leaned his hands on the door, either side of me. "Because—"

"I'll be gone tomorrow," I told him, quickly. "Alice won't know. It's not like you're betraying her."

He shook his head. "It was over with Alice before I saw you. I just hadn't realized it. But I didn't fall out with her yesterday just so that I could get off with you straightaway. I'm not like that."

"You don't want to kiss me?"

He groaned again. "Of course I want to!"

I smiled. I couldn't help it. He was so sweet, so unlike most of the boys I came across. "Then kiss me." I slid my arms up around his neck. "I want to know what it feels like."

His mouth twisted into a rueful smile. "So it's an

experiment. And I happened to be near by?" He leaned closer.

"No. It's my first kiss. And I want it to be with you."

His eyes widened, so did his smile. "You never kissed anyone before?"

"No. I never met anyone I wanted to kiss. I'm usually fighting the boys I meet, not thinking about kissing them."

"Thank goodness you don't want to fight me," he said, breathlessly.

"Are you going to kiss me, or what?" I said.

His hands moved and pulled me towards him. Our lips touched – lightly at first, until he wound his hands around my neck, pulled me even closer, and we kissed properly.

It took my breath away. I never knew it would feel like that. I forgot everything – the wedding, Milo, McCloud, Alice – everything except Gregory and the smell of his hair and the feel of his hands on my neck, and the touch of his lips. It was soft and strange and urgent, and it left me breathless and wanting more. But in the end we let go of each other, and he moved back and stared in wonder.

"Not bad," I said, when I could speak.

He laughed. "You've got nothing to compare it with, but I do. And I know that was amazing." His smile faded. "We've done it now, haven't we? One kiss is never going to be enough, is it?"

I leaned back against the door. "It's all there's going to be." I shook my hair back. "I thought if you saw me fight, you'd never want to see me again. I thought I could get over you that way."

"No. It doesn't have to be like your aunts think it should be. You'll be in the next town. I have a car."

"My uncle wants me to go to America. Everyone'll make sure I agree to go. They'll never let me get near you. I shouldn't even be here. I should be with Sabrina as she cuts the cake, or takes her first dance with Tyson." I pushed him away, even though I wanted to pull him closer again. "I have to go."

"Wait, I haven't told you yet," he said. "McCloud came to our house. He was ranting at my dad, saying that you and some of the boys at the site had climbed over the fence in the night. That you were trying to steal from the barns and the warehouses. That when you couldn't get in, you smashed the place up – did lots of damage. He took my dad up there and showed him the damage you'd done."

"We did nothing, he's lying. I bet he didn't report it to the police."

"He said he was giving you a chance, and that if you hadn't moved by tomorrow morning at the latest he wants my father to help get rid of you."

"He's a liar."

"I know. What's going on?"

"I can't tell you."

"Please."

"No."

As I opened the door, my hand shook. McCloud was covering his back. Making sure everyone thought we were thieves, so that I would never be believed. Granny shouldn't have mentioned the mullos. No matter how sunny the day was, I could feel it getting darker around me. I walked out into the corridor. He followed me and grasped my hand.

"You're shaking," he said.

"I know." I looked out of the window next to us. It faced the lawns. I could see Beryl and Queenie herding everyone inside the marquee.

I pulled my hand from his. "I better go back, or I'll be missed."

That's when I saw the magpies. Four of them sitting along the roof of the marquee. All in a line. One for sorrow, two for mirth, three for a wedding and four for a death.

Behind me Gregory's phone started ringing. He looked at it and frowned. "My dad. Wonder what he wants?"

Perhaps he was psychic and knew his son had been kissing someone he shouldn't. Gregory answered it and stood with the phone against his ear, looking shocked. "When? That's so weird. Is he ok? Shall I meet you at the hospital? OK, will do."

He ended the call.

"What's wrong?" I said.

"My great-granddad's been taken ill."

"He was OK this morning when he was having a drink with my granny," I said.

He looked bewildered. "I know. I saw him, too. Mum says he started gasping for breath, and rambling." He put a hand gently on my face. "I have to go. But don't leave tomorrow without seeing me. Please."

I didn't answer him. Something was bugging me. First Granny Kate starts acting strangely, and now the old man. Their only connection was that they were together this morning, drinking Granny's blackberry wine. I thought back to us picking the berries, and brushing the dust from them, and Granny saying, it's just their bloom. And in the background, Pony was hosing down the yard because a stack of sacks had fallen and scattered their contents everywhere. If McCloud handled stolen cars and weapons, maybe he handled drugs or dangerous substances as well.

Four magpies on top of the marquee. Four for a death.

A wave of panic swept over me. Something terrible was about to happen.

"What?" said Gregory. "What's wrong?"

"Everything."

I pushed past him and ran.

26

"Shoo!" I shouted, holding my dress up with one hand.

As I dashed outside, I bent down and picked up a plastic ball that had escaped from the ball pit, aimed and threw it as high as I could. The four magpies squawked and flew into the air, a whirl of black and white feathers. Everyone was inside the marquee for the buffet and the cutting of the cake. Only the children on the bouncy castle were left outside. They watched me run by, and then carried on bouncing.

And there was Hudson, of course. He watched me, but he stayed at his table. I had a glimpse of him, leaning forward, but at this time I didn't care about him. I rushed into the marquee. My knees were shaking beneath my white silk dress. I prayed that I was wrong. Nobody took any notice of me. Sabrina was having more photos taken at the wedding table as they cut the cake. Everyone was clustered round her. I could see Rocky and Bartley clapping and cheering as Sabrina cut the biggest of the fruit cakes. Cameras clicked, flashlights strobed, reflecting from the silk-draped ceiling. Even Beryl and Queenie weren't on patrol at the moment.

I looked through the crowd, hoping to see Granny Kate

there with them. Please let her be with them!

But she wasn't. She was at the back, where I'd left her. Her hands were folded in her lap, her head lolling forwards. She looked like an old lady taking a quick nap in the middle of a hectic day. Everyone must have thought the same, and left her to doze in peace. I threaded through the tables towards her. Please let her be sleeping, I prayed. Or unconscious at the worst. Please let me be wrong about the blackberry wine. I hitched up my dress and bent down in front of her.

"Hey, Granny Kate. Are you OK?"

Nothing. She still had the plate of sandwiches and cakes on her knee. They hadn't been touched.

"Wake up! Please. They're cutting the wedding cake."

I touched her poor old arm. It was cold beneath her lacy sleeve. I crouched down and looked up into her face. Her dark eyes stared back at me. But they weren't seeing me. They weren't seeing anything in this world any more. The vardo had come for her. She was far away now, going to wherever Smiths went when they died.

Someone tapped me on the shoulder, and I nearly jumped out of my skin.

"Me mummy sez, does Granny Kate want some cake?" It was Whitney Jade. She held out a napkin with a slice of fruit cake.

I sat back on my heels. "No. Go and tell Beryl I want her."

"But I'm supposed to be handing the cake around."

"Now!"

Whitney Jade took one look at my face and turned and ran. While I waited, I held Granny's cold hand, and going through my mind was only one thought: McCloud had killed me Granny. Whatever had blown out of the spilt sack and dusted the brambles had poisoned the wine. I had to find out what it was. It was too late for Granny Kate, but Gregory's great-grandad was still alive. He needed saving.

"What's wrong?" said Beryl, appearing at my side. "We're going to drink a toast with Granny's wine. I suppose we better wake her. She made it."

I looked up at her. "She's dead."

Beryl gawped at me. "Don't talk rubbish." She bent down beside me and took Granny's hand. "Come on now, Granny."

She let go of her hand as though it had stung her, and shot up like she'd got hydraulics in her legs. "She's dead! Do something! Granny's dead!"

It was a loud and frantic shout. Heads turned.

"Help!" Beryl shouted. "It's Granny Kate!" That brought people flocking over. I fought through them until I ran into Sabrina.

"What's wrong?" she said, her eyes panicked. "We're supposed to be having the toast."

Not any more. There wasn't going to be any more people poisoned. I hadn't time to soften the blow. "Sorry. Granny's dead."

Sabrina's mouth turned oblong, and she began to cry.

"No! She can't be. Not at me beautiful wedding. People don't die at weddings!" She pushed past me and ran, wailing, towards Beryl.

I headed to the drinks table. The bunch of little glasses that Alice had laid out earlier were full of blackberry wine. And she was now holding a tray of them, ready to hand them out to the family, even though she was craning her neck, trying to see what was going on in the corner. It had to be Alice, didn't it? I hadn't time to explain to her. How could I? What would I say? "'Scuse, don't serve the drinks. They're poisoned."

So I rushed up to her and kicked the tray from her hands. It flew upwards at speed. She screamed as the glasses turned somersaults, sending a cascade of deep purple wine over everything. I had this flash image of her standing there, purple splattered all down her and dripping from her hair. Any other time but now it would've been funny.

"Why?" she howled, as the tray clanged down, destroying her shoes with the last of the wine. "Why would you do that? I kept out of your way!"

"Sorry. It's not you. The wine's bad." I pushed her to one side and swiped my arm across the table, spilling all the little glasses before anyone could drink from them.

The marquee was in chaos. Alice's screams as she tried to wipe the splashes off her shirt were blending in with the screams coming from Granny's corner, as all my aunties and sisters realized there'd been a death in their midst. Tyson was trying to stop Sabrina from having hysterics. Bartley was trying to calm Beryl down. Rocky was trying to get through the crowd to me, but the manageress got to him first, demanding to know what was happening. The news was spreading fast. Even the children had sensed something was going on and were rushing in to stand and gape. None of us would be dancing under the twinkling starlight drapes tonight.

I headed for the exit. Gregory was hovering in the doorway.

"What?"

"Not now." I pushed past him and ran outside.

Hudson was nowhere in sight. Didn't matter. I headed for Pony's Jeep in the car park. He must've saw me coming, because he got out straightaway and squared up to me. Granny was right about him being a mullo. I looked into his eyes and I saw death in them. My death. But I was so angry, so desperate, I broke all my rules and ignored the goosebumps and the hackles rising and all the danger signs.

"What was in the sack that got spilled?"

He stared blankly at me. "What sack?"

"A few days ago. When you first saw me and me granny." He gawped at me. I wanted to hit his stupid face. "Answer me!" I thumped my fists on his chest. "You were hosing down something that got spilt. What was it?"

He still didn't get it. His eyes flickered past me, and a footstep sounded. Suddenly I realized the danger of what I was doing, but I didn't have time to spin round and save myself. Something cold touched the back of my neck. It felt like metal. I smelled Paco Rabanne again. It was Hudson, so close I could feel his breath on my neck. And he had a gun. Guns changed everything.

"Don't try anything, fighter girl," he said, quietly. He needn't have been quiet. There was no one in the car park except us. "I told them to be patient, that we'd get you on your own at some point, away from your ridiculous family."

"I'm not going to tell on you. I just need to know—"

He jabbed the barrel into the back of my neck. "Did you really think my dad was going to let you go free, after what you've seen?"

No, I didn't. I'd always known deep down that if they got me on my own, I was dead.

"Turn round," he said.

I spun on my heel, and Pony grabbed my arms and pinned them back. Surprise, surprise, Hudson was smiling at me. In his hands was a small, black revolver. A few feet away Milo was on sentry duty, making sure no one came over here. With his free hand, Hudson reached for the top of my dress. I kicked out at him, and he backed off, the smile leaving his face.

"I want your phone."

"I'll kick your head off if you try and touch me again."

"I said, I want your phone."

My heart began to thump. "Do I look like I've got room in this dress to be carrying a phone?"

"It's down the top. You're not as clever as you think. You

gave the game away earlier." His smile came back. "It'll be fun getting it out."

My skin crawled. "No. Or I scream and people will take notice. Tell that pig to take his filthy hands off me, and I'll get it out."

Hudson nodded at Pony, and I felt the grip on my arms release. I wriggled the phone out of my bodice. He looked smug.

"We couldn't let you keep photo proof, now, could we?" He held out his hand for the phone.

I hesitated. "So if I give you this, are you going to let me go?"

He pulled his little-boy-sorry face. "You're very pretty, but unfortunately, no." He glanced at Pony. "Get it off her."

He didn't get the chance. I threw it as hard as I could. For a split second their eyes followed it sailing over the cars and disappearing. A split second was enough.

27

I punched Hudson in the face. As he sank to his knees and slumped to the ground, I stomped my daggerlike heel into the arch of Pony's foot. He screamed and staggered backwards, hopping and swearing. I'd almost crushed the arch of his foot.

This was my chance.

I sprinted for a gap between a truck and a car, but I'd forgotten about Milo. He came racing round the back of the truck and sped towards me, his white potato face flushed now with savagery. He thought he was going to get the chance to repay me for the beating I gave him. Something glinted in his hand. A knife. Knives changed things, too – but not like a gun. Knives I could handle. I stopped. Waited. Then ran at him as he hurtled towards me. That shocked him. Milo's way of attacking people was to run up from behind.

It was like a game of chicken. For a couple of seconds we went racing towards each other. He flinched first. He stopped and brought his blade round in a wide sweep. He had no chance. My brain was speeding, my eyesight super-sharp, my hearing intense. The adrenaline racing through my veins was doing its job. I saw the knife, a kitchen one, probably nicked from his mama, the blade sharpened so much it had a curve, spots of rust on the edge. It was coming for my face but didn't reach it. One, two, three fast steps and I spun round in a semi-circle, a half-cartwheel, using my momentum to swing through the air with my feet flying in an arch. I kicked him in the head. I heard his jaw crack.

It was called a "jump spin hook kick". I'd mastered it by the time I was ten. It was spectacular and effective. It destroyed my dress, nearly ripping the skirt off, as it destroyed him. He hit the ground, out cold, his nose bleeding, his lips already puffing up over his crooked jaw. A tooth sparkled on the ground.

So now I knew for sure. If they caught me, they would kill me. I'd seen too much, and I'd signed my own death warrant. They'd never had any intention of letting me live. Rocky and Bartley weren't far away. Could I get to them? Tell them? It would mean danger for us all, but I didn't have much choice. I turned and headed for the marquee.

But then I saw Gregory. No. He mustn't get involved. I'd done enough damage to him. He was weaving through the cars towards me, trying to figure out what was happening. If they saw him, they might target him as well. This was all my fault, not his. I turned and ran back, away from him. To my left, I heard an engine roaring and the squeal of tyres. The Jeep came out from between two cars. Pony was driving it, his face a mask of rage. He put his foot down and aimed straight at me. I rolled under the nearest car and out the other side. The car park had a low wall at the back, and beyond it was a maze of narrow streets. If I could reach them, I could lose myself in them and find a place to hide. I glanced over my shoulder.

Hudson was back on his feet and after me. Could I outrun him in silver Jimmy Choos? I couldn't kick them off. The ground was too rough. I ran at the low wall, his footsteps pounding behind me.

But I'd forgotten one thing: leaping a wall in a ripped bridesmaid's dress is not easy.

I swung myself over but went flying on the landing, tripping on the trailing hem and tearing off the rest of the tulle underskirts at the knee. Good, it meant I could run faster. I picked myself up, untangled myself from the net and silk and raced off along a narrow street lined with empty buildings. There must be an alley or a yard there where I could get out of their sight.

I needed to find someone with a phone and call Rocky. It didn't matter if he knew now. Things had gone too far. I needed help. But Hudson didn't give me the chance. I heard him thump over the wall behind me, followed by Milo. I ran, but their footsteps were gaining on me.

I swerved into the first side street and took the first right, weaving in and out of parked cars. But they were fast like rats, and every corner I took I could hear them gaining on me. A car was coming at speed, too. It didn't sound like the Jeep, but I couldn't risk it. I swerved down another street, and slid under a parked car. I waited. I heard them shouting to each other.

"Where's she gone?"

"I don't know. Find her!"

Their footsteps got louder. I held my breath as Hudson ran round the corner and straight past me, followed by Milo a few seconds later. I peeked out. They'd rounded the next corner. I slid out and scrambled to my feet, but a car was bearing down on me at high speed. It wasn't the Jeep or the Subaru. It screeched to a halt inches from me.

It was Gregory in an old, battered Fiat. The window slid down, and he leaned over to fling open the passenger door.

"Get in!"

"Leave me! Drive off!"

He leaned over and grabbed my hand. "Get in. Or I'll drag you in."

I threw myself onto the seat and swung the door shut as Gregory slammed the gears into reverse, turned round and headed off up the street, away from the direction Milo had taken. But not for long. The window was down, so I heard a furious shout, and swivelled in my seat. Hudson appeared first, yelling into his phone. And then Milo, powering after us. Gregory put his foot down and we shot away from them. They chased the car like dogs for a few yards, then stopped and ran back towards Pony's Jeep as it slid round the corner and braked for them.

"Give me your phone and let me get out," I shouted as he careered round a corner. "Then drive away fast, understand?"

He shook his head as he slid round a corner. "No. Tell me what's going on. Who's chasing you?"

I was checking the rearview mirror, but there was no sign of them yet. "It's McCloud's son. I saw him and McCloud in the International Express yard, unloading guns."

Gregory glanced at me, confused. "Guns? McCloud? But he's—"

I had to make him understand, and quickly. "Gregory, I don't lie, not to you. He's a criminal. He handles stolen cars and guns. And something else, something that made me granny die, and made your grandad ill."

"But how could McCloud make them ill—"

"He did! Some kind of dust or white powder from his yard got on the blackberries. It could've been drugs, or poison. If he can move guns around, he's not going to worry about health and safety, is he?"

"How do you know all this?"

"I saw them. And they saw me. They know that I know. They've been following me ever since."

Gregory gave me a horrified look. "Jesus. Why didn't you tell anyone?"

"No one can help me. McCloud said if I told on them, my family would suffer."

He thumped the wheel. "No. You have to tell the police. Did you get proof?"

"I took a photo on my phone, but I threw the phone away so I could escape. If we go to the police, it's my word against McCloud's."

"I'll back you up. I saw that guy – the one with the hairstyle and the designer stuff – I saw him going for you. And the one with the ponytail who works for McCloud."

"No. They'll believe him, and then he'll get my family."

He didn't understand. How could he? "Stop and let me run."

"No."

He turned another corner, engine racing, changing gears fast and furiously, and gunned the Fiat along the road. "Just let me drive. I'm good. I passed first time."

"Please, Gregory. Let me get out, and then you go and fetch Bartley and Rocky."

"No. We stay together. We're not far from the police station now. They can raid International Express. They can find traces of whatever's making Pops ill. Your guys can't do that." He put his foot down. "Hang on."

An image of Granny's eyes staring down at me, sightless, dead, flashed into my mind. She'd survived for ninety years, just so that Mr McCloud could kill her. A wave of sadness and anger swept over me, but there wasn't time to grieve, not here, not now.

I took a deep breath and prayed Gregory was right.

"OK. The police. I want Mr McCloud caught," I said. "I want him punished."

"I know these streets. Leave it to me."

He hunched himself over the steering wheel. I could see a nerve twitching in his eyelid. One minute we were kissing. Now we were fleeing for our lives. All I'd done since getting here was ruin his life. He'd had a girlfriend and an unscarred face, and now look at him.

A motor turned out from a side street right behind us, but it was a transit van, not the Jeep. It was blocking my view, though, as it followed us down the road. I couldn't see whether the Jeep was on our tail. It could be catching us up. I didn't have to worry for long. At the next left Gregory braked, nearly sending me sliding through the windscreen, and headed off down a side road lined with warehouses, all of them closed for the weekend, the sort of place where I'd come for my fights. None of that mattered now.

"You should've run in the opposite direction," I said, as Gregory urged the little Fiat forwards.

His hair was damp and his face shiny. "So was I supposed to let them get you?"

"It's not your fight."

"Milo jumped me from behind, remember. They kicked me. They nearly broke my ribs."

"Because of me! This is my fault," I said. "I should've moved from Gypsy's Acre. I've done nothing but get us all into trouble."

"No! This isn't your fault. It's McCloud's." Gregory shook his head. "I can't believe he was there in our house, being all pally with my dad. Making out you were the vandals. Playing the honest businessman."

"Exactly." My stomach lurched. "Who's going to believe me?"

For a moment, I thought I heard the loud diesel engine of the Jeep, but there was nothing behind us. That didn't mean we were safe. These streets were like rat runs. There were side streets and turnings everywhere.

"They'll believe you. I'll tell them."

"You're still crazy," I said. "Coming after me."

He laughed. The adrenaline was running through his veins as well. Danger is like going on a roller coaster called something like Death Dive, and as it hurls you at the ground your brain thinks you're going to die, even though you're safely strapped in. And when you don't die and the ride ends, you get a high, and you bounce out of the carriages screaming and laughing. We were at that point now. We'd survived the first attack, and we were free and speeding towards safety.

He glanced at me. "Crazy? Yeah, that's about right. Crazy about you."

I took a moment out from checking the road behind us. Our eyes met. "Me, too."

Can you realize you love someone after knowing them for a short time? Does knowing that you might die make a kiss into something more? I did think I loved him in that moment, as he raced his rusty Fiat through the streets. He'd come to rescue me, even though he knew I was a fighter. It didn't matter that in the real everyday world – not this nightmare one we were living in at the moment – we couldn't be together. That I would be going back to our home behind the gym in the next town, and he would be doing whatever rich boys do – going to college, going to university, hooking up with girls like Alice. That didn't matter any more because there was only the nightmare world now, and me and him fleeing through the streets in a little Fiat.

He was a good driver. He braked and cornered, putting

as much distance between us and them as he could. There was no traffic around. No one to witness the chase. No CCTV. Nothing.

I kept screwed round in my seat, watching for the Jeep. Nothing.

"Maybe they've given up," said Gregory.

"No. Hudson's like his dad. He won't give up. McCloud hated me from the start. Now his son wants me dead."

Up ahead there were traffic lights. They were on green. He raced for them, leaning forward, hands gripping the steering wheel, knuckles white, but the lights turned red. He slammed on the brakes, nearly sending me through the windscreen again, but I stopped myself in time.

"Sorry," he said.

"Don't be. I'm used to it," I told him. "Sabrina brakes like that all the time."

"We're nearly there."

My heart began to thump. "I need to ring Rocky. I need to tell him."

"Here." He fumbled in his pocket and pulled out his phone and unlocked it.

I shouldn't have been joking about his driving skills. I should've been watching out for danger. There was a fast movement to my left, and out of nowhere the Jeep screeched in front of us and stopped, blocking us. Hudson was already leaping out.

"Reverse!" I shouted.

Gregory was already jamming the gearstick back, his

foot slamming on the accelerator. Too late again. Hudson wasn't just a pretty boy, he could move. He slid over the bonnet and dragged the driver's door open. I slammed my hand down on my door lock so they couldn't get in. But the driver's door flew open. Hudson's fist appeared. It smacked Gregory round the head, knocking him almost into my lap, and then Hudson grabbed his phone. The back doors shot open. Hudson threw himself in behind Gregory. Milo slid in behind me. My hand was already moving up and over my shoulder, my fingers stiffened, ready for an eye-shot.

"Don't you dare!" Milo growled. I felt a stabbing pain and blood trickling. His knife was already at my throat, his stinking breath in my ear. "You're in so much trouble, bitch," he growled.

I lowered my hand.

A bruise was flowering on Gregory's cheek as Hudson dragged him up by his hair.

"Drive."

I wished I'd told Gregory that I'd fallen for him. Maybe I'll never get another chance. We were in big, big trouble.

Milo had one arm around my neck now, leaning forward in his seat. The other hand held the knife to my jugular vein. It was giving me the stench of his sweaty armpit and a perfect close-up view of his upper arm.

That's when I realized he was more dangerous than I'd suspected. I'd thought him and his brothers were nothing more than thugs, trying to be tough guys like Pony to impress McCloud. But I could see a big sore on his bicep with muscle damage around it. I knew what had caused it. He'd been injecting steroids. There were fresh marks as well as the swelling. My father would've gone mad to see that. He chucked anyone out of our gym who used anabolic steroids. He says it's cheating and it's the easy way and all it does in the end is harm your body. But that's not all. It makes the users become aggressive because they're putting extra testosterone in their bodies. And he says that if you've got a fighter who's already got a temper on him, or who's hostile and violent by nature, then when he takes steroids he becomes a monster.

It's called roid rage. It makes nasty little fighters into psychos. It explained Milo.

"This your boyfriend?" said Hudson, as he forced Gregory to drive away in the opposite direction to the police station. He was leaning forward, keeping his hand around Gregory's neck in case he tried anything. He hadn't got the gun, or he would've used it by now.

"He's no one," I said, quickly. "He gave me a lift. Let him go."

"Liar." He peered at Gregory's face in the mirror. "I know him. He's from the big house. I've seen him a few times." He grinned and squeezed Gregory's neck. "Your father is going to be pissed when he knows what's happened. He should've told you to keep away from girls like her."

"I said, leave him alone. He doesn't know anything."

"Yeah, yeah, yeah, course he doesn't," Hudson jeered. "Should've kept his nose out of this, then."

Behind me, Milo laughed and began running the tip of his knife along my bare shoulder. "He's got the hots for her. I bet she's been all over him. Dirty bitch. His dad won't be pleased."

"Fathers. They don't understand true love." Hudson gave me a sly smile. "But so nice of him to take you for a drive, you being trash and all. Pity you're not going to have a long romance."

"Why?" I said. As if I didn't know, but at least we were alive while they were talking and bragging.

Hudson licked his lips. "You're going to die in a car crash.

262

Gregory's not long passed his test. It's what the kids do these days. Die in crashes." He pulled his fake sorry face. "Sad, isn't it? Such a waste. I bet there'll be bunches of flowers left at the spot. And little notes saying, 'Gone to heaven with the angels' and 'Forever sixteen.' Ahhhh."

"No, there won't be," said Milo. "Not where they're going to crash."

They seemed to find this funny. Clouds of bad breath wafted over me.

My heart began to thump, but you'd never know it. I kept the shock and horror inside me. So that was the plan. To get rid of both of us. "My family will never believe I left the wedding to go driving with him. Not today."

Milo's arm tightened around my neck. "Don't listen to her. She's a lying bitch. His mates know he's been hanging around with her. They'll tell everyone. Their families will believe it."

"I'll enjoy seeing her little face as she realizes she's gonna die." Hudson smiled at Gregory in the mirror. "Gypsy girls are bad luck, didn't you know that, boy?"

Gregory didn't answer him. He didn't look scared. He looked furious, two spots of red on his cheeks. He'd still got the injuries from when Milo beat him up, and Hudson had added to them with his punch. One of his eyes was swollen and closing up. And now he was being ordered to drive us to our deaths.

Good. If we were going to get out of this, we needed cold fury, not nerves.

"Turn here." Hudson pointed at a road that led out of town. Gregory crashed the gears angrily and swung the car round the corner. I could see him glaring into the rearview mirror, watching Hudson's face.

"Where are we going?" I asked.

Hudson licked his lips. "Langton Reservoir."

I froze. I heard Gregory swear under his breath. I knew the place. We'd been there for picnics when we were younger, even though we all preferred Alton Towers. It was a huge country park with miles of paths and roads and car parks, most of them empty and lonely, spread out around a huge lake that was so deep that when cars fell into it, it took them ages to get them back, if ever. Some people said there were lots of vehicles and dead bodies down there, and even a plane from the war, but all lying so deep in the pitch-black water that no one would ever reach them.

Not many things scare me. But deep water did. I can swim. I learned when I accidentally fell into a pool when I was young, according to me daddy. He rushed to get me out, but I'd come to the top and I'd started to doggy paddle to the side by the time he reached me. Since that day I've never forgotten the feeling of water coming over my head and my breath running out. I've had nightmares about drowning.

A picture flashed through my mind, of the Fiat going over the edge of the reservoir and hitting the water, and sinking deeper and deeper into the black depths. Another flash and the picture changed, a new camera angle, me and Gregory floating down and down, our lungs filled with water, the remains of my white dress floating ghostlike around us, holding hands as the Fiat settled next to the skeleton of the war plane, and the ghosts of all the dead people clustering around, knocking on the doors for us to get out and join them.

Hudson shouldn't have told me that's what they were going to do to us.

"Oh yeah, she doesn't like that," said Milo. His dirty finger traced along my collarbone. "I felt her shiver. The Gypsy girl doesn't want to drown."

"I'm not going to. You'll never get that far. My family will notice I've gone. They'll be looking for me by now," I lied.

"No. Nobody will miss you yet." He held up my phone and Gregory's. I couldn't believe he managed to find my phone after I threw it. I bet he'd wiped the photo from it. "But in the end they'll try and trace your phones, and that's good. The last known location will put you right beside Langton reservoir. We want them to know that you died together, in a tragic accident. It'll put their minds at rest." He smiled and threw the phones onto the back seat. "Turn here."

Gregory did as he was told, hitting the kerb and moving his head angrily away as Hudson swore and smacked him for daring to jolt them. Gregory jammed his foot on the gas and jerked the car forward. "Hit me again, and we might crash before then," he muttered, angrily.

I could hear the tension in his voice. He knew we were

far out of town now, far away from anyone who could help us. I saw a sign saying LANGTON RESERVOIR as Hudson ordered another turn towards it. He didn't hit him this time. And a mile further on, as we began to drive through thick woods, he said turn again. He wasn't taking us to any of the big car parks, but there were lots of others that were much more remote. For the last five minutes we'd seen hardly any cars, and no walkers. I kept getting glimpses of the reservoir through the trees, its waters black against the falling light of evening. Soon it would be dark. I made myself think of those dark waters crashing through the windscreen and hitting us in the face as we sank.

He shouldn't have told me that they were going to drown us.

I began to squeeze and release my muscles, so I'd be ready to move fast. The road curved and twisted, sometimes running close to the reservoir. In some places there was a barrier, but every so often there was nothing to stop a car going straight into it. Everyone knew there had been accidents here. There were warning signs. We went by a tree with a bunch of faded flowers tied to it. If you went another mile down the road you'd see another like it.

There could be no better place for Hudson and Milo to get rid of us and make it look like an accident.

As Hudson ordered another turn down a narrow lane, where the branches of the trees joined overhead, Gregory said, desperately, "Why are you doing this? This is murder."

"Blame her," said Hudson. He gave me that creepy grin. "My father's safety has been threatened."

266

"Do you always run around doing his dirty work?" I asked. "While he keeps his hands clean?"

Hudson reached over and smacked me across the face. No smile for me now. "Shut it. I've seen you in your slutty clothes. You're nothing but scum. This is doing the world a favour, I reckon."

"You hate girls?" I said, even though my mouth was smarting.

"I hate girls like you. You're less than nothing to me."

He didn't know anything about me, but he hated me all the same. He might have better looks than Milo and an education, but they weren't so different. Good. I took some deep breaths. I hated him, too.

I could see the black lake ahead of us now. We were running down a slope towards it. There was a small patch of tarmac at the bottom and a patch of grass with a burned-out circle where someone had camped and lit a fire. There were no tents now. It was deserted and overgrown. I bet we were the first people here for weeks.

"Stop at the bottom," said Hudson.

"Yeah. Brake like Sabrina," I said, quietly.

Gregory glanced at me. He got it. He knew. I braced myself. As the car ran down into the little clearing by the water, he let it pick up a bit of speed, and at the last moment slammed his foot on the brake.

The car stopped dead.

Milo flew forwards. I threw my head back and felt it smash into his face. I heard his nose break like a dry twig.

He screamed. I bit his hand and twisted the knife out of his grasp and threw it out of the window. And in the same smooth motion, I brought the edge of my hand sweeping towards Hudson's wrist as he flew forward and smacked into the back of Gregory's seat with an "oooph". If it had hit him, it would have snapped the bone, but it didn't. It missed, only grazing the skin, and giving Hudson time to push himself away from me. Behind me Milo was still howling in pain, flopping backwards onto the back seat, dazed and confused, his broken nose bleeding like a tap.

I was out of the car, the door snapping back as I kicked it. Gregory was even faster. He was fuelled by anger and revenge. He was already out and dragging the back door open, punching out at Hudson, all the pent-up fury powering his fist through the air. But he wasn't used to it. He wasn't trained, his punch had power but not accuracy.

His fist struck Hudson on the cheek, but it wasn't enough to knock him cold. Hudson might look like he spent his time buying expensive clothes and going clubbing, but he was McCloud's son. And he looked like he'd been in violent situations before. As Gregory aimed his fist again, silent and furious, Hudson ducked, swung round, bunched his legs and kicked Gregory in the stomach, sending him flying backwards across the car park. He rolled into the ashes of a campfire.

"Punch me, would you?" Hudson shouted, and he was out of the car, running and swinging his foot at Gregory.

I saw it in slow motion, as I ran. It was like a dream, the

air turning to treacle as I threw myself after them. Hudson's foot swinging back as Gregory rolled on the ground, gasping, all the breath knocked out of his body.

The setting sun lanced prettily through the trees, highlighting the shoe as it aimed at Gregory. I hurled myself at them, but there wasn't time. I heard the crack as his foot hit Gregory's skull. Gregory jerked in the air and lay still, but Hudson was swinging his foot again to make sure. He never made that kick. I smashed into him, thumping him in the back, knocking him forward, sending him tripping and falling to his knees. He was up straightaway, but now I was between him and Gregory. He was facing me, one of his eyes starting to close from Gregory's punch.

"Get away from him," I said.

I was a wolf protecting her pack. I had to tend to Gregory, but I couldn't while Hudson was close. I had to deal with him first. But he was hyped. He was bouncing around. Then he bent down to pick something up off the ground. Something steel? Not the knife, that was far away. A tent peg, a deadly-eight inch spike. His rage was building. But mine was already sky-high. He shouldn't have told me about the reservoir. When I'm scared, I get mad. He shouldn't have kicked Gregory. All that did was fuel my hatred of him. I let him see the fury in my eyes. I began taking deep breaths again. I needed oxygen. I needed all my strength.

But before I could strike, something hit my back and clung on. I staggered, before bracing myself. Blood trickled over my shoulder. Milo wasn't out cold. He was on my back, covering me with blood, breathing like a bulldog through his smashed nose.

"I'm gonna kill you! Bitch!"

He wasn't a threat. I grabbed his stinking, sweat-covered shirt and pulled him over my shoulder, elbowing his nose again, making him scream as he flew and hit the ground head-first, splattering the grass with blood, and rolling, and lying still.

It had given Hudson time to come at me, though. The steel tent peg caught the last of the light. It was twisted steel, sharpened to a point. He was holding it like a dagger, ready to stab me. Weapons make people feel invincible. They make them careless. People rely on them, but what happens if the weapon is knocked out of their hands, or the gun fails to go off? Hands and feet don't fail. You can't drop them somewhere, or get them taken off you.

I jumped, spinning round, and kicked, my foot coming up like a pendulum and smashing the tent peg out of his hands. It went sailing through the air. My blood felt as though it was on fire.

Hudson should've stopped there. He should've run off, or backed down. He didn't, because he was filled with uncontrollable rage as well. He roared and came at me. I lunged. We met in the middle. Arms trying to get a stranglehold, hands trying to find eye sockets and mouths, feet trying to trip each other. Stalemate. We were locked together, arms and legs and feet straining. A small moment of equality. Which one of us would give way first?

Once, I'd seen two lizards fighting in a glass cage in a pet shop. They were all about stillness. They'd each got their jaws fixed on the other, their legs braced, tiny muscles stretched to breaking point. And neither would give in. Neither could win. It was stalemate there in the steamy glass cage. Fighting over what? A tasty grasshopper? Or maybe one lizard didn't think the other lizard had a right to exist, or it didn't look the right colour or its eyes were the wrong shape, or it didn't build its nest in the right way. They were like statues as they strained and tried not to be the one that weakened first.

That's how me and Hudson looked. He knew what I could do. He'd heard Milo's nose snap like a dry twig. His skin was going slippery with sweat. I could smell the fear coming off him. He was at the limit of his strength, and if he failed today he'd have to face his father, McCloud. But he wasn't protecting someone. Gregory was lying behind him, and I saw his arm twitch, and then his legs. He was coming round. He rolled over and I saw his face, a pale oval in the growing darkness. He was blinking at us. I had to get rid of Hudson and go and help him. I forced my arms and legs to stay strong, to ignore the burn in their muscles, to push harder.

Hudson twitched first. So had the bigger lizard in the glass cage.

I'd watched those lizards for minutes, but it had ended quickly. The bigger one, with a frill around its neck the colour of emeralds, had twitched one of its claws. A tiny movement. In less than the blink of an eye, the other lizard, which had no bright colours, knew it had won. There was an explosion of teeth and claws — a dance of death — as it brought the emerald-frilled one down and chomped on its head, before lashing its tail in victory.

I had no tail to lash. But I felt Hudson's biceps weaken for a moment. I moved like a lizard — no thought, just survival in my mind. He knew he'd lost. But he tensed and swung himself away from me, trying to get his balance, trying to make a comeback, and I followed. Our own dance of death. We whirled across the clearing, me a step behind him, trying to get a grip on him. His muscles must've been burning after our power struggle. His knees would be beginning to shake as his blood sugar dipped.

It didn't matter, though. Because he'd got his eyes on the tent peg again. My kick had sent it flying across the clearing. As the sun dropped, a final ray sparkled on it. He threw himself at it. It would give him the advantage again. He didn't reach it. I didn't know where Gregory had found the strength — he'd been kicked in the head — but he did.

His hand reached out as Hudson scrambled past him. He grabbed Hudson's ankle, and yanked. Hudson fell, his fingers grasping for the tent peg as Gregory hauled him back. I thought for a moment that Hudson had managed to grab it, but he hadn't, because he squirmed round and did a feeble punch to Gregory's ribs instead. My muscles were still burning from the fight, my knees shaking, but I ran over, my foot lifting for a kick to Hudson's solar plexus.

I didn't get the chance. Gregory was up on his knees, his fist swinging back. He let fly. It was the punch to beat all punches, revenge for being jumped and thumped and threatened with death. His fist blurred as it smacked on the bone and flesh of Hudson's chin, sending him flying backwards to join Milo, out cold on the ground.

"You did it!" I ran to Gregory. He was still on his knees, swaying. I held out my hand. I pulled him up. Our eyes met, our arms went around each other. He leaned against me.

"Now who's the fighter," I said. I couldn't work out whether I wanted to cry or laugh.

Gregory let out a big breath. "Did I really just knock Hudson out?"

I laughed, and he joined in, but only for a moment. Suddenly his face changed. He winced, puzzled, and staggered back, his arms dropping away from me. He put his hands to his ribs. He looked down as he staggered again. "What the hell—?"

Blood was seeping out from between his fingers. I knocked his hands away and pulled up his shirt. A tiny, round wound. And on the ground beside Hudson's hand, the tent peg, slender as a stiletto. Deadly and glistening with blood. I was wrong. Not a feeble punch to Gregory's ribs. A stab with a deadly weapon.

Gregory gave a strange half laugh. "The bastard. He got me."

I ripped a bit more off the bottom of my destroyed dress, and bundled up the fine silk and pressed it to the wound.

"Don't worry. We're free now. I'll drive."

"You can drive?"

"My daddy taught me when I was thirteen."

I put my arm around him and turned towards the car. But it was never going to be that simple. A car was approaching at speed, a big one, the engine droning and echoing through the trees, getting louder and louder. I looked around, trying to keep Gregory standing.

"More of them?" he groaned.

I dragged him along. "Don't worry. We just have to get out of here."

But the Jeep was in sight now, raising dust clouds, power-sliding round the corner and gunning towards us.

"No, no, no."

"Shush."

He was going limp, but I hoisted him up, using all my strength. I glimpsed Pony's face through the windscreen. No way were we going to die by his hands. We were so close to the Fiat. The driver's and back doors were still open. I half carried Gregory towards the car. He helped, moving his feet, holding his breath against the pain.

"Nearly there."

But so was the Jeep. It came skidding into the clearing, pebbles flying, brakes squealing as it stopped inches from the Fiat. The driver's door flew open as Pony threw himself out. Two more steps – that was all I needed, and I could push Gregory in the back, throw myself in the driver's seat and get the hell out of there. Pony was coming towards us, but he was hobbling where I'd smashed his foot. Two steps, that was all, but I never made them. It turned out it didn't matter that he couldn't run at us and stop us.

"Don't move," he said.

It looked small in his big hand. The barrel was pointed straight at me. Pony had the gun now.

The light was fading fast. The setting sun had given the air a rosy glow, and the little campsite was bathed in pink. It shone on Pony's silvery hair, but it couldn't make his hate-filled face look any better.

"Let your boyfriend go," he said, twitching the gun.

I couldn't be bothered to tell him he was wrong to call Gregory that. I liked the sound of it, and anyway it wouldn't matter soon. It seems that me plus Gregory equals death – however hard we fight. His daddy had been right to warn him away from me.

"I said, let him go."

I took my arms from around Gregory and edged away from him. He sank to his knees, blood oozing through his fingers as he clutched his ribs. I made myself stare at the blood and think hard, because Gregory would die if I didn't get the gun out of Pony's hands. I was guessing he wouldn't shoot, not unless he had to. Bullets would give the game away. Hudson wanted it to look like the two of us had died as the Fiat ran over the edge and crashed into the water. Pony would probably try something similar.

Pony glanced over to Hudson and Milo. His eyes lingered on Hudson's sprawled body, and he almost smiled. Maybe seeing the boss's son get flattened pleased him. Maybe he was sick of that permanent smile as well.

I wanted to spit in his couldn't-care-less face. I let the fury rise in me. He'd picked the wrong person. I was a fighter. I wasn't going to let him point his stupid gun at me and pull the trigger. I thought of all the Smiths down through the ages, all the Samsons. I imagined them lined up, watching me. Arms folded, muscles bulging, wild-haired, fearless.

You're a Smith. You're one of them, I told myself. OK, they'd be a bit amazed that I was a girl, but it had to happen sometime. They'd understand there was no way I was going into that deep water, or taking a bullet. And there was no way Gregory was going to die before I told him I loved him.

Pony was hobbling closer to me, keeping the gun aimed but staying out of my reach. He wasn't Milo, he wasn't stupid. He wasn't Hudson, thinking he was God's gift. I concentrated on working out the distance between us. Near enough to jump and kick him? Near enough to do a hand strike, if I lunged forward?

"Put the gun away," I said. "Let's fight."

He looked me up and down. "Got to admit, I never came across a girl like you before. They're normally snivelling by now."

So he beat up girls, or worse. Good, I was glad he said that, because it made the fury rise even faster inside me.

He signalled with the gun. "Get in your car." It was

277

behind us, still with the doors open.

"You're joking. So you can knock me out and push it into the water."

His mouth curled up on one side. "You're going in there, even if I have to shoot you." He looked over my shoulder into the back of the car. "And if I do, the phones stay with me. They'll show your last location to be far from here. Your families will never look here for your bodies."

I had to keep him talking, while I found a way out of this. But delaying meant that Hudson would wake at some point. As soon as I thought that, there was a groan. Even with concussion and a headache, Hudson could be dangerous.

It didn't matter. What Pony didn't realize was that there was no way I was going in that water.

If I could kick the gun out of his hands, I could beat him, but he was too wary. In a fight you always have to look for a way to turn things to your advantage. His eyes were on me. I'd made sure of that because it meant he'd forgotten about Gregory. I hadn't.

I could see him out of the corner of my eye. He was still on his knees, one hand holding his ribs, looking like he was going to throw up. He was trying to tell me something. Then I saw. His free hand was swinging up. It was holding a stone he'd found on the ground. He let me see it and then he threw it at Pony.

It missed. It would never have hurt him. But it didn't need to. It gave me the chance I needed. As it sailed past him, Pony glanced round, only for a split second, but it was enough. I took my chance. I leaped for him, striking out with the side of my hand. It hit home, sending the gun flying out of his hand and out of danger. But his finger had already tightened on the trigger. There was a muffled bang. The gun went flying, glinting in the twilight. I saw Pony's arm recoil, and he staggered back, tripping and falling.

But I was falling, too. A force had got hold of me and was spinning me round. My arm flew out and a pain started up in my left shoulder. It felt like someone had hit me with a cricket bat. A dull thud that burned like fire, and froze like ice. It nearly threw me to my knees, but I couldn't stop to think what had happened yet.

The gun was spinning over and over as it fell to the ground. I threw myself after it, but Pony was doing the same, howling with pain from his injured hand, and holding it close to his body as he dived and reached with his good hand. He was too big, too hefty. I could move faster.

The gun hit the grass and bounced, and I was right after it. Pony got my ankle and pulled, but my fingers touched the gun. He scrabbled madly for it, all his cool lost. My hand closed around the handle, but he was inches behind. I had no time to aim. I'd never handled a gun. I threw it. It went up in a sparkling arch and hit the undergrowth beyond the trees. He would never find it in there. Now we were equal. He gave a roar of pure fury, and launched himself at me. I kicked out and hit him on the chin, knocking him back.

But something was wrong with me.

My left arm was useless. The pain in my shoulder was

getting worse. It was throbbing madly. I went scrabbling back, using one arm, and managed to get to my feet, pulling up the hem of my dress to wipe the blood from my face. My knees were wobbling. I could feel all the power leeching out of my muscles and limbs. He'd shot me in the shoulder. I was losing blood, and I was going to pass out soon.

But not yet, please not yet.

Pony was on his feet, shaking his injured hand, swearing, cursing, limping. Granny Kate was right. He was a zombie, shambling towards me, his good hand outstretched and reaching for my neck. He could snap it in a second; he had that strength. And I could do nothing about it. The weakness was creeping through my veins and sinews.

I was going to die just when Gregory had proved to me that true love did exist. And he was going to die as well. He was wounded, he couldn't fight now. He was here only because of me. I'd killed him.

I took a deep breath. I couldn't let that happen.

No time to get scared. No time to worry that I was getting weaker.

As Pony reached out to grab me, I stumbled out of his way, using the last of my strength. I had to stop this mullo, even if my muscles were freezing up. My right arm still had some strength. I lashed out, catching him on his chin. But it wasn't enough to knock him over. He came right back at me, grabbing me by the throat. I got my hand up and tried to pull his fingers off me, but there was no strength left in me. His foul face thrust into mine. His fist pulled back, ready for the finishing punch.

"Bye-bye."

Something moved on the edge of my vision. It was Gregory. Somehow he was up on his feet, his face no longer pale, his cheeks red with anger. He was holding something in his hand, like a dagger. The tent peg. Pony flicked him a look. But Gregory didn't seem much of a threat. He was a nuisance, nothing more.

"Leave her alone!" Gregory managed to croak. "Or I swear I'll kill you."

"Yeah, of course you will." Pony kept his hand on my throat, but he'd underestimated the danger. Gregory was blazing with fury.

It all happened in an instant.

Gregory gave a roar and lunged at Pony. The tent peg glinted in his hand. Pony saw him coming at the last moment and jerked back. I didn't know where Gregory was aiming for. I didn't think he did. It was a last-ditch burst of energy. But as he jabbed his arm forward and Pony turned round, the tent peg hit Pony full in the face. I saw it in technicoloured slow motion. The peg hit Pony's cheek and carried on right through, fuelled by the power of Gregory's lunge. Right through his cheek into his mouth, sticking through his flesh like an arrow.

Pony let go of my throat. His fist sent Gregory flying backwards. It was the last punch he'd ever give. I nearly crumpled, but I braced my knees. Pony clawed at his face, mumbling and swearing that as soon as he pulled the peg out, it would be going right through Gregory's heart. And he would be able to, because that punch had knocked Gregory half senseless again. He was on his knees but swaying and trying to find his balance.

Pony grasped the peg and psyched himself up to pull it out. He gave a tug, but it was jammed in his cheek. He screamed in agony and took a firmer hold on it. The attack had done nothing except make him want to kill Gregory. I couldn't let that happen. I took a few deep breaths, ignored the burning, freezing pain in my shoulder, and forced my muscles to work. This had to be the kick of my life. I wouldn't get another chance. I balanced myself, concentrated my power, and exploded into action with every last bit of energy I had left. My foot blurred as I kicked like I'd never kicked ever before.

I could've won the Olympics. I could've kicked a fly out of the air. My foot soared, turned, aimed, homed in on Pony's face. My harsh, desperate cry echoed across the clearing. He didn't stand a chance. Even if he hadn't been lame and one-handed, he couldn't have avoided that kick.

It hit him like a hammer to the face. I saw spit fly, his ponytail waving like a piece of dirty white string. The force sent him flying through the air, big as he was. His feet left the ground, and he smashed backwards and smacked into the ground, bounced once, and lay still, his arms and legs trembling as though he was having a fit.

My knees buckled and I dropped to the ground, the

weakness flooding right through to my feet. I was a ragdoll. I couldn't take my eyes off Pony. He was still twitching. If he recovered, I wouldn't be able to stop him. Gregory was sitting up, clutching his side, his face battered and bruised, one eye closing. He was staring at Pony, a strange look on his face.

"He's dead," he said in a voice that shook.

I wished that was true, but there was no way he was dead from a single kick. He wasn't even out cold, because his legs were still moving.

"Gotta get out of here," I mumbled. "'fore he comes round."

Gregory was looking at me now, his eyes so wide there was a rim of white all the way round.

"No, he's dead, Sammy-Jo."

As I struggled to my feet, my good hand clasping my burning shoulder, Pony gave a last twitch and his face turned my way. I wish it hadn't, because it will be in me nightmares for ever. Gregory was right. He was dead. It was the steel tent peg that had killed him. Gregory had stabbed it through his cheek, but it was my kick that sent it plunging up through the roof of his mouth, through his skull. His eyes were staring, his lips pulled back in a death grimace, biting on the tent peg.

I slid to my knees again.

The mullo's dead, Granny Kate. Dead and biting on steel.

31

So the wedding's over.

My beautiful bridesmaid dress is soaked in blood. Crimson on white. The tulle skirt's missing, and the strapless bodice ripped. My tiara is long gone. My hair is stiffening with dried blood, not mousse. My legs are crumpled beneath me, unable to move. I'm like a rag doll. The black water's lapping by my feet.

The magpies warned us. Granny warned us. Now she's dead and gone. I never thought I'd be seeing her again so soon. All my fault. Everything is my fault. I want to hug Gregory, hold him close, tell him I didn't mean to let this happen to him. But I can't move.

He'll hate me now.

I have a gunshot wound in my shoulder. I can't see it, but I feel it. It's burning like ice. I can't move my arm. Can't hardly think properly. Everything is really bright around me but distant as well, like I'm watching it, but it's not real. I keep blinking really slowly, and each blink is like taking a photo. A whole line of photos with nothing joining them together.

Blink – Gregory's leaning over me, his face full of fear. I think he's trying to stop the blood coming from my shoulder. "Lay down." That's not hard. He's putting something on my shoulder, pushing. He takes my right hand and places it on my shoulder. "Hold it there. Can you do that?" Uh-huh. He's turning round. Wonder what he's seen.

Blink – can't see Gregory now, but I can see Hudson. He's stirring, he's up on all fours, shaking his head, dribbling blood. No smile on his face now. Fear rushes through me as he gets to his feet and staggers towards me. But he's too late; Gregory appears. His hands are shaking, but they're holding the gun. He's shouting something, and Hudson turns away and heads for the Jeep, leaving Milo still lying as though he's dead. Maybe he is.

Blink – the Jeep's engine is revving. Dust is flying. Hudson's driving away. Good, I'm glad he's gone. Gregory's got a phone in one hand now. He must've found it in the car. I didn't see him get it. I think I'm missing chunks of time. I can see his blood-streaked hair. Bet I don't look much better.

Blink – I think I can hear sirens. Is it the police? Has anyone at the wedding missed me yet? Just now I thought I smelled blackberry wine and tears trickled down my cheeks and my heart ached. Maybe Granny's soul is floating around trying to help, and that's her way of letting us know. But I think maybe I'm getting a little crazy like Granny did before her death.

I try to sit up, holding my shoulder. There's just me and Gregory now. I can see him sitting by the car. His shirt is covered in blood, like my dress. He sees me watching him.

"Sammy-Jo," he says. He limps over to me, stumbling and tripping. "Just hold on. They're coming for us."

"Hudson?"

"No, not him. Don't worry. He's gone. Scarpered."

I can't answer him, but I'm so glad he's talking and he's OK. I watch every move he makes as he comes closer and closer. Milo is still out cold. Good. No more fighting for me. Can't move at all now.

"Hey," Gregory says as he drops to his knees beside me.

I say, "Hey" back to him with me eyes. That's all I can do. My mouth won't work. I'm silent for the first time in my life.

His face is bruised. One eye is closing fast, and will be black by tomorrow. But the wound in his side has stopped bleeding, I think. He looks like he's gone ten rounds in Maltese Joey's cage. I want to kiss his bruised cheek. I want to hug him, but one arm is useless. Instead he lays me back down and presses on me shoulder again. The sirens are coming closer. I can imagine them weaving their way along the side of the reservoir as the road twists and turns.

What will they say when they see the dead mullo? I can see his feet sprawled across the grass. At least they're not twitching now. I don't want to see his face, with the steel sticking through his mouth. That's how you kill a mullo. Granny must've known I'd need that information. Will I get done for murder? I've taken a life to save my own life and Gregory's.

The sirens are close. They're echoing between the trees, and I can see the reflection of their blue lights.

"I rang 999," Gregory mutters.

We stay together, me on the ground, him leaning over, protecting me, as we hear the sound of tyres on the track and the engines of two vehicles.

"You're shaking," he says. "But we'll get over this. Me and you. Both of us together."

I can feel my eyes watering, and I start to cry. I can't stop myself. No sobs, just tears, streaming from my eyes, down my face and onto the ground. His lips are against my hair. He's in shock. I can feel him trembling, too.

I don't think I'll ever get over this. I want to say sorry to him for all he's been through since he met me, but I can't speak. My chest is getting tight, as though a boa constrictor's wrapped itself around me. It's getting hard for me to breathe. This must've been how it felt for Granny. Did she think old age had come to get her, or did she know that she'd been poisoned? And now I'm wondering whether I'll see a vardo coming for me, or whether I'm too young for that, and it'll be a beautiful Airstream trailer, like Rocky's father has.

There's something making a horrible noise near me, though, blocking out most of the sounds and getting louder. Like someone gasping. I think it's me, gasping for air as the weakness gets to me lungs. I can just about hear Gregory shouting. He looks terrified, and he's crying. He looks more frightened than when Milo and Hudson were beating him up. He's shouting, "Hang on, hang on, they're coming!"

And I can see blue lights reflecting, and there's vehicles pulling in. An ambulance and police cars. Gregory is pleading with someone to help me quickly.

"She got shot in the shoulder. It went through. It's stopped bleeding, but she can't breathe."

Faces looming above me. Green uniform. Paramedics? Someone's ripping my bridesmaid's dress even more. Voices all around.

"Shoulder wound … substantial loss of blood … collapsed lung…" I can see a paramedic running over with an oxygen mask, and jamming it over my face. And at first I panic because I think they're trying to suffocate me, but Gregory's got my hand and he's squeezing it. Until the paramedics start on him as well, and tell him to lie down. We're side by side, and he's holding my hand, which is sticky with blood – mine or his?

I can hear him telling them about the bullet wound, and I can hear one of them saying, "It's all right, son, we'll sort you both out. Just hold her hand and keep calm."

I take a lungful of oxygen and my chest eases. It's still too tight. Another paramedic has a needle in his hand. I feel a sting on the back of my hand, and they're rigging a drip up at the side of me, and the blue lights are wonderful. It's like a disco as the night falls, and more blue lights join the ones already here. And there's more faces looming over us. I think I see Rocky and the spiky blonde hair of Miss Stroud.

"You in trouble again!" It sounds like Rocky's voice, but maybe I'm dreaming.

Gregory seems to be talking to him, though. He's telling Rocky to go and get McCloud, that all this is McCloud's fault. And that Hudson has escaped, and they have to get him as well. I see an ambulance man come forward and throw a blanket over Pony. But there's lots of police around, too. Will they believe our story? What if they investigate McCloud, and nothing can be found, and no one believes us? But I can't be bothered to think about it now. The paramedics gently lift me onto a stretcher, the drip still in my hand, and a blissful sleepiness seeps through me.

32

There's darkness.

And in the darkness there's a face coming at me all the time, and I can't get away. The face has a name. It's Pony. It's scaring me to death. For a long time I shiver and gasp for breath. Nurses hover beside me, topping up the drip that makes the pain in my shoulder go away. At some point they wheel me into a brightly lit room. Voices move around me, hands touch me. Needles, machines beeping. I remember shouting and struggling at one point because I think Pony's coming back to get me, but it's only a nurse trying to clean me scratches and cuts. Sometime in the night I stop shaking and my breathing gets easier. The boa constrictor's gone away. I don't know how long this lasts: me lying there as weak as a kitten for the first time in my life, but before I go crazy, it ends.

The darkness retreats, and it's morning. I open my eyes. I'm back, and I can feel my strength returning drip by drip. My brain starts to work again. I'm Sammy-Jo Smith. It'll take more than a shark-eyed businessman and his grinning son to plan my death.

My first words?

"Where's Gregory? Is he OK?"

"Yes," says the nurse. "He's even eating breakfast."

They won't let me see him, though. He's in Room 10, I'm in 18. Same floor, but at different ends of the corridor. She tells me there's a policeman outside guarding the corridor. I don't know whether it's to stop me getting out or to stop anyone getting in to me. The policeman tells me that they've got McCloud but not Hudson. Sometime in the night there was a police chase, but he got away in his boy-racer Impreza.

I've seen Gregory's father and mother passing by. They went straight past here, they never looked in at me. His wound has been stitched. The nurse says he's lucky, because the tent peg missed anything important inside him. They're keeping him in because he's got concussion. His great-grandaddy is on the floor above us. The nurse says he's going to be OK, unlike my granny.

I'm sitting up in bed in my little room. There's a couple of chairs and a bedside table, and that's it. My hair is still sticky with blood. They've taken away the torn and filthy remains of my once beautiful bridesmaid's dress, and I'm wearing a hospital gown that doesn't do up at the back. My shoulder has a dressing on the front and one on the back, where the bullet came out. The wounds are very small, considering how painful it was. They're going to scar me for life, but with every minute I lie here, propped up on pillows, I can feel myself getting stronger again. I'm no longer like a kitten, but my brain is still haunted by Hudson and Pony. Every time I shut my eyes I see Pony's face again.

Don't think about his face.

When the nurse comes back in, I demand to see Gregory again, but I'm still not allowed. They don't care that Gregory saved my life, and I saved his. They just keep on giving me tests. I've had so many needles stuck in me, I swear, I'd leak like a sieve if they ever gave me a proper drink. Instead, I have to take small sips of lukewarm water, even though I'm dying for a Diet Coke. I've tried explaining to the nurses that I'm a chief bridesmaid and I have to go and find out what happened to the bride and her groom, but they ignore me.

I'm not sure what the time is, but with everything that's happened, time doesn't matter any more. Especially for Granny Kate. Her time has run out, and although my heart aches for her, this still isn't the time to grieve, not here in this place. But there will come a time when I will weep for her. And a time when I will get revenge for her pointless death. Just thinking about revenge makes me want to move, however much it hurts. I'm thinking about sneaking along to Gregory's room when I hear Sabrina and Beryl outside having an argument with someone. I think it's the poor policeman. He's telling them that I should only have two visitors at a time, but Beryl's taking no notice. She bustles in, followed by my father, Bartley and Sabrina.

"Here she is!" she shouts.

"Oh my God, get me out of here," I say straightaway.

"I'm going crazy. I'm suffocating. And everyone's asking me questions, but no one's telling me what's happening."

Beryl plonks down in the nearest chair. She's still in her wedding outfit, with her fascinator sagging from one side of her hair. Sabrina sinks into the other one, smoothing her white going-away outfit, her face miserable. Bartley and my father loom over the bed, staring at me.

"Well, this is a mess," says Bartley.

"That's what I've been trying to tell the police," I say. "They've stuck a policeman outside my door, but they should be protecting you, and everyone else as well."

Bartley looks horrified. "We don't want the police hanging around us."

They don't understand. "You're all in danger. They've got McCloud but not his son!"

"Calm down." Bartley pushes me back onto the pillows. "It'll be fine. McCloud is helping them with their enquiries, so are his men. His business is finished. He's got more to worry about than us."

I sit straight up. "You've got to make sure they arrest him and don't let him out."

"I knew that man was evil," says Beryl. "Every time we drove into the field he was there, glaring at us like we were the criminals. And now it turns out he is one!"

"Leave it, Beryl," says my father. "She's wound up about it enough as it is." He turns to me. "Why didn't you tell us he'd threatened you?"

I look from him to Bartley. "Because he said he'd get my

family if I told anyone. I thought if I stayed in the crowd and kept them at a distance, and showed them I wasn't running off to the police, that we could just leave after the wedding and never come back."

"No one is going to get us," says Bartley. He leans down and strokes my hair back. "Seriously, you were worried this man was going to get away with hurting the Smiths?" He smiles. "Just let him try. I've alerted everyone, and I mean *everyone*. We're all on the lookout." He pats my good shoulder. "I think we can get on with our lives without worrying about McCloud."

He looks so strong and capable standing there that I do start to relax. I almost feel like smiling, but then I see my father's face. I know what's coming.

"There's something else we've got to straighten out, haven't we, Sammy-Jo?" he says.

I slump back on my pillow and try to look weak. "The fights?"

"Yes, the fights, you little madam. You're never going to fight in those places again, do you hear me?"

I give a small nod. "Yes."

"We're better than that, Sammy-Jo! You're better than that!"

"I know."

But he can't shut up. "Running wild and sneaking out without me knowing. Maggie would die of shame. And now look at you!" He shakes his head at my cuts and bruises and the bandages on my shoulder. "I'm at my wits' end with what to do with you. Rocky's told me all about it. He's going to have a word with you as well."

I roll my eyes. "Can't wait."

"Why did you do it, Sammy-Jo? Tell me that!"

"It was exciting." I'm not going to tell him the truth, that I needed the money for the wedding.

He sighs. "I've not been taking enough notice of you. From now on, you're not going to go running off all over the place. I'm keeping my eye on you, girl. And no more fights until you're eighteen and you can enter the legal ones."

I shrug. "I don't want to fight in competition any more. I'm not interested. I know I can win them, that's all that matters."

"Good. I'm glad you said that," says Beryl, quickly. "Because Bartley's got an idea."

I bet I know what it is, but suddenly Sabrina comes to life. "Shut up, all of you! Sammy-Jo's recovering from a trauma, and you're all shouting at her."

This is something new: Sabrina sticking up for me. And the shouting does stop, because a nurse has popped her head round the door to have a word with my father. Beryl and Bartley follow him, which leaves me and Sabrina alone. She's looking dangerously close to tears.

"Don't ever do that to me again," she says, blinking madly. "I couldn't cope. We all thought you were going to die. First Granny, then you."

"Sorry. And sorry your wedding got ruined."

She wipes her eyes carefully, so she doesn't disturb her

eyelashes. "And our wedding night. That was a disaster as well. We didn't go away on our honeymoon, as you can see. It turned into a wake for Granny Kate and you."

"I'm not dead."

"You nearly were! We took it in turns to be at the hospital. Everyone else went back to Tyson's house. We weren't alone for two minutes, I swear."

"Very romantic," I say.

"Some bridesmaid you turned out to be." She stops, bites her lip and starts winding her hair around her finger. Something's up with her, something more than a ruined wedding night. I wait. Eventually she glances up at me through her lashes, and whispers, "You paid for the wedding, didn't you? From those fights."

That gives me a jolt. "Who told you that?"

"No one. I just figured it out. I'm right, aren't I?"

I relax again. "Yeah. My choice. But don't tell anyone."

Her face crumples. "I'm going to cry."

"Oh God, no, please don't."

Her lip trembles. "I was such a bitch…"

"You were you. Now shut up about it." I have to distract her, and I know just the thing. "Do you want to see the bullet wound?"

That perks her up. "Go on, then."

I lift the dressing. She peers at it. "Urgh. That's disgusting. It's going to scar you for life."

I can't help but smile. It's good to hear her back to normal. Yesterday I thought I'd never hear her moaning ever again. But the others haven't finished with me yet. The nurse has gone, and they have returned to my bedside. Beryl comes straight to the point.

"Bartley, tell her your plan. It's the answer to everything. Listen."

Bartley sits on the end of the bed, which creaks under his big frame. "Come to America for a holiday. It's going to take a while for them to investigate McCloud and catch the son. You need to get away from it all for now."

My daddy's nodding and saying, "Bartley's right. Go back with him. We can get a ticket next week, after the funeral." His face looks strained. I can tell he's been worrying all night. "You'll be safe in California. No one will ever touch you again."

"No." I have to put my foot down now. "You've got to let me live my life. I don't want to get out of the way. I want to get back to normal."

Like hell I do. I want revenge, but I'm not telling them that.

Now Beryl's chiming in. "And the best place to do that is America. Tell her, Bartley!"

"Quiet, Beryl! I'm trying to tell her. I want you to join the training courses I run out in the desert for the contestants. We're thinking of having girl contestants, so you'd be the guinea pig. You'd be doing me a favour."

"I can fight already, Bartley, I don't need to go to America."

"It's not just fighting. It's boot camp. It's about surviving, and it's worse than military training. You think you're tough, but you need discipline. You've been running wild for too long." He narrows his eyes at me. "It'll be the hardest thing you've ever done—"

"You're not selling it well, Bart," mutters my father.

"—but it's better than being injured in one of these illegal fights," he finishes, quickly. "Say the word, and I'll get you a ticket."

"And you can be with family, instead of hanging round with people we don't know," says Beryl.

"She means Gregory," interrupts Sabrina. "She's been glaring at his mum and dad in the waiting room, and they've been staring at us."

Beryl's face goes stubborn. "Well? He's not family."

I can't let her get away with that. "He's my friend, OK?" I slide down my pillow and let my eyes droop. "Anyhow, you've got to leave me alone, all of you, and not nag me, the nurses say. I've been shot. I'm still recovering. But I'll think about your offer, Uncle Bartley. I really will. I'll decide after the funeral."

They have to put up with that. It's been a long day and an even longer night as well for them.

Finally, after they all kiss me and hug me, they leave me alone. But there's no peace for me, and no chance to sneak off to see Gregory, because soon as they disappear, Rocky bounds in, followed by Miss Stroud.

33

Rocky throws himself into the nearest chair. "About time. I've been here most of the night."

I push myself back up against my pillows, ignoring the pain in my shoulder. "Why is she here?"

"Miss Stroud?" He gives her a glance as she sits in the other chair. "She's helping with the investigation. She's not really my probation worker."

"You don't say." So I hadn't been dreaming, when they both turned up at the reservoir last night.

"Too right, I'm not." Miss Stroud has cool blue eyes, and she's pretty enough. She's lounging in her chair, tipping it back onto two legs, her feet in biker boots sprawled across the floor. "I'm CID."

That makes me blink. Rocky hanging round with a plain-clothes woman detective? I turn to him.

"I swear I'll need emergency treatment if you tell me you've joined the police."

He pretends to look offended. "Heaven's sake. Of course I'm not a gavver, Sammy-Jo. Never was, never will be. I'd sooner chew off me own leg."

"That's the truth. He's definitely not the police," says Miss Stroud. "He wouldn't last a day." She looks at him like he's some naughty boy. "We're both investigating illegal fights."

I hadn't expected that, but then my brain starts ticking over. That must be why people knew him when he followed us to the fight the other night. And how he got to hear my name, Gypsy Girl.

Rocky looks smug. "The police were getting nowhere, so I had to help them out."

"Don't push it," says Miss Stroud.

He laughs. "OK, the truth is I'm helping them and they're helping me. We're going to stop all the illegal fights before more people get killed, or crippled."

I remember him going mad at me that night, telling me about his mate who got crippled. "Is this because of Billy Lee?"

He nods, the smile fading. "Of course it is, Sammy-Jo. Me and him were like brothers. It was my fault he got into fighting. He came to the gym with me one day and got hooked on it. When he got crippled, I went a bit crazy and started doing stupid stuff."

Miss Stroud gives a small smile. "I was the one who arrested him. When he told me his story, I realized we could be of use to each other."

"That's why I went mad at you at the fight. I don't want anyone else injured." Rocky glances at Miss Stroud. "Me and her have got the same aims. She's doing it for the police, and I'm doing it for Billy."

"But it's still taking a long time," she says. "We'll never close the fights down until we find the one man who runs everything, even though no one ever sees him."

I suddenly realize who she's talking about. "Maltese Joey?"

"That's the name he's trading under. But no one knows who he is or where he lives. He's at the centre of all the deaths and injuries. Plus he sells steroids, and gets kids hooked."

All this talk of Maltese Joey is getting Rocky riled. His hands are in fists, and he springs to his feet and starts pacing. "He was the one who got Billy taking steroids. And that's how he made him keep fighting."

He goes on and on, pacing and ranting about the fights and how dangerous they are, and how Billy Lee will never walk again, and how stupid I was to get involved with it. "You were all being exploited. Maltese Joey is clever. He sits back and rakes the money in from idiots like you."

He's making my head ache. "I knew what I was doing. Nobody forced me or any of the other fighters."

He throws out his hands. "You were exploited!"

"How?"

Miss Stroud's keeping out of this. She's sitting back, watching, as Rocky sits down again, leaning forward, counting on his fingers.

"Steroids, DVDs of the fights. Pay-per-view Internet sites. The numbers of hits on the Internet for some of these files are in the millions! No proper referees, no medics, no first aid of any kind. There's been deaths, permanent injuries and brain damage at his fights." He shakes his head at me. "And you went and put yourself at risk."

I shrug with my good shoulder. "I made money. How else was I going to do that? There's no jobs around for girls like me."

Rocky throws his hands in the air again. "And Maltese Joey made lots more!"

He's forgetting one thing. "There's always been bare-knuckle fights," I say. "And our men are the best. It's our history."

That makes him even angrier. "So? It's time to change. Do you want to get crippled, or killed? Do you want to knock someone out and then find out there's no first aid to help them?"

I don't. I'm hearing what he's saying, and I've probably always known the truth about the fights. But I want Rocky to shut up.

So I make up my mind. "Scar-face," I say.

He stares at me. "What?"

"The last club we fought in. Remember the manager, the one with the scar where someone put a knife in his mouth and pulled, so he looks like one side of his face is always smiling?"

"Yes."

"That's Maltese Joey."

Total silence falls. Miss Stroud is staring at me. Rocky sits down. He's frowning. "How could you know that?"

"Because he told me."

Miss Stroud leans forward. "Why would he do that?"

I can tell she doesn't believe me. "Because I'm a girl and he's a creep. He hit on me the first time I went there. He started talking big, trying to impress me. He thought I was just this girl, that I'd never be a threat to him."

I've stunned them both. Miss Stroud shakes her head, a smile appearing. She looks over at Rocky. "Simple as that. The idiot keeps himself out of the limelight, then tries to impress a girl young enough to be his daughter!" She gives a laugh. "Girls should be ruling the world because sometimes men are so stupid." She looks at me, and I think I can see admiration in her eyes. "Thanks. This could be our lucky break."

"I can come and help you get him," I say.

Rocky grabs my hand. "No. This is our fight now. You keep out of it. Go with Bartley. Get away from here."

I pull my hand away. "Everyone's telling me to do this, or do that. I've got my own ideas."

He frowns. "What are they?"

I might as well tell him. Maybe he'll understand. "I'm going to find Hudson McCloud and get vengeance."

Suddenly they're both sitting bolt upright.

"No. You forget him," says Rocky.

"He tried to kill me. He's a psycho! And I'll get him, you'll see."

Miss Stroud leans forward, no smiles now, and points a finger at me. "You do not do that. You leave him to us."

"The police let him get away!"

"I know. Unfortunate." She scowls. "Bloody boy-racer cars. But you leave him to us. We'll find him – not you."

I've had enough. "You can't tell me what to do," I tell her.

"Yes, she can," says Rocky, deadly serious now. "It looks like McCloud is running something big. At first I thought you were just being your usual self and annoying the neighbours."

"Thanks."

"But when Bartley told me someone was following you, and I saw that Jeep at the church, I got suspicious. I called Miss Stroud. She came over, took the registration number and got a glimpse of the big guy with the ponytail."

"I went and checked. His real name's Victor Polanski," she says. "He's from Eastern Europe originally. Everyone calls him Pony. He's been suspected of all sorts of gang-related stuff, fights, manslaughter, blackmail, never got charged with any of them. Until his luck ran out yesterday."

Mustn't think about Pony.

Rocky sees my face change. He takes my hand. "You could've got killed. Don't scare me like that again."

"International Express is part of a police operation now," says Miss Stroud. "McCloud is helping us with our enquiries. When Milo regained consciousness, we arrested him. He's talking in exchange for a lesser sentence. He doesn't know much about McCloud's business, but he's told us about the plan to kill you and Gregory. He's blaming it all on Hudson, of course."

"So McCloud will pay for what he did?" I ask her.

"Yes."

I see Hudson grinning at me in my mind. "And what about Hudson?"

"He's gone to ground somewhere. You don't have to worry about him. He's not going to risk coming anywhere near you." She points a finger at me. "So forget him and leave it to us. You're tough, but you're not tough enough to go after him, do you hear me?

Seems that everyone's got opinions about how tough I am today. None of them know the truth, though. I collapse back onto my pillow. "OK. Don't go on about it. I get it."

Miss Stroud nods. "Good. We'll find him, don't worry." She gives me a reassuring smile, but I'm not interested in being reassured. I change the subject.

"They poisoned me granny. Did you find out what it was?"

"We're thinking one of the new designer drugs. No one knows what's in them. Mephedrone's been out on the streets for a while, but they change all the time. Some of them are probably more harmless than alcohol. But the problem is they're not like cocaine or weed, which have been around for years. You don't know what you're buying, it could be mixed with something poisonous, it could be lethal. The people who make them don't care."

"Granny found that out."

"We've got forensics going over the barn and the other buildings. Soon as we find traces of the drug, we can match it with your granny's blackberry liqueur. McCloud will get done for this, don't worry. We've already found evidence that the company is shipping stolen goods."

"So all you have to do is stay out of trouble now," says Rocky. "And leave Hudson alone."

This time I don't argue. "OK."

They don't look as though they believe me, but what can they do?

"I thought you were going out with each other," I say, to change the subject. They both laugh.

"She wishes," says Rocky. "But seriously, me go out with a gavver? Leave it out."

"He wishes." She grins at him. "He insists on calling me Miss Stroud. I think he's got a teacher complex."

They've only been here minutes, but Rocky is already looking twitchy. He hates hanging round indoors. He's like me. He likes to be outside, doing things.

"You can go now," I tell him. "I'm tired."

He stands up, fixes me with this stern look. "No more fighting, Sammy-Jo. It's over for you now."

In my mind I see the bright lights above the cage, the people crowding round, shouting me name, "Gypsy Girl!" The thrill of walking into the centre and waiting, not knowing if this is the time I get beat. Bouncing on my toes, getting myself ready, and the roar as we start fighting.

"You sure you don't want me to help you get Maltese Joey?" I say.

"No!"

Rocky looks like he wants to shake me. I don't push it.

"OK, don't go on at me."

Rocky looms over me. "I'll know if you start hanging around the fights again. I'll tell Samson, and he'll go crazy. Even worse, he'll be disappointed in you again."

I nod. Anything to shut him up. "Gypsy Girl doesn't exist any more. Maltese Joey's clubs will never see me again. I hope you catch him."

Rocky still doesn't look totally convinced, but Miss Stroud drags him away. I expect she wants to start planning how to get Joey. Soon as they disappear I find a dressing gown and creep out, telling the policeman I'm going to the toilet. He watches me as I shuffle along towards the ladies'. My legs are shaky, but I can cope with that. Soon as I'm level with Gregory's room I take a quick peek inside to check that his parents have gone for now, and sneak in.

He doesn't see me at first. He's lying with headphones on and his eyes closed. The bruises on his face are murky purple, acid yellow and sickly green. The nurse told me that his cheekbone is cracked. And I have a horrible feeling his nose might be a little crooked from now on. For some reason, I think it will suit him. I have the urge to go and kiss his wounds and stroke his hair back from his forehead, but I don't. I perch on the edge of the bed. When he opens his eyes and sees me, his face break into a smile and then stops, because it must hurt.

"You should be mad at me," I say. "I got you into that mess."

"No. I'm not mad at you." He attempts a smile again. "Mad about you."

I don't say anything to that. He holds my hand. I start crying. It's seeing him looking so battered. Sixteen years and I hardly ever cried, and now I can't stop. We carry on holding hands, but nothing has changed. Even though we'll be staying around for Granny Kate's funeral, sometime soon we'll be leaving. And sometime after that the summer will be over and Gregory will be going back to college.

And me? Where will I be? I think I know now.

I hold his hand. It's warm and dry, fingernails bitten, the knuckles scraped red raw, the back tanned to a golden colour but covered in scratches. For now this is enough. I'm too tired to think of the future.

Later they come looking for me, and I have to go and have more tests, to see if the nerves in my arm are OK. They put little stickers all over my body, and a net of them over my head, all attached to little wires that lead into a machine. They stand around the machine, two doctors and a couple of nurses, "oooh"ing and "ahhh"ing, and tell me my reflexes are off the scale, and so is my muscle strength. They tell me I'll have to have physio and take it easy for a while. No fighting. That's what they think. I can already feel the strength coming back to me.

When they wheel me back to my room, I look into Gregory's, but he's gone.

A nurse tells me his parents have taken him to a private hospital.

34

A couple of weeks have gone by. It's still sunny. I walk up the drive to the big house, and knock on the door. The last time I was here I got thrown out. I wonder if it's going to happen again. I'm not dressed so extreme now. Jeans with a check shirt that covers the bandage on my shoulder. I've tied the shirt at my waist, though, so there is a bit of my tanned skin showing above the top of my jeans. No heels this time, only sandals.

The door opens immediately. It's not Gregory. I never thought it would be. It's his mother. She looks nervous and hostile, and I'm not surprised. A war has broken out between Mr Langton and my father. Gregory says we're the opposite of Romeo and Juliet. When they died, it brought their families together. But we lived and now ours blame each other for what happened.

"Yes?" she snaps, with a face like she's been drinking vinegar.

"We've just had my granny's funeral," I say.

The horses and the funeral carriage left from the field this morning, to go to the church. It was a proper Smith funeral.

Granny Kate went to her final rest in a glass coach pulled by two black horses with black plumes on their bridles. Smiths from all over came to pay their respects.

"Yes, I know," she says. "And I'm sorry for your loss. But really, we can't have you coming here and bothering Greg—"

"I'm not," I tell her, quickly. "I want to ask you a favour." She looks likes she's got a bad smell under her nose now, but I carry on. "See, it's an old tradition to burn the trailer when someone dies. We want to take Granny Kate's trailer into the field next door and burn it. My auntie says I have to ask your permission."

The burning is my idea. In the days since I got out of hospital, I've helped me sisters to clear out Granny's trailer. We've looked through all her old photos and put them in a box to keep. We've carefully wrapped up her old Crown Derby plates and cups, and stored them in boxes. And now the empty trailer stands with its door open, and the Queen Anne stove cold, never to be lit again. The old mirrors no longer reflect Granny Kate, just the dusty air and the bare shelves and cupboards.

But whenever I walk by, I swear I can smell blackberries. I thought it was just me, until Sabrina grabbed my arm and said she could smell them, too. Somehow, even though Granny is dead and gone, it didn't seem as though she was resting peacefully. I remembered when she used to tell us about the old days, and how the burning of the trailers would allow the departed souls to carry on roaming.

Granny needs to be able to go on her way.

Mrs Langton doesn't know what to say. She wants us gone. I think this is the only reason she doesn't argue. "I suppose that'll be all right. But you've still got to leave afterwards."

"Yes, I know." She starts to shut the door in my face. "Wait. There's one more thing. Would old Mr Langton like to come to the burning? He knew Granny Kate. He remembered her."

"And her wine nearly killed him," she snaps.

If she thinks she can make me ashamed, she's wrong.

"She would never have made poisoned wine if it wasn't for Mr McCloud – the man *you* sold the barn to. You thought you knew him. Just shows you can't always judge people by the way they look, or what job they do." I peer over her shoulder. "At least your grandfather is out of hospital and getting better. Not like my granny."

Mrs Langton's eyes narrow. "How do you know he's out of hospital?"

Oops. "I'm guessing. Didn't see no funeral here."

She doesn't believe me, but what can she do?

I back away. "Anyway, tell him he's welcome to come and pay his last respects."

As I reach their gate, I glance back at Gregory's bedroom window and smile to myself.

We hitch the old trailer to the Mitsubishi and drive it to the centre of the field, everyone following behind. We've taken out the beautiful old mirrors because we're going to fit them into the gym back at our place, so that we can remember Granny Kate when we look in them.

We gather in a ring around the outside. There's a big crowd of us. There's Bartley next to Beryl. And Rocky standing with Miss Stroud. She's changed her leather jacket for a long black coat. We're all in black. My father and Bartley go inside the trailer with cans of petrol and soak the seats and the floor. But before they can throw a match and run, we hear someone shouting.

It's Mr Langton. His car's parked at the gate, and he's striding over to us. I suspect he hasn't been home and he hasn't spoken to his wife.

"I told you to pack up and go after the funeral," he says, striding up to my father.

"The funeral's not finished yet," me daddy tells him.

"Looks like it is to me. I've given you enough time, but now you have to move." He sniffs the air. "Why can I smell petrol?" He notices the matches. "You cannot seriously be going to set fire to that caravan!"

"We are. We're not doing any harm. It'll be cleared up afterwards."

"He's right," says Bartley, coming over to them. "Come on, let's not argue. It won't take us long."

But Mr Langton's not happy. "I'll call the police. I mean it."

Which sets my father off. He pokes Langton in the chest. "You do that. See where it gets you."

"Is that a threat?"

"Oi," shouts a croaky voice. "What's going on here?"

Coming across the field is old Mr Langton. He's being pushed in a wheelchair by Gregory, who looks at everyone except me. "You can't be shouting and arguing at a time like this," the old fella says to both men. "Now let's get going. I've come to say farewell to the old lady."

Which gives my father the chance to stride away striking a match, which he throws into the trailer. It goes up with a *whump* straightaway, the windows smashing and the flames shooting out. Soon the flames are licking into the sky and roaring loudly. Everyone's standing back because the heat is scorching our faces. None of us imagined the trailer would burn that fiercely. The smoke's so thick that we can hardly see each other. Which gives Gregory the chance to park the wheelchair by his father, who's standing with his arms crossed, but not saying anything now.

Gregory creeps to my side under cover of the smoke and takes me hand. I can smile at him now. His bruises are starting to fade. His stitches have healed. But I knew that already. This isn't the first time I've seen him since his parents took him away. When he was spirited away from the hospital, everyone thought I'd never see him again. But I knew I would. It's as though we've got a thin silver chain – so fine it's invisible to the world – joining us together.

That first night I got out of hospital, I lay in my trailer all alone. Sabrina was with Tyson at last, enjoying being in her new home with her new husband. I didn't think I would sleep, but I did. I wished I hadn't. I dreamed of mullos biting on steel, and Pony's face coming at me, and I woke shivering, wanting to scream, my skin crawling. So I got up and went out in my shorty PJs, with a fleece blanket pulled around my shoulders like one of Granny Kate's shawls. I made my way to where the yellow police crime-scene tapes fluttered across the wide-open gates of International Express. There were no cars or lorries in there now. The forensic teams had worked on it for days. All the stock had been taken out of the barn and the other buildings. All paperwork and computers had been seized. The place was empty. I ducked under the blowing tape and walked towards the barn.

The night was full of that silvery light you get when the moon's full and the sky's clear. More tape criss-crossed the barn doors. I ducked under it and went inside. I had to face my fears. This was where Pony had worked but not any more. He was dead. I stood in the centre and bear-hugged myself, wrapping my fleece blanket tight. The night wasn't cold, but the atmosphere in here was. Most of the space was taken up with ceiling-high racks to hold all the boxes and crates. But to one side there was an old leather sofa, and a table with mugs and a kettle, where the workers and lorry drivers took their breaks, I supposed.

"Sammy?"

I spun round. It was Gregory, standing in the doorway, one hand clutching the doorpost. He was wearing old joggers and a creased T-shirt, his hair mussed up. It looked like he'd been in bed, too. It was the first time I'd seen him since they whisked him away, but it was like we'd never been apart. He must have felt the tug on that thin invisible chain that bound us.

"You couldn't sleep, either?" he said.

"Not unless I want to have nightmares."

He groaned. "Me, too. If I see Pony's face again, I'll scratch my eyes out."

"How did you know I was here?"

"No idea. I just did."

I folded my arms. "Yeah, right."

He laughed. "OK. I was lying in bed looking out of my window. I can see the field and the barn from there. I saw you come here and jump the police tape."

"Good. I'm glad."

He walked over and put his arms tight around me, and we stood for a long time, bathed in moonlight coming through the high, dusty windows, not having to say a word, until his arms crept up around my neck, and I looked up at him, and he kissed my cheeks and eyes and finally my lips. And Beryl could say what she wanted, but it wasn't wrong to fall in love with another human being, wherever they came from.

When at last he moved and unwrapped my arms from around him, I said, "Stay with me. Don't leave yet."

And he smiled and said, "Don't worry, I wasn't going to." He pulled me over to the sofa. I wrapped my blanket around us both, and rested my head on his shoulder, and curled my feet up.

"It's like staying in a haunted house," he said, stroking my hair, his warm breath tickling the side of my face. "We'll get over our fears. We'll cast out the evil."

I think he was right. We stayed there all night, and in the end we both slept, and I didn't dream of mullos biting on steel. I dreamed of Gregory, forbidden dreams of lying beside him, of passion and thrills and him pinning me down but not to fight me, to love me.

I don't know what he dreamed, but when we both woke with a start as a police car drew into the barn yard, he looked at me for a moment, and in that moment I saw the same love and passion.

Before anyone could discover us, we crept out and ran.

Whatever happens in the future, we had that night together.

And now, as we watch the trailer burn, he squeezes my hand. Maybe he's remembering that night, too. I can see Beryl peering through the smoke at us, but it's too thick. It seems to blow our way so that no one can see us. Maybe it's Granny Kate sticking up for us. She wasn't that keen on housed people, but I reckon she was sweet on old Langton at one time, so she'd understand.

"Look!" Gregory points through the smoke to a couple of tall trees near the hedgerow.

There's a whole bunch of magpies sitting in a line on the top branch, as though they're watching the trailer burning. Not four of them this time, more than that.

"There's ten of them," I tell him. "I don't know what that means. Granny only told me the rhyme up to number four."

"There's lots of different versions. I asked my mum. She says there used to be this television programme when she was younger, called *Magpie*. Everyone knew the rhyme back then. Her version goes like this: "One for sorrow, two for joy, three for a girl, four for a boy, five for silver, six for gold, seven for a secret never to be told, eight for a wish, nine for a kiss, ten for a time of joyous bliss."

"So this is going to be a time of joyous bliss."

"It was the other night," he says, playing with a strand of my hair.

"And now I've got to make my mind up about my future. There's nothing blissful about that."

The fire is dying down. Old Mr Langton has started to cough. I think the smoke's got to him. And people are going to see me and Gregory standing together. Already Gregory's father is looking over here, his face like thunder.

"I better take Pops home." Gregory reluctantly lets go of me hand. "I'll see you around."

"I'll be gone later today," I warn him.

He doesn't look convinced. "And I start at college next week. It's twenty miles away. But this isn't over. They can't stop you being here, in my heart." He gives me one of his deep, deep looks. He crosses his fingers. "Me and you. We're entwined now. You won't get rid of me that easily."

And he leaves me. It's only just in time. Beryl and Queenie are on their way over, with Bartley.

317

Before they reach me, I say goodbye to Granny Kate. I watch the last of the flames licking through the trailer windows. And just for a moment everything goes quiet around us. And I hear very faintly the clip-clop of hooves as the vardo comes to take Granny away.

"Did you hear that?" I ask Beryl as she reaches me.

"What?"

"The sound of a wagon and a horse."

She looks at me as if I'm going crazy. I'm not. Granny Kate told me I was the seventh of the seventh, and that I was special. Maybe I see and hear more than others.

"Never mind that," says Beryl. "Have you made up your mind? Bartley's all ready to get you a ticket."

Behind them I can see Rocky and Miss Stroud watching. Everyone wants me to go to America.

"How tough is this boot camp?" I ask Bartley.

"You think you're fit and strong now, this will make you unbeatable."

That's what I wanted to hear.

"OK. I'll go." Rocky looks surprised. Beryl looks relieved. "But only if my friend Kimmy can come with me."

Beryl doesn't look pleased. "She's the one who helped you go to those fights – and kept it a secret!"

But Queenie nudges her. "Shut up and let her take a friend with her. Stop being mean." She turns to Bartley. "Quick, go and get the tickets before she changes her mind. You'll have to make sure neither of them get into any trouble over there."

He gives me a smug smile. "After the *CAGED* boot camp,

she and her mate won't have any energy left to get into trouble."

That's what he thinks.

He wants to drag me off and sort the flight out straightaway, but I hear the peep of a horn from the road.

"'Scuse. I've got to go and speak to someone."

I leave them discussing my trip. A car has drawn up at the entrance to Gypsy's Acre. It's a battered old Golf. I make my way to it and get in.

"You didn't make it to the funeral, or the burning," I say to Kimmy.

She grins at me. "I watched. I was keeping out of your dad's way. He's still mad at me. He says if he ever catches me taking you to fights, he'll ban me from his gym for ever."

"Good job there's more exciting things for us to be doing."

She's dying to ask me. She can't wait any longer. "So are we going?"

"We are."

"Yes!"

Everyone is trying to order my life for me. But I'm going to do things my way.

"And when I get back, and I'm stronger than ever, I'll go and find Hudson, and make him pay for what he did to Gregory and me."

Gypsy Girl doesn't exist any more. No more fighting in cages for me. I've got boot camp training to get through. And after that I've got a war to fight against Hudson McCloud.

I'm Soldier Girl now.

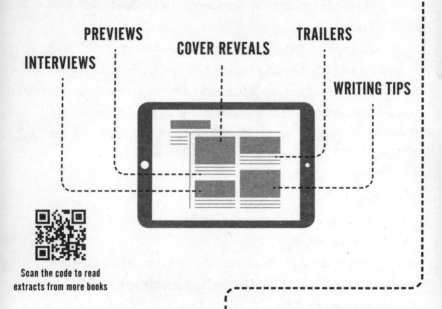